COMPASS and BLADE

**Available from Rachel Greenlaw
and Inkyard Press**

Compass and Blade

RACHEL GREENLAW

COMPASS and BLADE

inkyard PRESS

ISBN-13: 978-1-335-01232-6

Compass and Blade

Inkyard Press
22 Adelaide St. West, 41st Floor
Toronto, Ontario M5H 4E3, Canada
www.InkyardPress.com

Printed in U.S.A.

For Rosie and Izzy,
I love you to the moon
and back and all the stars
in between

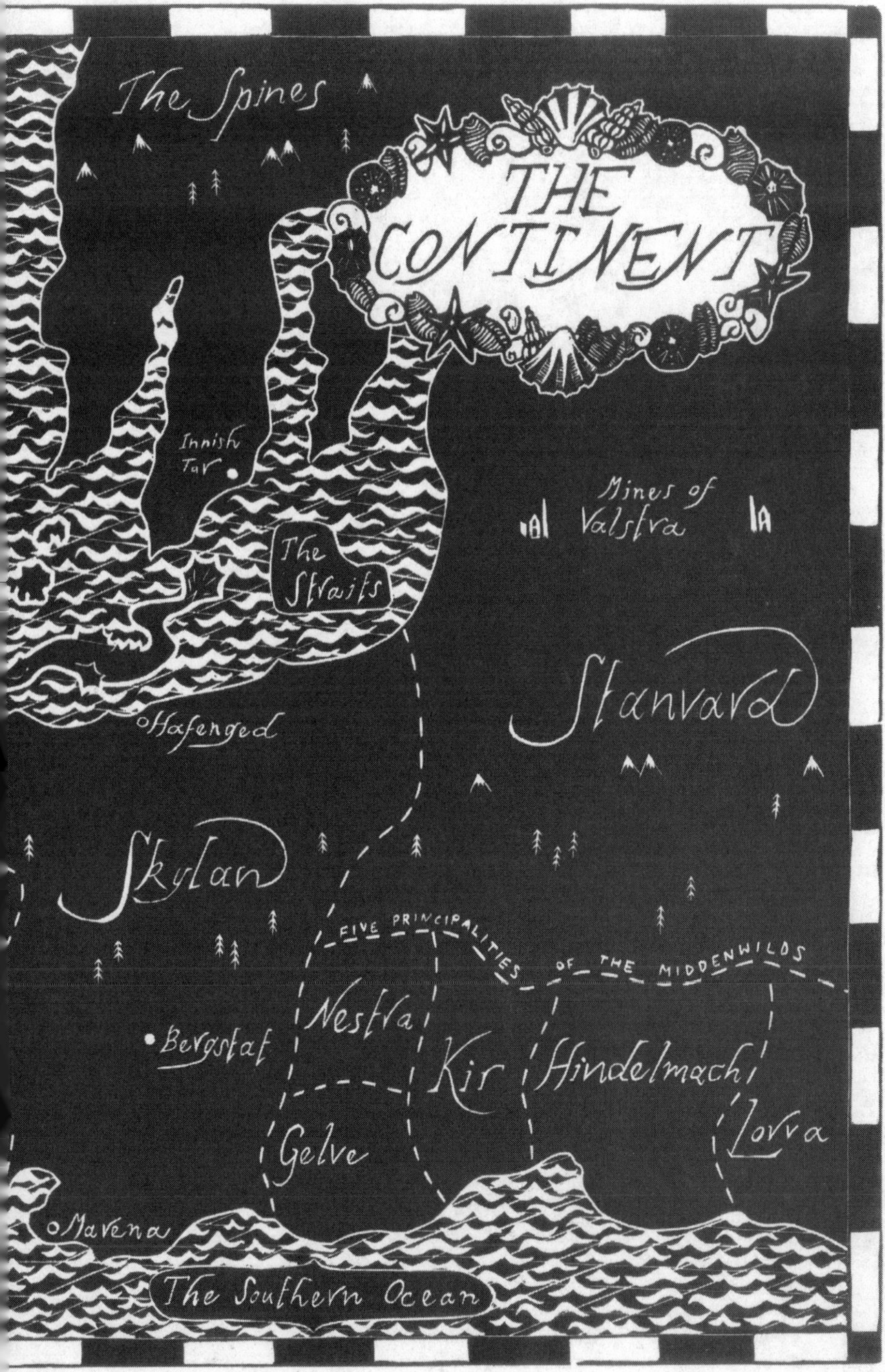
THE CONTINENT
The Spines
Innish Tar
The Straits
Mines of Valstra
Hafenged
Stanvard
Skylan
FIVE PRINCIPALITIES OF THE MIDDENWILDS
Nestra
Kir
Hindelmach
Bergstaf
Lorra
Gelve
Mavena
The Southern Ocean

CHAPTER ONE

THE THUNDER SENDS ME RUNNING. AS LIGHTNING cleaves the sky, casting a flash across the sand, I see the ship. An outline. A struggling beast in the water. Its carcass is spilling cargo, wood splintered and swollen. I gasp, pulling in a breath as I stumble over the rocks. The wind whips the rain against my skin, a sharp spray of cold dashing across my cheekbones.

"Am I too late?" I ask as I reach the group on the beach. A hand reaches for mine, calloused fingers gripping my own.

"You're cold, Mira," my father says, blue eyes hidden under the folds of his hood. "Take my gloves when you go in."

I nod, avoiding the fact that we both know I don't need them. That as soon as I hit the water, I will no longer feel the cold. Moving toward the line, I find my place along the length of slick rope. Six others are with me. Six other island-ers who have the song of the sea in their blood, and can last in the ocean and not succumb to her ways so easily. But none of them can last as long as I can. None of them can find warmth beneath the waves.

I touch the rope, the rasp of the twine biting into my palms. Waking me. Igniting the fire in my blood. I look out at the ship, imagine the dying gasps of the sailors. My heart lurches, prickles of heat shivering through my veins. I was born for this, the tide and the foam and the cold. I am ready.

I will save as many as I can. We all will.

But we will never tell them the truth. That *we* light the fires along the cliffs. That we are the beacon their helmsman followed. That we wrecked their ship on our rocks to plunder all they have, to take any cargo we can eat or trade.

This is how we survive.

Agnes is just ahead of me, her fist gripped around the rope like a promise. It's her job to cut the cargo from the ship so it floats toward the crew on the shore. I look behind me, catching Kai's wink. He'll be with me, saving as many as we can.

The roar of the sea echoes in my chest and I beat my feet against the sand, in step with the others. We work as one and I match my rhythm to theirs. We haven't lost any of us, any of the seven who swim out to the wrecks, this season. Or last.

"On three! All together!"

The answering call goes up all around as we shout back his words. *All together.* My father appears beside me as we walk, tugging his gloves over my hands, gripping my shoulder.

"I'll be fine," I say, turning back to the tide. He says nothing, but I feel his love, the ghost of it lingering as he disappears into the night. It wraps around me, a little too stifling.

The first lash of sea batters against my thighs, reaching for my chest. I take a deep breath, keeping the rope tangled in my fist, then in a rush of fire and ice, I dive under. Agnes surfaces first, just ahead of me. Her red hair flashes, float-ing like a beacon. I keep her in sight as I work through the waves, feeling out their song. Feeling for their pull and beat. The sea is a fickle creature and on a night like this, she can be wicked and cruel.

I fall into a rhythm, keeping the rope tucked in on my right, feeling the knot of the spliced twine, which is tied around my waist and attached to the main rope, digging into my middle. Wood floats past, cargo released from the hold. Perhaps they were already sinking before we lured them in. The rocks are like teeth, hidden in the gums of the ocean. And surrounding our islands there are rows and rows of them, far more than we can chart on our maps.

I dive once more, catching my rib against something heavy. A thumping ache dulled by the water flares across my side. I bite my lip, stilling the hiss behind my teeth as my body instinctively curls inward, losing the rhythm of the others. I stretch out, hauling my arm overhead to cut through the water, bubbles escaping my lungs as the dull ache sharpens to a point. I surface, panting, my legs tangling with the rope. Letting the others carry me for half a breath. I consider hang-ing on to the rope in my hands, allowing myself to be pulled to the wreck—there's no way of binding my side until we reach the shore again—but I can't throw the others off. We're a team, I have to pull my weight. I carry on, sipping the air before diving down to push more flotsam away. My side grates angrily, pain roaring up my arm. I hope my ribs aren't bro-ken. That I'll still be able to haul in any survivors.

"Mira!" calls Bryn from near the front. "Mira and Kai, you're with me!"

I look up, finding the ship looming above me. She's keeled

right over, a gaping hole in the starboard side, the ocean roaring as the waves claw at her. Wood and crates float past us and I scan them for bodies. For eyes and limbs and hearts, anyone that I can save. But there's no one gripping the crates, clinging to their floating backs.

I hope we aren't too late.

I release the rope and move toward the hole in the ship's side. My hands scrape against the splintered wood and I'm grateful for the gloves my father gave me. They protect my palms as I drag my body up, leaning on my elbows as I slither forward on my belly. Pain explodes along my side, stars snapping behind my closed eyelids. I try to ignore it as my feet find the ship's edges. Bryn keeps the rope lashed to his waist, the rest of us untying ourselves as he directs us, calling orders as he stays by the gaping entrance we clambered through. We have to keep him in sight in case we need to leave quickly. He's our leader and our escape route if the ship caves in around us.

Agnes peels away with three of the others, and I see a flash in her fist as she pulls out her blade. She makes her way deeper into the ship's belly, searching for plunder. Searching for anything this ship carried: food or fabric or perhaps more precious things we can trade. This winter has been harsh and long, and fewer ships have graced our shores. The ache in my heart at the thought of these sailors' deaths is nothing compared to the ache in my belly. A ship like this is a bounty with the right hold. I only hope there's more than salted fish.

"Got one!" Kai calls to me, his voice echoing through the dying ship. The wood groans as I dart toward the sound, his voice the only thing guiding me through the dark. Kai and I are always assigned to finding survivors while the others search for cargo and precious keepsakes. Kai is the strongest;

he is Bryn's second. And I cannot stand to leave a beating heart behind. I lean down to the body on the floor, breathing hard.

"I hit my side, the debris—" I gasp, sinking next to the body. Kai glances at me with his wide brown eyes, all traces of his usual ease and warmth erased by this wreck, this night. He places a hand on my arm and I look up at him, all broad shoulders and steady strength. He assesses me with the barest sweep and I know what he'll say.

"Check him over, then lash yourself to the rope."

"But—"

"Take no chances, remember? We can't lose you," he says firmly, before standing to move farther in. "I'll go through the rest of the deck. Don't try to move him."

Before I can argue, he's gone. I bite back my frustration. There's no time to disagree; we have to work as one. And Kai's right. I would make the same call if it was him instead of me. I turn to the body, gripping the sailor's shoulder to heave him over, onto his back. I feel for any wounds, any gashes, and when lightning flashes illuminate the ship, I blink down at him. I'm sure this is the face of someone my age, or just a little older. Brown curls frame wide, unnerving eyes and freckles crowd like constellations over his tanned skin. He's staring right back at me, the whites of his eyes gleaming in the dark. A fleeting spark lights my veins, making my breath hitch. He's striking in a way that isn't quite beautiful, and yet I know that his face, the shape of his eyes and cheekbones, will haunt me. His lips flicker upward, as though he's trying to smile. With that smallest hint of warmth, his features align in a way that is handsome, like this boy was made to be forever laughing and smiling. Then his eyes close, his mouth slackening.

"Are you awake?" I ask as the ship moans ominously. I shake his shoulders, his breath rasping as he fights for air. He must have fallen overboard and pulled himself back onto the ship. "Can you stand?"

He coughs, spitting up seawater as he draws himself onto his side. I lean back on my heels, putting a little distance between us. Watching him.

"I can help you up—"

"Leave me be. I can do it." His voice is husky, burned by the salt in the water. I wonder how long he lay here as the rest of the crew abandoned ship.

"Kai," I call into the dark as the ship lists slowly, sickeningly. "Kai!"

"I'm here," he says, emerging. "Didn't find anyone else."

He takes in the survivor, leaning down to grasp his arm. A frown pinches his face as the boy says something I don't quite catch. Then Kai releases the boy's arm, letting him fall back to the wooden boards.

"What?"

"Leave this one," Kai says, already making his way back toward the rope.

I look at Kai, already lashing himself beside Bryn, then turn back to the survivor. Confusion pools inside me. Why would Kai want to leave him? Is he a threat? The boy is sitting up now, watching me. Waiting to see what I'll do. He blinks once, slowly, and I feel that spark again, flickering in my chest. There's something about him. Something dangerous. But as much as we work as a team, I won't do as Kai says, not without good reason. I won't leave this survivor. There is too much blood on my hands, on *all* our hands already to leave behind someone I could save.

"Lean on my arm," I say to the boy, helping him stand. He's taller than me, all rangy and slim, towering up to stare down at me. He sways, forehead dipping, and I catch him, crying out as the pain in my side twists a little deeper.

"I said to leave him!" Kai calls as I haul him toward the rope. I want to ask him why, but there's no time.

"I can't do that." I find Kai's eyes in the dark, and hold his gaze. "You know I can't."

I lash myself alongside the others, tying the boy one place behind me. The rope bites into my middle as the others converge. Bryn's sharp whistle pierces the storm, twice, short and clear. It's the signal.

It's time to leave.

I turn, checking on the survivor, this boy with freckles so dense they remind me of a winter night. He looks back at me as lightning splits the sky once more. The shape of his face, the depth of his eyes, burn into me and I feel a tug. Something strange, something like the pull of the tide. Like a song that is at once familiar, and yet evades me however hard I listen. I open my mouth to say something, but then the rope drags me forward and I find myself in the water.

The sea is in a frenzy, churning with fury. I lean on the rope, my side on fire, and kick with all I have left. I picture my father scanning the shoreline, hauling the rope that guides us in. Agnes is just ahead, Kai a few places behind her, and as my feet hit the sand, I turn to look for the survivor.

But he's gone.

"Wait!" I shout, turning, searching. "The sailor we found! Kai, where's the survivor?"

The group on the beach stop hauling the rope and I struggle out of it, loosening the knot around my middle. I cast around, but I can't see him. A hand slips over my arm, but I shake it off and dive under. I search and search, raking my hands through the waves, twisting as the current pulls and punches, my heart near bursting with the need, the desperate need to find him—

I surface.

Choking on the air, I no longer feel the tug. As I make my way back to the beach, to my people, I know. The sea kept him. I should be grateful for the wreck, for what we took tonight. But all I see is his face, his freckles, like a map of the starry sky. His eyes, the whites of them. Burning as they locked with mine.

They say we are lawless on Rosevear; that we're not all human, and maybe that's true. But when the storm clouds bloom, casting darkness over our islands, I can hear the song of the sea. The call of the deep, the answering beat in my heart.

They say we are wreckers; that we take and plunder and kill. And maybe we are what they say.

But we call it survival.

CHAPTER
TWO

"MIRA!"

I stumble up the beach, the wind and rain snatching at my skin. The others are still gathered, hauling cargo across the sand. My father finds me, running his eyes over my face, my clothes. Making sure I came back from the wreck safely.

"I still think of her…" he says, so softly I almost don't catch it. I nod, turning away. I love my father fiercely; it's been just me and him for so long. But I can't handle his grief as well as my own. Not tonight.

"We've got a few hours 'til dawn," Bryn says, addressing us all. "Reckon we can haul it all on the carts? Get it stowed before the watch hears of it."

We nod, dividing into groups. Agnes is at my shoulder, wringing the water from her hair. She grins at me, her teeth pearls in the night, and I catch the flash of her green eyes, brimming with relief that it's over. We're safe. I grin back, glad she's unscathed. She's a year older than me, but we're almost a match in height and curves. Her skin reflects the pale moon's glow as mine does, turning tan in the summer. But her hair is the fiery sun as it sets on the water, whereas mine is the color of the wheat that grows in the fields. I am the one that should have been born with hair the color of flame though. And she the sweet, flaxen color of the fields.

"Any survivors?" a voice calls across the beach, lantern swinging from a fist.

Bryn bows his head beside me, scraping in a breath. "Not tonight."

A silent sorrow steals over all of us. We grow still for a moment, searching the sea. Some say we are heartless, that we pillage and murder with purpose, but if we don't fill our bellies, this life will end too swiftly. For us, our people, our children. I wish it wasn't so harsh, but every winter is long and bitter. Hard to fish, harder to trade. The only way to survive is to take what we can from the merchant ships passing through from the mainland ports of Arnhem, down to the shores of Leicena on the continent. I wish it wasn't us or them.

I wish, more than anything, that I had saved that boy on the ship tonight.

Agnes and I work as a pair, loading up the first cart. The cargo is sea swollen and heavy, weeds already gathering at its edges. I pull off the worst of it, shouldering it up onto the boards of the cart. Old Jonie watches us, chewing slowly on the end of her clay pipe. It's unlit, but she's never without it. Her hair snakes around her shoulders, hiding her face.

"This better be worth it," Agnes says, panting as she helps me haul up a crate. We're both shivering, our limbs moving in spasms and bursts as the cold burrows deep into our bones. I was warm in the sea, but it's too wild now to slip back under the waves and feel the blood-hot heat under the surface. "Remember the last haul?"

I nod. It was barrels of salted pilchards, hundreds of them. They only kept us fed for a few months and the watch were on us like rats. Questioning and following us, handing out Wanted posters. We burned them when they weren't looking. Tore them down and used them as kindling. The watch don't know what it's like. They never suffer hunger or spend cold winters hunkered down in old cottages. But they do take bribes, these men from the mainland with their scarlet coats and writs and warrants, holding all the power. They take whatever they can get. Which makes them more dangerous than the sea, in my eyes. They like to steal people in the night and see them swing from their gallows.

When the last cart is loaded, Bryn whistles. Our signal. We melt into the night, leaving no trace of ourselves behind. No footsteps, no cart tracks. They're all washed away by the tide.

Our village on Rosevear is silent and watchful the next morning. The sun peels away from the horizon, bathing the island in a wash of warmth. With spring comes hope, green life, fresh food. But underneath all that is the heaviness of what we have hidden. Our haul, carefully stowed where no prying hands can snatch it. Father is mending the nets, squinting into the sunlight, so I settle beside him, drawing my knees under me, and pull some of the netting into my lap. We work in companionable silence, trading sections of the netting as our people pass to and fro. It's always like this the day after a wreck. Like we're all walking on scorched earth, terrified the watch will descend and start their questioning.

"You looked like her last night," my father says, flashing

me a look. "She had golden hair plaited like you wear it too. In a long rope over her shoulder. You've even got her eyes now. Dark blue. Never seen the like. Well, you know."

I picture her, that old familiar ache pressing on my chest. She had eyes like the ocean, my mother. The deepest blue I'd ever seen. Father's are a light blue, like so many others on Rosevear, but I do not favor him. "I know."

"Sometimes I wish…"

"What?" I say, impatience building beneath my skin. "You wish what?"

"Did you get your side looked at?"

"It's just bruised. It's fine today," I say quickly, frowning down at the nets. Father never goes fishing the day after a storm. He says it's bad luck, that any catch will be cursed. "What do you wish?"

He sets down his net and stares at me. It's the first time he's really looked at me in ages. I know why. I grew up too fast, shed my childhood like a second skin. Now I remind him of all he has lost. All he could still lose if anything were to happen to me. "I wish you weren't like her. Wild. I wish you didn't have the song of the sea in your blood. It's more than the others that go out on that damn rope. Not like Kai or Agnes—or even Bryn. It's different. You… *You're* different."

And there it is. The real thing he's been making his way toward saying. I took her place on the rope when she died. Just as Agnes took her mother's. Both of them were lost in the same storm, the same shipwreck six years ago. Bodies given back the next morning all wrong and broken on the shoreline. I was twelve when I took my place. Agnes was thirteen. We've grown up with the rasping feel of the rope in our hands.

What I don't tell him, what I can't tell him, is that I *live* for it. Even six years on, when Bryn whistles through the village, the signal for a wreck, I come alive. And in the sea when I hit my rhythm, when she folds me into her wild embrace, I am at peace. More than anything, I want to wake with the sea surrounding me. To find a crew and a ship to take me on, and sail away into the iron-gray abyss.

I can't tell him that though. My dream would lead me even deeper into the water—farther from him, my anchor to this island. He would unravel. He would never understand.

"Father, you..." I bite my lip as the worry floods me. I want to reassure him that nothing will happen to me. But I can't give him that. Not when I am one of the seven. "You always said you would give me the key to her chest when I turned eighteen. That was two months ago," I say quietly. It's been calling to me, the sea, like it always does. The song of the waves, the steady slip and tumble of them. But not from the cliff edge. From the wooden chest in my father's bedroom, the one he keeps locked. The one holding all my mother's things, her keepsakes, her notebooks. The song luring me to that chest is sometimes so loud, I wake in the night in a fever.

I tried to pry it open two years ago, breaking my nails on the wood. But it wouldn't budge. "I can't change my nature, but you have to know I wouldn't... I won't leave you. Not like that. I... I just need to know about her. I need to know why she seemed different. Why I'm different."

He works the words around as though they pain him, as though they weigh too heavily on his tongue. "I've changed my mind, Mira. Give it more time."

I laugh bitterly. I've known for a while now that no amount of prodding will make him give up that key. More time will turn into a year or five years and I will still be on Rosevear, waiting for him to be ready. Every time I lash myself to the rope and swim out to a wreck, it feels like he adds an anchor to my shoulders. Weighing me down. Keeping me on this island. And yet I can't shake the feeling that there is more beneath the surface, answers to be found inside that chest. "You can't keep her secrets forever. What's in there? What are you so afraid of?"

"I think you know what I'm afraid of." He gets up, not meeting my eyes.

"Father—" I reach for him, regret and bitterness coiling in my throat. I don't want to hurt him. He's more precious than jewels, the last of my kin. But he just shakes his head, like he always does. My fingers find his jacket, the rough-spun feel of the wool rasping against my skin. He looks down at my hand, his brow knotted, and I think I see a tear forming at the corner of his eye. It's the same look he gave me when he passed me those gloves last night. Like I am his everything, and if he gives me the key to that chest, I could slip away.

"Father…"

He sniffs, shaking me off with a smile that doesn't seem true. "Get along with you. We'll discuss it in a few months."

I nod, knowing it will be the same answer, and swallow down my disappointment. Over his shoulder I catch sight of Agnes, rounding the corner of the next cottage, and I stand, walking to greet her. I try to forget about my mother's chest, about my father's unwillingness to accept who I am. Agnes has heard the fears and frustration spilling from my lips too many times. And today is a good day. The day after a wreck always is, because we are richer than before the storm brought it to us. Her red hair is pulled over her shoulder, freckles drift-

ing like tiny stars across her white cheeks. With a fleeting
jolt, they remind me of the sailor's. The one I couldn't save.

Her mother had blond hair, a few shades lighter than mine;
it's her father she favors. And as she takes my arm now, leaning
her mouth toward my ear, I catch the sweet scent of pound
cake, made from the sugar we plundered a year ago when it
was on its way to Leicena to be spun into whisper-thin tarts
and delicate creations that I've only ever heard tell of. She's
always smelled like this; she sells the bread and cakes her father bakes. Pasties too, when we can get the skirt for the filling. Cows are valued for milk though, so it's rare we butcher
them for their meat.

"Bryn's called a meeting. Let your father know. I'll save
you a seat."

I nod as she winks at me, passing me a bun studded with
apple pieces. "Don't tell."

I grin, and watch as she makes for the next cottage, spreading the word. Her soft singing washes through the silent
morning as I take a bite of the bun, eyeing the row of four
granite cottages huddled together in this part of our village.
The tart apple bursts across my tongue and I quickly hide the
rest before the two boys living in the farthest cottage in our
row can run out and pry it from my hands. I'll pass it to Father later. They are his favorite.

The meeting house is on the other side of the village. It
serves as everything: church, sanctuary, the place we ready
our dead for burial. Our village on the isle of Rosevear isn't
like the isle of Penscalo, where the watch live with their high
walls, glass windows, and imported mainland finery. Penscalo
is like another world. Or at least, it is now the watch have

taken over. On Rosevear, we make do with what the sea gives us. With old weatherworn cottages, slender fields covering layers of harsh granite and months of scratching a living from almost nothing. We hide our stolen bounty.

The sea gives. The sea takes. That's what we say. That's what we believe. But this place, this island, is in our blood, our bones. It's everything. If you cut my veins open, I would bleed all the colors of Rosevear. The delicate pink of sea thrift growing along the cliffs, the pale golden sand, the deep navy of the roaring sea in winter. I would do anything for my island, my people.

Father shoulders his way over to his set, the other fishermen he grew up with. They stand against the side wall, arms crossed under sun-weathered faces. I feel him tracking me, measuring whether I wince whenever someone bumps into my side. Agnes narrows her eyes at another girl a year older than her, Gilly Matthews. Whereas Agnes and I wear breeches and rough white shirts, anything we can move in, swim in, Gilly likes to wear delicate dresses and lace. She twists her hair into curls, pinches her cheeks to make them glow. Sometimes I want to look like her, to care as much as she does about pretty things. But then I remember that I want to look like me. I slip past her, squeezing into the place Agnes kept for me. Gilly rolls her eyes and flounces off, earning us a snigger from Kai on Agnes's other side.

"She'll dump fish heads on your doorstep," he says, dark brown forearms exposed as he leans forward to rest his elbows on his legs. "Gilly never forgets."

"Let her try," I say. "I'm not afraid of Gilly Matthews." When the storm wind blows, I'm not afraid of anyone. There's only one thing that sends fear shivering through me—the thought of losing anyone else. Of finding another body I love on the shore, broken and cold. I glance up, finding Father's eyes still on me. I smile and his frown deepens before he looks away.

I wish... I don't know what I wish. I suppose I wish he would trust me. That this anchor I feel, the weight of his love, wouldn't hold me back so much. I wish he would trust me with my mother's secrets.

Bryn stands at the front, nodding to a few people, patting Old Jonie on the shoulder. He draws his hands behind his back, raising his chin. And as if a spell has been uttered, we fall silent.

"The sea gives," he calls.

"The sea takes," we all call back, holding our fists to our chests.

"And the watch can wait!" a voice shouts from the back, sending a roar of laughter through the room. Bryn holds up a hand, a smile twitching his mouth, and we all fall silent once more.

"The watch has been out on the beach this morn," he says, his voice flecked with gravel. "I know what you're all thinking. That we shouldn't be bothering with them. That the likes of them aren't a scare for us. But they've got rifles now. *Rifles.*"

A muttering sweeps through the room, the heat from all our packed bodies making my cheeks flush. I've heard of the rifles, but never seen a man of the watch with one. I've heard they're long and heavy, that they take time to load and shoot. They're being made on the mainland, somewhere far north of the capital of Highborn, where the wilds are being beaten back to favor the progress the ruling council wish to make. Somewhere in big factories they're building them from the metals they mine and ship over from the other side of the continent. A place called Stanvard. These rifles might be cumbersome, but if a shot catches you, they're deadly. I bite my lip, turning this information over like a copper coin. I'd still like to see the watch try.

"There's a new captain, Captain Spencer Leggan. There's tell that he was in the Far Isles last. Brought them to heel. Made them suffer." A chill creeps over us. We've all heard what happened to the Far Isles, the cluster of islands to the east of here. "The watch say the law is clear. That the ruling council and no one else set the laws of this land. No smuggling. No taking from a wreck. That any bounty belongs to *them*.

"They sit there in that far-off capital, with their tall town houses and their paved streets and carriages, telling us how to live our lives. Sending their men here to stamp on us. But we can outlast them. If we stay strong, stay silent, they won't catch us. Not this time, not ever. Terry, Lish. Bring the first one up," Bryn says, quieting the mutters.

A man and woman sitting on the front bench get to their feet, moving toward the crate Bryn points at. It takes them a good minute to wrestle it to the front, and we're all craning to see. This is what we all came for, to find out what we hauled last night.

Agnes's fingers reach mine and we watch together, barely breathing as Bryn levers it open. I half stand, heart thumping like a rabbit caught in a trap.

And then I can see.

Glass beads.

Hundreds of them. All glistening and beautiful, catching the light through the window. A myriad of shades and colors—greens and silvers and mauves and golds. Glitter, they call these beads. Manufactured like the rifles up in the north, from what we've heard. Sewn into fine gowns, or looped around throats, even hanging like glistening teardrops from the fine merchant ladies' earlobes. A cry runs through the room, quickly followed by whoops and cheers. The flush in my cheeks blazes. All that wealth.

All that beauty.

"You know what this means, Mira? You know what this means?" Agnes says urgently, fingers tugging on mine. I nod. I can't speak. People clap us on the back, hug us, wipe away tears. Because if there's one crate filled with these beads, there's bound to be more. We haven't had a haul like this in a decade, and there could be enough to trade for years. It means more than a full belly. It means freedom. It means choices. And this time, Agnes and I have a stake in it. Most of it belongs to the island, and Bryn as our leader will direct the spending. But we were two of the seven on the rope.

We have a claim.

CHAPTER THREE

WE LEAVE THE MEETING HOUSE AS THE SUN climbs high in the sky. I try to contain it, all my joy, but it bubbles up my throat, spilling over in breathless laughter. That wreck was a blessing, and I can't help but think it was given to us. Offered up, like we deserve it. Like we deserve so much more than aching bellies. We don't celebrate much anymore, but we used to share feast days with the isle of Penrith. They would come over on their skiffs, or we would go to them and share any bounty of the season. We would sing and dance and light a bonfire to warm us long into the night. But we haven't seen the people of Penrith this winter, with precious little to celebrate. I'm so ready to cast off this cold and hunger, to sing our island songs in celebration and eat my fill.

But as Kai wraps an arm around Agnes's shoulders, walking her back to her father's bakery, I feel a tug. That same one I felt when I found the survivor on the ship last night. I know I should follow Agnes and Kai, to sip on the cider we pressed

last winter and swipe a loaf of bread to tear at with my teeth.
But that tug is a tether, leading me away.

Calling me down to the shore.

I follow the path along the cliffs. The breeze pulls at my
hair, sending it flying around my shoulders. The tang of salt
stirs through my chest and I lean into it, wanting to be near
the sea. Wanting to find the end of that tether and whatever
is calling me down to the water.

"Not celebrating with Agnes?" a voice calls behind me. I
stop, turning to find my father coming along the path. He
has his hands in his pockets, stubbornness etched in the lines
of his face. He might be happy about the haul, but he's not
happy that I was involved in finding it. That I risk my life
every time I swim out to a wreck while he watches anxiously
from the shore.

"I'll go over there in a bit. I just want to—"

"Follow in the footsteps of your mother?" he asks, stepping toward me. My throat grows claggy, heart picking up
a faster beat as I stare at him. "You know she always went
back to the sea after they brought in a good haul off a wreck.
She said she didn't, but I knew where she went. Back to the
water, every time. Never to celebrate with us."

A fleeting look passes over him before he blinks it away.
I pull in a breath, wondering how I can reassure him that
I'm not her. That I won't vanish every few months, returning with seaweed tangling my hair like green jewels. I suppose it was never enough for her, this quiet life on Rosevear,
however much she loved us. She always longed for the ocean.

"I only need a moment. A moment alone with my
thoughts," I say gently, holding out my hands. "I won't be
long. I promise."

He nods gruffly, glancing away. We both know what's underneath our words, the undertow threaded through every conversation we have.

"I'll see you this afternoon. Don't be too long alone—the watch will be abroad."

He turns on his heel, shuffling back toward the village. I watch him go, the faded green of his wool jacket blending with the heather. I should go to him. Find his hand and remind him that I am a constant; that I can resist the urge to follow my heart into the ocean. But I don't, *can't*, say any of those things. Because I'm not sure if it would be the truth.

The beach is littered with wreckage. The stripped-bare carcass lies on her side by the rocks farther out, the tide flowing around her. I wince as I catch sight of her side, still spilling wood and debris. In the harsh daylight, she looks like a dying animal. I clutch my shawl tighter, silently calling to the sea to care for those souls. We do not mean to do harm and yet we do. Over and over.

A bitter thread grows inside me, twisting and turning in on itself. I try to shut my mind from it, and most of the time I can. But when that sailor looked up at me last night, his face as old as mine, I couldn't breathe.

The sand is soft as powder and I bend down, scooping some into my fist. It shifts in my fingers, spraying and glittering in the sunlight. I want to swim. Right now. I want that same wild freedom as last night, with the sea surrounding me. But I can't stand Father wondering if he'll lose me one day to the ocean, like we lost her.

I've never felt that bone-deep cold in the water, even in the depths of winter. That's why I was chosen for the rope, I can stand it for far longer than the others. Even as a girl I could swim farther, dive for longer. It was like breathing—I never needed to be taught how. The others were chosen for the rope because they're strong swimmers. Because they know how to handle a blade and how to work as a team. No one ever mentions how different I am, but occasionally I'll catch someone watching me as I wade out of the water.

My mother used to say that like calls to like, and maybe we were both born of the sea. She came here on a ship, a smuggler's drop in the dead of night, and never left. But there were periods when she would be away, when it was my father who'd tuck me in at night and tell me stories of witches and wild creatures, like the ones found in the north of Arnhem where the factories are being built now. He told me that magic comes from the corners of our world and the witches know how to wield it. It's only now that I'm beginning to realize that he didn't know where my mother had gone when he told me these stories of magic, or when she would return. But she always found her way back to us. Back to him.

Now that I'll have my share of the wrecked ship's cargo, I could travel to the mainland of Arnhem and pay for an apprenticeship at one of the port towns. I could join a crew and cut my own path. Find out who I am, away from this tiny island, like she did. The shipping routes go to the continent, circling the vast territories there, even as far as the mines of Stanvard to the east, where the metals are chipped away from the hot earth.

I draw in a breath, picturing the vast world beyond the Fortunate Isles. Beyond the world I know, and have always known. I trace the horizon with a fingertip, imagining the cluster of the Far Isles to the northeast, then farther still to the straits where the merchant ships pass through, hugging the

Spines to the north, Skylan to the south. The wrecked ship
will have come from Skylan. It will have traveled along the
straits from Stanvard, past the Far Isles to anchor at one of the
port towns of Arnhem. The merchants will have emptied,
then refilled the hold before setting a course south, for Leicena. Right past the Fortunate Isles, where we were waiting.

I push the thoughts of my father from my head, allowing
myself a moment to give in to the dream of crewing on one of
those ships. Seeing every corner of the ocean, perhaps even seeing with my own eyes the wild creatures that lurk in the deep.
I've heard tales of the kraken, of sirens and wraiths that lure
sailors and claw out their hearts. It's so close, this dream, I can
wrap my fingers around it. If only it wouldn't end in his broken
heart. If only a rich cargo could buy my mother back for him.

Very few leave Rosevear. In the calling season every ten
years, when Arnhem seek a champion to represent our nation
in The Trials, where they'll compete against the champions
of the other nations from the continent, occasionally someone will travel to Highborn and try out. Sometimes they return, bloodied and battered, and there are tales passed down
through the generations warning us not to answer the call.
Sometimes they don't return at all and our island receives
the news of their passing during tryouts. The calling season
is soon, but no one from Rosevear will answer this time. No
one wants to represent a nation that is trying to stamp us out.

As the sun shifts, hiding its face behind a slow-moving
cloud, I turn back toward the cliffs.

There's a body on the sand.

I freeze. It's turned on its side, its back a curve of spine and
sodden clothes. Between blinks, I find myself and run. Five
steps, ten, twenty and I'm there, kneeling next to it. Blood

beats in my ears, drowning out everything except this body, this person, this moment.

It's him.

I know as soon as I touch his face. I know before I've turned him over. That tether inside me snaps taut, making me shudder. I pull on his shoulder, moving his face up to mine. His eyes are closed. Brown curls sweep his forehead, in direct contrast to the deathly pallor of his skin. His lips hold the near blue tinge of the lifeless. When I run a hand along his jaw, the cold reaches up my wrist. I steel myself for death. For this survivor to die in my arms.

I place my hands on his heart.

There's a flutter, a warming. I bend my face down to his, as close as a lover, and feel the slight huff of his breath on my skin. My hands move to him and I don't hesitate. I bring my lips to his. I breathe, heat filling me as our mouths touch. His lungs expand like wings and I feel his body shift beneath me.

He chokes.

I pull back, throwing myself onto the sand as he convulses, retching a stream of sea from his body. My heart beats so fast, so hot in my chest as I watch him come back to life. He sucks in air, searching around...and he finds me.

I clear my throat, hardly daring to breathe. "Are you...are you all right?"

"It's you," he says, eyes burning into mine. Searing in a way that makes my heart leap in my chest. "It's *you*."

Then he collapses.

I rap on the door of the healer's cottage. Her eyes widen when she sees him, whistling in that close-lipped way we all do. Two men, her brothers, appear, rushing toward me.

"He...a survivor," I gasp as they lift him, carrying him inside. I press my hands into my thighs, doubling over. My lungs are on fire and I breathe and breathe until the ragged rasp in my throat is gone and my heart has slowed.

His body was limp and almost too heavy for me. But I heaved him, the weight bowing my bones, and dragged us both along the sand. It took an age to get him up the cliffs and I was scared I would drop him. But I made it back, stumbling and cursing until I reached the healer's cottage. I straighten out, wipe my forehead and follow them inside. It's only a small room at the front of the cottage and she's got him on her kitchen table. Her brothers are standing near the hearth, watching the boy like he's got evil inside him. I cross straight to him as the healer carefully checks his bones.

"You on the rope last night, Mira?" she asks, pushing a strand of hair from her eyes. They're a piercing, pale blue in the folds of her brown skin. She's older than Father, maybe as old as our village, I don't know. What I do know is that she's not a witch. There's never been any magic on Rosevear, or anyone to wield and shape it, and I think maybe that's our problem. If she was a witch, if *anyone* had magic, maybe we would have prospered. Father used to say in his stories that the covens in Arnhem are generations old, their coffers running deep as the sea. Maybe if there was a coven on Rosevear we wouldn't have to wreck to survive. But Mother never liked the witches. She used to say in her stories that they were full of greed, that they drained magic from the world. So perhaps Rosevear is better off without magic.

"I was," I say, placing my hand over the survivor's protectively. He's still so cold. I flex my fingers around his, wanting him to wake up. And suddenly, strangely, wanting his hand to curve back around mine. We always try to save them, but if they accuse us, or mention the watch, or if we think they know too much...some islanders get suspicious. Just like Kai did aboard the wreck.

"And he was inside the ship? Did you see him?"

I balance a lie on my tongue. But her old eyes see everything and I know I won't get a false tale past her. "He was in the ship. I tried to save him, but he slipped from the rope on the way back."

"So he saw you? Only you?"

"I think so. And Kai."

She nods, satisfied. I look up at her brothers, great hulking men with graying beards and wide-set shoulders. They meet my gaze steadily and it's clear why they stayed. We don't trust the survivors. Not until we know they won't talk or that we're sure they believe us their saviors.

"He'll live?"

"If he stays warm enough, he might," the healer says, pursing her lips. "Jowan, stoke the fire. Ethan, get some more wood in here. He has a fever. We need to sweat it out."

His fingers twitch, suddenly gripping mine, and my stomach flips over. Then his eyes fly open, unfocused and wide. I lean down, hardly daring to breathe, and catch a fever-whisper.

"Don't let them kill me."

I blink up at the healer, and she avoids my gaze. I shift away from his body, reluctantly releasing his hand as she busies herself with her work. She brews a tonic, cradling his head to help him drink it. I lean back against the sideboard, watching as he chokes on some of it, as the healer coaxes him to drink it down. His eyes sharpen, darting over the cottage walls. Taking in the healer, then me, and finally the door in the corner. I shift, placing myself between him and the exit, folding my arms. I want him to live. Now, in daylight, I can take in every inch of him. The way he brushes his tongue across his lips, the slow blink of his wide-set eyes. As he shakes his head, his curls settle back in a new pattern, gleaming in the light from the hearth. My heart flutters, beating against my ribs, and I slowly look away. I need to stay focused. I don't want him getting out before we have the measure of him.

"What's your name?" I ask, the words coming out sharper than I intended.

"Seth." It scrapes from his throat and he coughs, covering his mouth.

"Where are you from, boy?" the healer asks, shooting me a warning look. We can't make them feel like we're interrogating them, but we need to taste the burn of any lies they tell. We need to know if he'll turn on us after he leaves. She pads back to the stove.

He sits up, slowly, like his bones are old and frayed. A near drowning does that to you. "Everywhere." He winces, rubbing a hand in slow circles over his chest. My eyes track the movement and I swallow. "I was born at sea."

"On that ship long?" the healer asks.

"They just took me on. I was part of a different crew before. But the merchant never paid us."

The healer nods, handing him a mug. The scent of broth wafts toward me and my stomach twists. She clucks, ladling me a mugful too, and I cross the kitchen to take it from her. Her eyes soften a fraction as she watches me take the first sip, warm and woodsy with last year's dried herbs. She brought me into the world. She brought most of us into the world:

Kai and Agnes and even my father. Now she's training Gilly Matthews to take her place and I know her hands will never be so gentle and sure. You can't train a heart to be softer.

"You'll want to be getting back," I say, eyeing the boy. He's staring at me too, both of us weighing the other up. I wonder how much of last night he remembers. And whether he remembers my mouth on his at the beach.

He shrugs, wincing again as he sits a little straighter. "I'll need to go to the nearest town. Find a new crew, I guess."

"Is it hard? To get taken on?" The words tumble out before I can stop them.

His gaze rakes slowly over me. Taking in my breeches, the shirt I'm wearing, the wild tangle of my hair. Then up, past the curve of my chest, along my slender throat, to the flush coloring my cheeks. My lips part and I look away, furious with myself for the way my heart is thumping.

He turns back down to his mug of broth, a small smile flickering on his features. "You look strong enough."

"I… No, I mean—" I cut myself off, annoyed that I let the question slip out. That I was even thinking it. A shadow falls across the window, blocking most of the light in the small room and I narrow my eyes. The healer's brothers are running, lumbering toward the cliffs, away from the village. I move quickly to the doorway and a shiver slips down my spine, every piece of me suddenly alert.

"What is it, Mira?" the healer asks, moving to stand beside me.

"I thought—"

A whistle, shrill and long, cuts through my words. I thrust my mug into the healer's hands, rushing outside.

It's the whistle. The one we run for. The one that stirs my blood.

It's Bryn calling us, rallying us.

There's another wreck.

CHAPTER FOUR

MY FEET HIT THE CLIFF EDGE BY THE SECOND whistle. I pound along the stone-strewed path, leaping over the bracken and gorse. The sun marks the time as just past midday, and it's blazing up there in the wide sky today. Bryn's up ahead, Agnes on his heels, and I turn to find Kai gaining on me. He's got a gleam to him, like he's finally found some hope. We all lost it so long ago, it tastes sweeter than berries.

"Second time in two days," he calls, flying through the bracken. I match my pace to his, loving the way my body sings with anticipation.

"Bet you five pound cakes it's gold," I shout over the wind. He laughs and I grin, skidding to a halt by the beach. Quickly, I pull off my boots, wrestle with my socks and leave them at the edge of the path. I don't need them on the beach; the sand is so fine my feet sink into it.

"No talk of gold—we don't want to tempt fate to turn her back," Bryn says, but he's grinning too. He eyes the ship through his spyglass and hands it to me. I balance it against my cheekbone, leaning in to squint through. I can see her, guts already spilling on the rocks. No cargo though. Only swollen wood and sails. I hand it over to Agnes and glance at Bryn. He's got a wary look around the folds of his eyes, but in a blink, it's gone, replaced by a grin. I wonder if I mistook it.

"You heard of this one?"

He shakes his head. Bryn travels to Port Trenn a couple of times a year, the closest port on the mainland where a lot of the merchant ships sail from. It's the only way to hear the murmurings and rumors that we survive on. We learn the watch's movements and tactics from seafarers and smugglers and we trade coin for information on the routes of the merchant vessels. It's also how we hear most of the tales about the wild creatures, the ones with magic coursing through their veins.

"My contacts don't know about all of them though." He slaps my back. "You too jumpy to go on the rope or something?"

I shove his hand away. "You've got to be joking."

"That's what I like to hear."

More people arrive from the village and I turn to him, wanting to tell him about Seth. But Bryn's already walking away, organizing people into groups, moving among the old and the young, bolstering them, setting a feverish tone. It'll keep for later, after we bring in our haul and find any survivors we can. I warm myself with the knowledge that we didn't lure this ship in. It came to us, so if we swim out, we are only doing good. And if we keep hold of their cargo, well…it's only right and fair, despite the watch and the laws of Arnhem saying otherwise.

The rope is unfurled, carried down the beach, and I join the throng hauling it to the ocean's edge. It's still wet from last night, heavy with salt and seaweed, and the twisted strands cut into my palms as I drag it. The ship is farther out than the one last night and smaller. She's more of a schooner, run aground on Hangman's Rock. I frown. We all know about Hangman's; it's how it got its name. Too many ships run aground on her, so it was added to every map, every merchant captain briefed. It's one of the few half-hidden rocks that's well-documented.

Who has been foolish enough to run *this* ship aground?

"Are we ready?" Bryn calls.

I shove my worries aside, tying myself to the rope with Agnes in front of me and Kai at my back. I draw in a breath and relax my shoulders. There's still something about this ship that needles me. I'm becoming like my father, a worrier. I can't allow that to become a trademark of our family name.

Bryn whistles and we're off. As the sea slaps my skin, all I feel is warmth. Like the sun has sunk down into her, warming her through in the night. I cling to the rope and as the tide rises up above me, I leap.

We keep a rhythm, swimming as one toward the wreck. The sea is restless today; it jostles and pulls at us. I feel her tugging at my chest, my legs. As the distance widens between us and the shore, I can't help but feel it's a warning, as though the sea is trying to hold us back. I shake the salt from my eyes, finding my feet as Bryn hauls himself up onto the deck of the ship. The wood is splintered and old, but the hole in her side is clean. I make my way to the cabin door that leads below, checking for survivors. But there's no sign of anyone, or any cargo. Running a hand along the inside of the hull, sniffing

the scent of old wood and mildew that's been too long in salt
water, I frown. She's too old and bloated to carry passengers;
this is scrap floating. I can feel the ghost of her. She's like the
ships in Father's stories, the ones that sail through the mist,
unmanned and full of ill omens.

This doesn't feel right.

"She's empty," Bryn says from the cabin door above my
head. Agnes crouches beside me, taking my hand. She's shivering and it's not from the ocean. I purse my lips, the disquiet
in my heart rattling too loud to ignore. We go back on deck,
joining the others.

"This wreck is no accident," Kai spits, rubbing the sea from
his face. "No sailors, no bodies or cargo, but full sails. It's as
if she's been guided by ghosts." His eyes dart everywhere,
then back to the shore. I release Agnes's hand from mine and
turn to look at the beach. We're all thinking it. Although we
don't have magic on Rosevear, we've heard of the spells the
witches cast, the potions the apothecaries sell in their shops.

The curses you can buy for the right price.

"She's a ghost ship," Bryn says softly.

I scan the shore. There are our people, scattered, watchful.
But coming toward them—

"The watch," I breathe.

Bryn lunges for the rope and we all scramble after him. It
falls loose in the sea and I watch in horror as the men holding it on the beach drop in slow motion. A shot pierces the
air, cracking like a whip.

"Rifles." Not bothering to tie myself to the rope, I leap,
heart bursting with fear, and push my body through the water.
The world turns soft, just me in the vast expanse of ocean,
bubbles fleeing my lips.

My father.

He was holding the other end of the rope on the beach.

It takes three minutes to reach the sand. It takes three hours. As I fight against the current, whipping through the tide, all I can see is his face. He can't be one of the men that fell. He can't be.

I reach the shore, wringing the water from my hair. Smoke shrouds the beach, panic erupting in pockets, screams and shouts punching the air. I start for the bodies, but none of them are him. There are three fallen, two with wounds in their legs and screams in their throats as others drag them toward the rocks to hide. One, a woman, lies in a sickening arc of blood, unmoving. He's not here.

The watch are swarming the beach, islanders abandoning carts to pick their way back up the cliffs to safety. Bryn hits the sand beside me, shoving me to follow them. But I can't. Not without my father. As the red coats of the watch trickle down the sand like blood, I run toward them. Everyone else scatters, the others who swim out on the rope hiding from the watch and the rifles. But I have to find him.

"Father!" I scream, searching for him, raking the beach left and right. "Father!"

More shots crack open the sky and I drop to the sand, pulling my hands over my head. I still, my breath coming in panicked bursts. Is he dead? Where is he? Did he escape?

Then I hear him.

A voice, calling me. Warning me. I rise, spinning, searching.

I see him and my heart cracks. The watch have him. They have him and Bryn, hands pulled behind them, clapped in irons. I swear, already moving toward them. There are so

many, so many of the watch with their red coats and rifles, their grim, blood-thirsting faces. I count at least fifteen,
most of them standing around my father and Bryn, some still
searching the beach with rifles balanced against their chests.

I crouch down, grabbing a rock from the sand. I can free
them. I can fight.

"No!"

A body barrels into me and I hit the sand again, landing
hard on my bad side. I cough, raising the rock, ready to pummel whoever stopped me. But it's Agnes. Her hair smothers
my mouth, my nose, as she pins me to the sand. Grips my
wrists, whispering urgently.

All I see is red.

"Let me up! They're going to take them. They're going
to—"

"Stop! There's nothing you can do, Mira."

"My father. They've got my *father*!" I lunge to the side,
but she's too quick. She slaps me and I turn dizzy, reeling
with shock.

"*No,*" she says fiercely, bracing her body against mine.
"They haven't seen us. Stay down. I won't lose you as well."

I release a desperate sob as the men of the watch push my
father across the beach. They do the same with Bryn, shoving them hard with their rifles, making them stumble and
trip over the dunes.

Then one of the watch steps forward. It's the new captain
we've heard tell of, Captain Spencer Leggan. He's got his
hands behind his back, his nose cutting the air as he peers
around the beach. He raises a hand and the men of the watch
fall silent and still. None of us hidden behind the rocks dare
to breathe.

"My predecessor tolerated you, people of Rosevear. Even seemed to have a certain fondness…" His lip curls as he flicks his hair from his eyes. "You will find things very different now. I won't tolerate wrecking. Or smuggling. You will learn that none of you, *none of you*, are above the law of this land. The laws the ruling council sets. And to let this message settle in…" He takes another step forward and my blood turns cold. His eyes rake the beach, as though he can see through the plumes of rifle smoke, through the rocks we hide behind. "I will take your leader. And I will take the man holding the rope on the beach. And if I find those of you who swim out to the wrecks, you'll join them in the hanging square."

My father splutters, suddenly struggling against his captors, his eyes searching for mine across the expanse of sand and smoke. Then a rifle butt comes down hard on his shoulder. Blood-hot hate simmers in my chest. I take in every inch of this watch captain. The way he holds himself, the sneer plastered across his clean-shaven face. His straw-colored hair, the way his chest rises and falls. My rage rattles against my ribs, choking me.

No, no, no, no…

"Be smart, Mira," Agnes whispers urgently. "The watch *want* you to run after them. They want to see our faces, know who the seven of us are. Don't give in."

"They'll hang them. *He'll hang,*" I gasp as the watch shove Father and Bryn off the beach. The rest of the men and the captain follow, scarlet coats trailing away, leaving the few of us still huddled on the sand to stare after them.

Agnes releases her grip on me, rolling onto her back. I sit up, wincing as pain shoots along my side. It's still tender there from last night. But I have to move.

I have to go after them.

"Mira, *think*!" Agnes yells as I stumble up the sand. Kai appears, grabbing for my wrist but I shake him off, baring my teeth.

"What if it was your kin?" I shout over my shoulder, sniffing. "Would you hide and do nothing?"

"I would make a plan! I wouldn't just rush in holding a rock. What are you going to do, Mira? They've got rifles!"

I slow, the fire in my blood cooling to ice. The rock, smooth and dark in my fist, falls away. I take a breath and close my eyes.

I want to scream.

"Come back with us. They won't do anything straightaway. You know how this goes." Kai's firm hand falls on my shoulder. I look up into his solemn eyes, the troubled pinch of his mouth. I bow my head as a sob escapes my chest. His arms, warm and wide, close around me and I lean into his chest. My tears mingle with the salt from the sea, still clinging to his clothes as all my fire, all my fury drains away.

Leaving nothing behind but fear.

CHAPTER
FIVE

I CLOSE MY FINGERS AROUND THE MINIATURE. IT'S oval shaped, silver framed with a tiny portrait that is smudged by age and tide. One of Agnes's treasures. I release it, running my hand over a peacock feather, a broken piece of crystal. Her room is covered with things she's found in the sea, the things from wrecks we cannot sell or trade for fear the watch will take us. She's a magpie, feverish with delight every time she finds something new. Every item whispers a story, holding memories of lives that are lost now.

Holding memories of every time we've swum out on the rope together.

I picture my father, how he has stood at the shoreline in every storm, clinging to the end of the rope, waiting for me to return. A shudder creeps along the back of my neck and I step away. I've never kept a single thing I've found from a wreck. Agnes delights in tokens from beyond our island home, the small windows into the wider world. But I need more than a window, a glimpse. I need a door. A way to get out there, to see it all for myself. And these found objects remind me of that bitter swirl of longing. The frustration I feel toward my father for anchoring me here, then the inevitable guilt for not being a better daughter. If I surrounded myself with these treasures, they would shout too loudly.

I would never find peace.

"If we sell all the beads, maybe we'll have enough coin to bribe the watch into letting them go?"

I turn to Agnes, who is holding a steaming mug out to me, and take it, the scent of tea pluming around my face. The warmth stirs a little life into my fingers.

"If we sell the beads, they'll have all the evidence they need," I say. "It's too risky for whoever goes to Port Trenn to trade. All that glitter... Someone will link it to the merchant ship, then to us."

"Not necessarily. Bryn's contacts—"

"Were probably the ones who betrayed him. Betrayed *all* of us."

We can't allow anyone to go and trade those beads. The watch will be monitoring every island, and might even be searching ports on the mainland, like Port Trenn, for evidence to damn my father and Bryn with. They have us well and truly by the throat this time. And we walked into their trap like the greenest of them all.

Agnes sips from her mug, slipping into a chair in the corner. I blow the steam from my own tea, drinking it slowly. She likes to add lavender when it's in season; I can taste it in the milky swirl. I close my eyes, savoring the normality of it, the ordinary nature of this moment. Because I know that every moment after this will lead me away from Agnes, away from her mugs of lavender tea and her safe world of treasures. I'm ashamed to admit that I wanted it, this parting. But not this way. Not with my home hollowed out in my wake as I say goodbye.

But I cannot rest until my father and Bryn are free and safe. Even if it means that I must bang on every door in Penscalo, bribe every member of the watch until I get an audience with the captain and persuade him to free them.

"First things first. I will travel to Penscalo. I have to make the captain of the watch see me. Bargain with him, find some way to…"

Agnes's face cuts me off midsentence. The sadness, the *pity* crowding her features makes my breath catch.

"You believe there's no hope? That he won't grant me a hearing."

"I… I'm not sure he would see you. No captain of the watch has ever agreed to meet with us before, not for anything. I don't want to give in, but…when it comes to the watch, is there any hope? Kai's sure they're going to make an example of them. That they've been waiting to catch us on the beach. You saw the way that new captain was, how he spoke to us. I'm afraid he means to do what he did to those in the Far Isles. Remember what that sailor told us of them?" Agnes bows her head, voice catching. Her knuckles gleam white as she holds her mug.

"I remember."

The Far Isles were lawless once. Free. Much like our isles. But then the watch arrived and started issuing arrest warrants, putting up Wanted posters. There was no more wrecking or smuggling. And half of those islanders starved by the next winter.

"And that was *this* captain. Captain Leggan." I swallow, the fight I have clung to since the beach cooling, leaving only weariness behind. "What can I do? What can any of us do to free them both?"

I wanted independence, to carve my own path, but not like this. I wanted to be free to make my own choices and not be tethered to the Fortunate Isles. But I never sought it at the end of the noose. Or at best, at the mercy of the watch.

Captain Leggan didn't look much older than me and Agnes. Which means he's ruthless. It's the only way he could have risen through the ranks so quickly—he is not afraid of spilling blood and trampling people with his boots. I'm sure that Agnes is right, that he wants to make a name for himself here, just like in the Far Isles. At the expense of *my* people, *my* island. I raise my chin, staring out the window at the wide sea and sky. The mysteries just beyond my fingertips. So close, yet just out of reach, always. But I won't give in to a bully. I will find a way.

I will not see my father hang.

The door rocks open and I step back. Kai walks in, his shoulders so broad they almost graze each side of the door frame. He runs a hand over his close-cropped black hair as he looks at me then Agnes, still sitting in her chair. There is an unspoken weight in the room as Kai crosses his arms, focusing on me. He's a boatbuilder, but he also builds the coffins. Just like his father and uncle before him. He and his brother craft our pilot boats, the gigs we use to cross to Penscalo and Port Trenn for supplies, but the coffins are what he pours his heart into. He says it's a mark of respect, his way of saying goodbye. Each one is carved with roses or vines, waves or rocks. Whatever he feels depicts the person best, so they are wearing their soul in every inch of the wood as they are lowered into the earth.

I picture what details he will whittle into my father's coffin. Whether it will mirror my mother's with frothing waves and stars, or if it will feature the sea thrift that grows on the island's cliffs in spring, the sun that warms the front step of our cottage, where he sits to mend his nets. I bring my fist up to my heart as sorrow threatens to overwhelm me.

"It's not time yet," Kai says quietly, as if he's reading my thoughts, eyes burning into mine. "It isn't his time."

I nod, willing myself not to cry. "Thank you."

He sighs, uncrossing his arms to run a hand over the back of his neck. "There is something though. The survivor, he's asking for you. Saying he wants to leave."

I blink, realizing I had forgotten about him. It's approaching dusk, and the long day settles over me. "Can't someone take him to Penscalo at first light?"

Kai shrugs. "He won't speak to anyone else. And we need to make sure he only remembers what we want him to remember before we send him off."

"I know. I just forgot..." I run a hand over my face. "I'll deal with him."

"Be careful. I would bet my entire claim on that catch of beads that he's no sailor. You know when we found him? He said something. He said he had friends who would know where he was if we left him there. Friends who would come for him."

I pinch my lips together, twisting my hair over a shoulder. Only a few hours ago, this would have rattled all of us enough to call a meeting about what to do with him. But now that Bryn is gone there's no one to call a meet. No one to draw us all together. Kai is his second, but this matter is minor compared to Bryn and my father being taken.

"Probably an empty threat so we would rescue him. But I hear you. I'll tread carefully."

With the image of my father's coffin firmly planted like a nettle in the grass, I shift my feet, making my way from the room. Something catches my eye, one of Agnes's treasures. It's a notebook, frayed and worn, half the pages detached from the binding. It's as big as my palm, the ink almost washed away, barely legible. But it reminds me of something. And of someone. I bring my fingertips to it, tracing the pattern of an anchor, the compass points north, south, east, and west woven around it. It's a nautical guide, the kind sailors keep to track coordinates on their journey. My breath hitches, remembering a notebook just like this held in my mother's hands. I curl my fingers into a fist.

Her chest.

"I… I'll go and speak to the survivor in a bit. I just have to do something first…" I leave Kai and Agnes to their whispers, and set off at a run for our cottage. With Father gone, I can find the key. I hope more than anything that he didn't have it with him when he was taken.

My father's room is neat, as always. His bed sits under the window, his things in a simple set of drawers. And her chest rests at the foot of the bed, its curved lid carved with waves and stars. I swallow, throat growing thick as I run a hand over it. It reminds me of her coffin.

I have a reoccurring dream, where I am flying. Flying through the night, a hand gripped in mine. I know I am safe, that I trust the person whose hand I hold. And flying like that, through a vast ocean of night, is intoxicating. I told her

about my dream once, before she died. She said that she would
carve stars into this chest, so whenever I looked at it, whenever I saw the stars, I would remember the dream of flying.

I move away from the chest, swallowing down the lump in
my throat, searching his room for the key. It's not in the places
I've searched many times before, the pots he keeps tobacco
in, the drawers where his clothes are folded with dried lavender tucked in to keep them fresh. But I recheck them just in
case. I wander into the main room of our cottage, checking
the inside of the fireplace in case the key is tucked in a hidden groove. I rifle through the pots in our kitchen, tapping
floorboards for hollow places under my feet. I could never do
this when he was here for fear he might discover me looking.
The last thing I wanted was an argument to flare between us.

"It's not here. It's not here…" I whisper over and over,
upending chairs, feeling the lining in the curtains for any
bunching. I know he will have been clever with his hiding
place. Either it's not in the cottage at all or it's somewhere so
obvious that I could pass by it every day…

My thoughts snap back to his bedroom. To the bed, the
sheets I strip on wash day and the blanket I air out in the sun
during summer. And I wonder if he keeps it close to where
he sleeps.

I say a silent apology, then lift the blankets on his bed, running a hand over the slats. Then I check the headboard, but
still nothing. It's only when I grow desperate, pushing back
the bed itself, that I see it. A floorboard, its corner slightly
worn. As though the perfect shape to slip a finger inside. I
pull back the floorboard, heart hammering as I check the
small space beneath. It's a dark hollow, seemingly empty,
but I run my hand around it to be sure. My fingers catch on

something, something cold. Metallic. I close my hand over it, barely breathing, and pull it out. My heart thumps in jagged leaps, pulsing in my ears as I hold the key. It's small with a copper sheen, and I've only seen it once. When my father locked the chest the day after the funeral.

The chest opens with a faint click, the hinges creaking as I lift the lid. I lean close to find at last what's been hidden from me all these years. Her clothes are folded neatly on the left. The shirts she wore, the dark jacket that we would both cuddle under in front of the fire on cold nights. I pick up one of the shirts, the simple spun fabric scratching against my fingertips. It's worn in places, mended with careful, tiny stitches. I remember her sitting by the light of a candle, the mending pile in her lap. The way her smile caught the light as she laughed at something my father said.

I draw in a shaky breath, shifting the clothes aside to see what's underneath. I unroll a tube of parchment and find a portrait of her. It's drawn with charcoal, simple sweeps of gray and black capturing her likeness. She's staring at the artist, fearlessness gleaming in her eyes. We don't have any pictures of her in the cottage. It's been so long since I last saw her, I'd forgotten the way her hair fell across her cheekbones. The way her eyes glittered when she was happy. A small tear rolls down my cheek and I wipe it away, blinking back the memories.

Then I draw out a dagger. It's a sharp, spiny thing, so unlike any we use for fishing on Rosevear. I hold it up to the thin light coming through the window, its jagged sides glinting silver. I don't remember her carrying a weapon. The covering has a stain blooming across it, the color of rust. Or old blood. The back of my neck prickles, cold flushing through me. I hastily wrap it back up, wondering what she used it for.

Wondering why she needed something so deadly when my father has knives if we need to defend our island. Why it was hidden away in a bloodstained wrap.

The rest of the chest is filled with her notebooks. Some are wide, covered in sketches of the island, or of me and Father and the sea thrift. There are pictures of the wild creatures she and Father used to tell stories about: narwhals and pixies and wyverns with their pointed fangs and bat-like wings.

I reach for another notebook. It's small, filled with her precise handwriting, dates and thoughts and accounts of her days. I flip through, losing myself in her world. In a time I thought was permanently shut off from me.

The song that has haunted me for six long years prickles beneath my skin. Luring me toward one of the notebooks in particular. I fish it out, the leather cover warm in my hands as I turn the pages. It's almost empty. But when I skim to the last page, the song only I can hear suddenly stops. I am bathed in a sweet, hollow silence as I stare at the image on the page. It's one of her illustrations, an eight-pointed star with numbers woven around it. And there, underneath in a flowing script is my name.

Mira.

My whole body trembles. This is what was calling me. This illustration. Almost as though my mother was begging me to find it. But I don't know why. I don't know what the numbers mean, or why it would call to me so insistently. I run my fingers over them, trying to slot them into my memories in a way that will reveal what they are. Dates? Is she marking the passage of time in some strange way? I keep my fingers on the ink, imagining a connection between us that bridges the last few years. As though this ink is fresh and she isn't really gone.

My mother was taken by the ocean in the depths of winter. It never snows here—the air is too briny, so it won't settle on our shores. Except on that day. On that day, the snow thickened to a blizzard, coating our island like a blanket, freezing what little was left in our stores, spreading glitter and white over everything and everyone. Including the ship we knew was traveling past.

Bryn set the fires one by one to lure the ship toward the ragged stone teeth waiting just beneath the waves. We could barely see past the first circle of rocks, but still we huddled on the beach, frost gathering in our hair and along the folds of our cloaks. When the whistle pierced the night, my father begged her not to swim out with the others. But she had a flame in her eyes that had smoldered for too long. She craved the ocean in a way that he could never understand. And so she bound herself to the rope as one of the seven, and I watched with my father from the shoreline.

Only three made it back.

Only three, and they whispered of ghosts. Of a ship that wasn't really there, of red eyes in the water. Hunting them. That's when I learned that the sea could be murderous. That she could turn on us.

I refused to allow the sea to have her without a fight. I ripped free of my father's grip and dove into the water. The sea was a balm under the waves, the water too calm. Too merciful to be cruel. I swam out, farther and farther, raking the seabed. I saw red in the ocean. Even now, I'm not sure if it was hair or eyes or blood. But I saw a scarlet trail, a glimmer at the edges. And I followed it, screaming her name.

When minutes turned to hours, I returned to the shore without her. My father held me so tightly and, in that moment, I knew what it was to love so much it could suffocate.

My father broke that day and I found the only way to mend him was to promise to never leave. To tamp down the embers in my chest that flared and blazed whenever I swam in the sea's inky depths. I have tried so hard to do that—to stop longing to sail away and forever be surrounded by the water. To not break his heart as she did. He told me once that the scent of snow still haunts his dreams.

But I've never told him my secret. That the scent of the ocean fills mine.

CHAPTER
SIX

AS THE SUN CLIMBS THROUGH THE CLOUDS THE next morning, a single sheet of printed paper is passed from hand to hand. The ink is smudged at the edges by all our overeager thumbs and fingers, wanting to hold it, to read it. To see if it can really be true. A single tear escapes Old Jonie's beady left eye and she brushes it away, glancing at me. They're all looking at me, stealing furtive little glances. As if to check I'm still here, still breathing. Not yet unraveling under the weight of the piece of paper.

"Nine days," the healer says, stepping up to the front.

She spits on the floor and it's so out of character, so full of anger, that it jolts me. I've been drifting through this meeting as though caught in an undertow. Unable to take any of it in. But now I hold my hand out for the paper. I have to let the words sink into me, to let the ink travel through my veins until it reaches my heart. Maybe then I will feel the same anger as the healer. Maybe then I'll feel anything at all.

"We can't leave them!" shouts Kai and there's a rumble of agreement. "If we leave them in that prison to await the trial, they won't be fed. They'll starve."

"But the bail... Look at the coin they ask of us."

"...a trap, all along."

"They wanted to make an example of us. Well, damn it—"

"Stop." My voice comes out stronger than I intended. "Just stop! All of you." I stand up, still holding the paper in my hand, and face the rows of eyes, all hollowed out, all brimming with fear. I swallow, wondering if mine look the same. "Even if we trade all the beads, the entire catch, it still won't be enough to grant them both bail *and* buy their freedom. And the watch will expect that. They're baiting us. They're waiting for us to make that mistake."

Silence smothers the meeting room. No one interjects, not even father's set standing along the back wall. In this room full of people and opinions and loud voices, it scares me more than anything else that none of them have a single word to utter. Like all our hope has already died.

"We can't make the bail. They know that." I take a breath. "They mean to break us. To stop us wrecking. To bring us to heel and look away as we starve."

A few mutters pepper the silence, eddying like a current.

"Which means one of the seven must go and offer ourselves up as a trade for them." I close my eyes for a beat. "*I* must go."

The meeting room erupts.

Shouts of "*no*" intermingle with calls for Bryn's release. People break off into huddled groups, discussing who is most valuable to us. Whether it's me, one of the seven; or my father, a fisherman; or Bryn, our leader. Agnes's fingernails dig into my hand as she tugs me back down. I sink into my seat, my whole body trembling. None of this feels right.

"How could you," she whispers fiercely, "how could you even *mention* taking their place?"

I grip her hand right back, turning my face into the halo of her red hair. I'm trying to be strong, trying to push away everything I am, the fear pumping through me. I breathe through it, telling myself not to be scared for my own skin. Berating myself for even thinking that. How can I be afraid to take their place when it's my own father's neck on the line? I grit my teeth as the shouts around us become angrier still, people shoving each other's shoulders, flecks of spit frothing at the corners of their lips. The scent of desperation is thick as fog.

"It wouldn't work anyway," Kai says, cutting through the squalls of conversation. "They'll just take Mira alongside Bryn and her father. As soon as this captain knows she's a wrecker, that'll be it. A third for the noose."

The murmurs of agreement grate inside my skull. I sniff, realizing how very hopeless my plan was.

"I need air," I whisper in Agnes's ear and wait until she releases my hand. She closes her eyes, creases forming on her eyelids as she pinches them tight together. Kai wraps an arm around her, nodding to me. His gaze threads through mine, hard as stone. Hard as the chisel and hammer he works with on his coffins. He can see what will happen as I can. If they hang, the watch will win. And it will break our island apart.

I sip the quiet air outside and tilt my face up to the sun, the heat warming my skin. But their voices, their fear, follow me as I walk through the village. I can't shake it off. Each opinion whirls through my mind, pulling me this way and that until

I have to stop. I was so sure when I stood up, so convinced of my plan. But what if the watch want more than my blood? Or what if they don't want it at all?

I begin to run.

I match the pounding in my head with each fall of my footsteps until the village, the voices, all fall away. My feet carry me to the only place I feel peace. I scramble down the dunes, the sand giving way beneath me, the pale green marram grass scratching at my legs. I pull off my boots, my socks, then my shirt and breeches. I don't stop running until the first wave hits my chest.

I close my eyes and let go.

The waves part as I move through them, allowing me deeper and deeper. She's so calm now, this ocean, and I wonder how she knows that I needed this. For her to embrace me and let me through. I find my way to a current, snaking through the hidden path of rocks, and tread water gently. I dive down to the silence of the seabed, running my fingers through fronds of seaweed. My heart quietens. The silence here is heavy and ancient, as old as the water that carved its way into the land. It soothes me, slowing my mind until I can think clearly. I close my fist around the grains of sand, letting it scatter all around me as I release it.

The world down here is watchful. As though waiting for me to make my decision. I kick off from the ocean floor, striking like an arrow. As I emerge—the tang of sea and salt clinging to my skin—I am myself again.

Then I hear it.

The song, *her* song, wends its way through my veins, guiding me back to shore. It echoes inside me, sorrowful and calm, and I remember the first time she sang it to me. It was

underwater and we were swimming on a bright June day. I
fell in love with the ocean, with the ripple of her voice. She
never sang with my father, or the other islanders. Only with
me, underwater in the muffled, perfect quiet. I followed her
voice then, and I'll follow it now.

When my feet hit the beach, I know what I must do.

I empty my pockets, then press my finger into the last page
of the notebook. Breathing softly, I whisper the numbers
folded around the eight-pointed star. It's so simple, so obvious, I don't know how I didn't realize it before.

They are map coordinates.

Even now, my mother is reaching a hand back to me across
the years that divide us and showing me where I need to go.
When I am lost, she is giving me a path to follow.

I dress quickly, pulling my hair into a hasty plait over my
shoulder. Mother always said that if I needed her, if I was
ever in trouble, to listen for the sound of her voice. To follow
her song, and there I would find her. I know she is dead, her
body long cold in the ground, but her song still calls to me.
And I need her more than ever. My father needs her. I take
a breath, walking back toward the village.

Before I knock, I tuck the notebook back in my pocket. I
can't risk anyone knowing about this and taking it from me
before I can find my own way.

When I enter the healer's cottage, Seth, the survivor, is sitting up, tearing into a hunk of bread with his fingers. He's
next to the fireplace, the wood spitting and glowing purple
from the salt on the logs. The healer is sitting in the corner
of the room, scarcely moving. I move toward Seth and she
rises and steps out of the cottage, eyeing me with that same
pity as Old Jonie did. I close my eyes briefly, wishing I could

wind back time. Wishing I had trusted my instincts on the beach and persuaded Bryn to hold off swimming out to that old schooner. How different this day would have been.

"Your fever's broke then?"

He's wearing the clothes I found him in on the beach: I can see the collar poking out from underneath the blanket, the trousers as he moves his legs. But they are no longer salt stained and torn. The healer or one of her brothers must have mended and washed them for him. They obviously don't believe he's a threat and I wonder if he's spun a lie, or if it's true.

He clears his throat and rests his hands next to his meal, giving me his full attention. I hesitate, noticing the way he's sitting in the chair, commanding and yet totally at ease. I pull my shoulders back, forcing myself to focus on what I have come here for. Not his mouth, nor the way his shirt pulls taut over his lean frame.

He smiles at me knowingly, as though I am a book he can easily read. And despite myself, a flush blooms over my skin. "Only thanks to your healer. And you, of course, for finding me."

I sit on the chair opposite him, holding my hands out to the hearth. I can't be distracted. "How are you planning on getting off Rosevear?"

He shrugs and in my peripheral vision I catch his face twisting. "I was hoping you would help me. Or someone would lend me a boat."

"It's interesting, you know, how the watch knew of the wreck. Or at least, suspected. Does that seem interesting to you?" I turn to him, wanting to see the way he absorbs what I have said. If there is any change in the way he holds himself. I find myself leaning forward, as if drawn to him, to the

way he shifts his head to the side, the light of the fire casting his features half in shadow, half in light. And I notice his
confidence slip slightly.

"The watch? I wouldn't— I know nothing of the watch."

I settle back in my chair, watching him choose his words.
The healer might trust him enough to care for him, but I
need to be sure myself before I ask for his help. The way he
seems to make my heart beat a little faster means I cannot
trust my own judgment, not the way I usually can. I have to
lure the truth out of him.

He frowns. "We don't tangle with the watch. Only leads
to trouble."

"Which merchant ship did you say you were with, again?"

"Fair Maiden," he says, leveling his gaze. "Before that,
Golden Hind."

I nod, satisfied. I've heard of the *Golden Hind* from Bryn's
dealings. It's a merchant ship that sails from a mainland port
farther up the Arnhem coastline. At least in this, Seth is telling the truth, I think. "How are you with navigating? Could
you get me to Port Trenn in a skiff?"

"Better to go to Ennor if you're looking for a smoother
journey. Rough seas between here and Port Trenn."

A smile twitches my lips. He knows the waters at least.
Bryn is the only person on our island with enough experience
to guide one of our boats to Port Trenn and back. My father
and his set fish to the southeast. There's no one but Bryn I
would trust to navigate us to Port Trenn safely.

"You can get to the Isle of Ennor?" I don't know it as well.
Bryn avoids it, talking us all around in the meet if we ever
suggest trading there. There are rumors about Ennor, stories
passed along from sailor to barkeep to fisherfolk. They say

that the island is owned by someone dangerous; someone who controls half the seas from here to the Far Isles and beyond with his crews. There have been whispers of magic, a kind not created by witches, or found in the wild corners. We've heard tell that the owner is as dangerous as Captain Renshaw, with crews of smugglers and worse. Even the watch avoid Ennor, which should make it a draw for islanders like us. But if Bryn is wary, I should be too. Except now I don't have a choice.

"I can get there, yes." He sniffs, his confidence seeming to return as he considers me. "I'll need the stars to guide me, but I can find a new crew to take me on there. If you give me a boat, I'll be away."

"I need to get there."

His gaze sharpens and he leans forward, most likely realizing I haven't mentioned Penscalo and nor has he. Neither of us wants to travel to the isle where the watch are based. His voice pitches low, so low it sends a curling whisper along the back of my neck. "Trouble with the watch?"

"Nothing you need to know about," I counter, gritting my teeth. "One night's navigation for passage off the island. What do you say?"

He smiles for the first time. It's more fox than boy, his cheekbones stretching wide, exposing a wicked grin which is at once warm and unsettling. "They took someone, the watch, didn't they? And now you're trying to find a way to save them."

I say nothing.

"Got something to trade, have you? Maybe something from the cargo? I heard some of the sailors whispering about a catch of glitter. Glass beads if they're cut just right capture the light, you know? I heard there are fancy folk over on the mainland going wild for them. As precious as gems to the right buyer. I heard even the ruling council want them."

I hiss, standing abruptly, not wanting to talk about this with him. If he knows about the glitter…he knows too much.

"Fine, fine. No more questions. I'll navigate," he says, holding up his hands. "I'll get us to Ennor, and you can keep your secrets."

"Deal," I say, turning back to him. His features have settled back into a knowing smile. I cross my arms, narrowing my eyes. "Midnight. Be ready. Tell no one."

My hand is on the door handle when he speaks again, his voice velvety soft and treacherous. "You don't belong here, do you? It's not about the watch. I can feel it—you're different to the rest of them. Were you born here? Were your parents?"

I hesitate, nearly turning back. Nearly trusting this stranger with a piece of my heart. He has found the crack inside me, the fissure that will never smooth. That I don't belong here. That this island was never meant to be my end and my beginning.

People are brittle. We break and we fall apart, our edges flaking away until we're perfect copies of one another. All except me. Why can't I fall in like I'm supposed to? Why do I feel like I don't fit, like I don't belong with my feet planted here? The sea calls me. And this boy, this survivor from the wreck, sounds like a poet. There's something about the way he talks. It's all woven and pretty, like he's reading lines. It leaves a bitterness in all the honey at the back of my throat. As though there are lies woven through all that pretty. And I can taste them every time he speaks.

"Tell me. Maybe I can help you."

My hand tightens around the handle, wanting to share that

nagging feeling with this stranger, that I don't quite belong. That I'm different, even from the other six that swim out on the rope. That my mother held too many secrets and maybe I've been lying to myself all along that I'm an islander, and only an islander. I nearly say all this. But then I picture what's at stake. I picture the noose and the moment shatters like a spell around us. I can't trust this boy. I can't trust him an inch.

"Just be ready."

CHAPTER SEVEN

WE LEAVE AT MIDNIGHT UNDER A BLOOD MOON. She's full and brimming, casting an eerie glow, the ring of red blurring her edges. I shuffle my feet against the path, trying not to look up. A blood moon brings bad luck. It brings curses and hunger and death. But there's no time to wait for a more favored night. I push it from my mind. I have committed to this plan, to steal away with Seth when the stars pepper the night sky for him to navigate by. I won't back down now. I can't, with so much at stake. Not just my life, or my father's and Bryn's, but our whole island and its ways. I adjust my pack, containing only some clothes and essential items, a little higher up my shoulder. I couldn't risk my mother's blade being discovered on me, not with how strange it is, so I left it in her chest and packed hurriedly.

I don't need a light to guide me as we walk the trails running across the island. I know these paths like I know the creases in my palm, but Seth stumbles and trips behind me.

More than once I pause, holding up a hand to silence him, sure I can hear the soft pad of footsteps behind us. But when we stop, all I hear is the sea. The tumble and rush of the waves, a gull as it circles and cries to the night. Those footsteps must be the echo of my own heart, beating in my ears.

The boatyard is down a set of stairs, the treads carved from the side of the cliff. They're narrow and riddled with trick steps, still used for smuggling when someone pays us well enough to hide their haul. Some are shallow, some deep to force a stumbling foot. A curse under the breath. The warning we might need that the watch have planned an ambush.

"Kai has a skiff. We'll take that," I say, making for the small boat pulled up past the tide line. It has a small sail, oars, and enough room for Seth and me to sit. But I can't see it taking me onward to the coordinates my mother left me. From looking briefly at the map on the wall in the meeting house, I believe I will have to travel farther than Port Trenn. Almost to the edges of the map, my known world, far out into the sea toward the straits to the southeast.

I will have to find provisions on Ennor, maybe even a bigger vessel. The thought leaves me divided, at once thrilled and uneasy. I have only ever sailed to Penscalo, seldom to the other small inhabited isles and islets close by. Sometimes those islanders have visited us on feast days, but it is rare now that we all risk a big meet. Port towns on the mainland of Arnhem and on the north and western coasts of Leicena are the talk of sailors, of people that travel regularly to places like Port Trenn and only sometimes stop on Rosevear, usually with smuggled goods in the dead hours of night. Now I will get to see one of those ports for myself. But now it's after midnight, I only have eight days before I must return for my

father. Before he will hang in that square on Penscalo. I will
have to travel swiftly.

Seth grabs one side of the skiff as I grab the other, and we
start pushing it down to the water. I brace my feet against
the sand, feel the rasp of the wood under my fingers. Then
a shadow moves beside Seth. I gasp as he's knocked to the
ground. Kai towers over him.

"I told you he wasn't to be trusted!" he calls over his
shoulder. I rush around the skiff, shoving him aside as Agnes
emerges from behind the boat shed.

"We knew he was planning something. We *knew* it," she
says, holding a blade that glints in the moonlight.

I help Seth up off the ground, turning so my back is to him.
"You've got this all wrong. He's helping me—"

"He's tricking you."

I blink as Kai crosses his arms, glaring at Seth over my
shoulder.

"No tricks, honest."

"Shush, Seth," I say, shaking my head. The last thing I need
is his voice added to theirs. "He knows how to navigate, and
I made a deal with him. He's showing me the way to Ennor."

Agnes's eyes widen. "But what about your father and
Bryn?"

"This *is* for my father," I say fiercely, stepping toward her.
I glance back at Seth, then pull Agnes out of earshot. I trust
Seth to get me to Ennor, but beyond that I have my doubts.
"I found the key to my mother's chest."

"But how, where?"

"It doesn't matter," I say, pushing aside my guilt for having
ransacked the cottage as I pull the notebook from my pocket.

Kai crowds in, keeping a wary eye on Seth. "I found this. These are coordinates. Look."

They both bow their heads, tracing the illustration by the light of the moon. Agnes bites her lip, glancing up at Kai, then at me. Worry plasters her features.

Kai shakes his head. "You don't know that it's anything. Your mother could have just noted an interesting rock, or a place she dropped anchor once. You know she was with a smuggler crew before she landed on Rosevear."

"No," I say firmly. "No. It's more than that. I can't explain it, but this notebook…it was calling to me. All this time, locked away in that chest. It's haunted me for six years and now that I hold it in my hands, I have to listen. There's something at these coordinates, something my mother left me. I'm sure of it. And she wouldn't have gone, she wouldn't have kept leaving us if…if…"

Agnes places her hand over mine, closing the notebook. Of anyone on Rosevear, I hope she will understand. We both lost our mothers that day. We both had to inhabit the spaces they left overnight, for our community, for our kin.

"Your mother was different to us. She wasn't born on Rosevear. She wasn't an islander true. And maybe she did leave you something. I would do the same, if I were you. I would find this place too. If I thought my mother had left me something—" she huffs a pained breath "—I would rake the ends of the ocean to find it."

I sniff, nodding slowly. "Right now, we have nothing. Nothing to offer the watch but our own blood. And even that won't save them. She has to have left me something I can save him with. Something the watch would want, something of value. I know it. I *know* this is what I'm meant to do to save them."

Kai frowns. "I don't like this, Mira. Not one bit."

"You don't have to like it, Kai. You don't even have to like *him*. But you do have to trust me." I sigh, running a hand over my plait. "If I can't fix this, then it isn't just Father and Bryn, is it? They'll just be the start. The watch will come after all of us. You heard the captain on the beach—he means to break us. They'll destroy us."

Agnes looks as though she might cry, her eyes shining.

"I have to do this. I have to know if I can fix this without anyone else getting hurt, or worse. If I fail, if my mother left nothing behind that I can use to free them, I will bargain with this captain of the watch to take my father's place. I will find some way to free him with my own blood. Surely I'm worth more to the watch than he is. You can't stop me."

Agnes sniffs, looking away. I want to reach out to her, tell her it's fine. But I don't know that. None of us do.

Kai uncrosses his arms, throwing them up to the night. "I've never known anyone so stubborn."

I grin at him, feeling the tension ease. "I'll come back, I promise. I'll free my father and Bryn and make sure the watch can't hurt us. Any of us."

Agnes nods, turning her blade in her fingers. She was given that knife when her mother died. It's a reminder of her mother's love, and all she lost. It's what drives her every time she swims out to a wreck. And now she holds it to me, offering up the handle. "Take this. If that boy so much as *looks* at you funny, you cut his throat."

I hear Seth choke behind me, but I only have eyes for Agnes. I take the blade, tucking it away. In her way, this is her going with me. Protecting me. It wouldn't be the first time I've held a blade to someone's throat. We all do what we have to on this island.

Kai smiles, sorrow painted along the lines of his mouth, and moves to help us get the skiff down to the water. Seth grabs the other side, as though putting as much distance as he can between them.

"Take this too," Kai says, passing me a cloth bag. There's a scattering sound as the contents move inside, like a stream over rocks. "Your share from the wreck. And also my share. And Agnes's. We want you to have it."

I bow my head, my heart feeling too big for my chest. I know it's full of the glass beads, all that precious glitter. A small fortune. This could have meant so much for Agnes and Kai, for their futures, for their kin. I grasp the bag, my fingers trembling. "You never came here to stop me."

"No," he says softly. "That would be like trying to stop the tide from turning. We just wanted to make sure you had a plan."

"And, Mira," Agnes says quietly, her eyes seeking mine in the dark, "be careful who knows what you can do. I mean with being in the sea and staying underwater." She glances at Kai. "We know you're different. I've known it ever since we would go swimming together as children and you could stay underwater for so long. Anyone else would have turned blue. And don't mention that dream you have sometimes. The one where you're flying. Just blend in, all right? Be careful."

"All we're saying is…you're one of us. Whatever your mother left for you out there, you'll always be one of us. Stay safe," Kai says. "And if you can't stay safe, be faster than them."

I climb into the skiff, carrying their words in my heart as I hide my face. I don't want them to see my tears. I don't want them to see me any less than brave and certain. Because if I fall apart now, I'm not sure I would be able to leave.

"Come back to us!" Agnes shouts suddenly, wading into the sea-foam, and I hold out my hand to her, our fingertips grazing. "The sea gives."

"The sea takes," I reply, my voice cracking on the last word.

She sobs, bringing her hands up to cover her mouth as the sail fills and we move away from the shore. I hold it all in, my fierce pride in them, my fear, my hope. It's all so huge inside me, almost overwhelming. I keep my eyes on the beach, on Kai and Agnes, on the isle of Rosevear, the only home I've ever known, until it is all consumed by the night.

And we go into the tide.

"Thanks for what you did back there."

Seth's voice startles me. I'd almost forgotten he was in the boat. But as I turn to him and look out to sea, I see the glint of his eyes, the way his curls fall into them, the foxy tilt of his cheekbones. And I can see why Kai was so wary of him. "It wasn't for you."

"Still, he was going to—"

I'm on him in a second. The blade is in my fingers, my hand gripping his throat. All the fear rising as fury up from my chest. "If you are tricking me, if you can't get us to Ennor and this is all a lie—"

I feel a pinch at my side. I look down and there's a knife angled at my rib cage. When I look back up, our faces are inches apart. And he's smiling. I loosen my grip on his throat slowly. But the knife at my side sharpens against my skin.

"Listen. Let's get one thing straight. You can trust me.

But," he says, his eyes boring into mine, "no more pulling blades on me."

He removes his knife from my side and my chest rises and falls with quick shallow breaths. His teeth gleam, catching the moonlight as he grins, still just inches from me. The scent of untruths wraps around us along with something deeper, wilder, like the pine trees scattered in the northern fields of Rosevear. His mouth is so close to mine.

"If you try anything, I *will* kill you," I breathe. I almost believe it. Almost believe I could pull out Agnes's blade and plunge it between his ribs.

I unwind myself from him, sitting back on the middle plank.

He points to a constellation overhead. "We follow this for a time, then take a quarter turn to the west. Ennor is a fickle island—she likes to dance in the twilight hours. But we'll find her at dawn. You should get some sleep."

"I'm fine."

He shrugs, taking a deep breath of air before settling against the stern. "Suit yourself."

We don't speak for some time as we navigate the midnight ocean, scattered with reflections of starlight, all its secrets locked within.

CHAPTER
EIGHT

THE ISLE OF ENNOR EMERGES WITH THE DAWN. I lean toward it, tracing the pale shapes of rooftops and walkways snaking away from the quay. It's solidly built, this place, with shimmering glass windows and polished granite walls. I can't see any signs of disrepair or hard times. Perhaps they have found other ways to survive the long winters of the Fortunate Isles.

Although it's early, their fisherfolk are already up, swapping out lobster and crab pots, checking over nets, whistling to one another. Just like my father and his set would be. It's strange, finding a place so new, yet with the same familiar rhythms of island life.

"Don't tell anyone where you're from," Seth's voice taps, startling me.

"Why not?"

"Why do you think?" I turn and he smiles slyly. "Not everyone takes kindly to wreckers. I would wager some of the cargo you have stolen over the years belonged to the lord of this isle. Everyone here knows what you do on Rosevear. Even if the watch haven't caught you all yet."

"Isles don't have lords."

"This one does. You see that castle, up on the hill?" I look up, casting my gaze over the evaporating mist. Towering over the town is a castle shaped like a star, hewn from pale gray granite. It's sprawling and magnificent. I can just make out the nearest points, the ramparts, the arrow-slit windows and the wider, glass-paned windows shimmering as they catch the early sunlight. I can't help the feeling of being watched from one of them. I remember the whispers about the owner of Ennor, how Bryn avoided this isle.

"The lord of Ennor's stronghold. He's a young lord, came into his inheritance tragically early. But the castle has been in the Tresillian family for generations. Impossible to break into, sadly."

"Why do you say that?"

Seth busies himself with the sail. "There's magic there. And riches. More than you'll see in a lifetime of wrecks."

I shrug. "If somewhere has a door with a lock, you can pick it and take whatever's inside."

Seth snorts. "Spoken like a true wrecker. Don't say anything like *that* while you're here either."

I turn my attention back to the quay and the buildings beyond. I've never had to hide in plain sight before. It makes me uneasy, how others will view us. And with Kai and Agnes's warning to hide what I am capable of, I'm doubly anxious suddenly.

"I'll get some provisions, find a crew and a bigger boat.

That's all I need to do here," I say, keeping my voice neutral. I don't want him to know I'm rattled by this place.

"Sure."

"I'll be gone by midday. No need to hang around."

"All right."

"Nothing to add to my plan? No other words of warning?"

He shrugs, as though he couldn't care less. "It makes perfect sense."

I frown, feeling rather than hearing the stirrings of a lie. It prickles under my skin as we tie up alongside the quay and I hop out, climbing the sea-washed steps. Either I truly am my father's daughter, a worrier, or Seth is hiding some details about this place.

"Thanks for letting me join you in the skiff," he says, shoving his hands into his pockets. "I guess this is where we part ways."

"I guess it is. Thanks for navigating."

Seth kicks a stone along the ground, his curls falling in front of his eyes. My heart patters as he looks at me. "Good luck with everything."

"Thanks," I say, wondering what it is he isn't saying.

He sighs, leaning his forearms on the railings that loop around the quay. "I suppose we're even now? You saved my life—I brought you here."

Shading my eyes from the sun just emerging, I take him in, noticing how much taller he is than me in his shirt and patched-up jacket. The casual way he leans against the railings. I wonder where he conceals that blade he carries and whether I could take him in a fight. I remember how close we were last night with our blades drawn. Mere inches apart. I swallow, biting my lip.

"Take care of yourself. Hope you find a new crew to take you on," I say hurriedly, turning on my heel and striding up the quay. Before I slip around the corner into town, I glance back at him. He's still leaning against the railings, head tipped to one side with a smile playing across his mouth. Watching me.

The town fills quickly as the sun climbs higher. I follow the sounds of gossip and mild griping until a market square opens up from one of the lanes. Stallholders are setting up for the day, women lingering for a chat with great baskets slung over their arms. Small children weave in and out, clutching lumps of bread and sticky sweet buns with dimples in their cheeks. Seagulls cluster on a rooftop, cawing for scraps. The scent of breakfast lingers everywhere and my hand strays to my belly. I need to trade some of these glass beads and buy myself a meal. Then I can get my bearings and make sure I find the provisions I need. These are island people far better off than my own. I can already see a thriving trade, coin changing hands, fabrics worn on well-fed backs. This is not a lean island like Rosevear. Ennor somehow sustains itself.

A girl with long dark hair and an eye patch is playing a fiddle nearby, coaxing a few passersby to toss coins into her case. The velvet lining is a bright, screaming scarlet, but it's old and worn, as though well loved. I hover nearby, listening to her play a familiar tune that we dance to on celebration days. Her eye snags on mine and she winks. It catches me off guard; she reminds me of Agnes.

I melt back into the crowd as my belly rumbles. I shouldn't linger too long; they might notice I don't belong here. Seth's warning rings in my mind and I realize I don't want to fall into conversation with anyone, however casual.

I wander past the shops lining the market square and find myself outside a real apothecary. I've never seen one before. I press my hand against the window, examining the display of potions in glass bottles and jars, the jewel-bright colors glinting with an inner glow. There are labels slung around some of them, listing names like Dew Radiance and Nettle Sooth.

The apothecaries make these potions from raw magic, I know, mixing them with other ingredients. I've heard they even mix curses. They get the magic from the witches, weaving it into their potions and tinctures for the general population to buy. I don't know if the witches create raw magic, or if they get it from a source. All Mother and Father said in their stories is that they wield it. We've never been able to afford an apothecary's potions on Rosevear, or the services of a witch. The healer gets by with homemade remedies. A woman brushes past me, pushing open the door, and I move along. The last thing I want is for someone who creates curses from raw magic to notice me.

I make my way over to a dusty shop with a magpie assortment of objects and curiosities displayed in its windows. I clutch my pouch of glass beads in my fist, weighing them. I have traded on Penscalo under the careful eyes of the watch on market days, spitting on my hand to seal each deal, Bryn's hand clapping my shoulder when I did our island proud. But this shop, these people, are unknown. And Bryn is not here to guide me.

A bell chimes over the door as I cross the threshold, echoing through the silence. A counter, long and polished, sits at the back, a doorway behind it. But that's not what holds my attention. The walls are lined with shelves full of treasures from days gone by. Piles of citrine gems pool next to mirrored pillboxes no bigger than my thumb. There are hats trimmed with the inky feathers of exotic birds lining one wall, and sitting to my left on a low table, there is a jar containing what looks like tiny jet-black beetles. It's the oddest collection of objects I've ever seen, even stranger than Agnes's treasure room.

There is a long and spindly key the color of the deepest ocean sitting on a shelf. It shimmers, holding light within it, almost dripping with a coating along its edges. I walk toward it, my fingers reaching, wanting to touch it, to know what it unlocks.

"I wouldn't," a voice creaks.

I whip around, finding a man standing behind the counter. His hair is cloud white, his eyes ancient and knowing behind a pair of spectacles. "Forgive me, I—"

"No, no," he says with a chuckle, bracing his hands against the counter. "It is for your sake I say that, not because I think you will steal it. That key holds a curse. A rather specific, witch-made curse. If you hold it without being the true owner of what it unlocks, it will coat your veins in poison."

I look back at the key, finding the glow surrounding it no less alluring.

"The last person who touched that key had scorched nightmares for a year. Drove her to madness, then into the sea to wash them away. She was not the true owner of what it unlocks, and I am still uncertain of what that is. Perhaps a door? A safe? Who knows? So, you see—" he pauses, shuffling some papers "—you do not want to touch that key."

I purse my lips, retreating from the shelf. There are things

on Ennor, like the apothecary shop, like this key, that fall beyond my understanding of the world. "Why do you display
it then? If it is a cursed thing?"

A line burrows between his brows and I wonder if I have
asked the wrong thing. "This isn't a shop of peculiarities or
jewels. Well, sometimes it is. I take whatever walks through
that door. I pay a fair price and the owner may come back to
claim the item for a bigger price within a month. If not—"
he shrugs "—then it is mine to do with as I wish. And when
it comes to that key…maybe I'm hoping that the true owner
will find it one day and I will finally learn what it unlocks."

I nod, marking his words as I step farther from the shelves.
If he's interested in items for their own sake, will he be interested in my stolen haul? My fingers tighten around the bag in
my hand, calculating quietly, weighing up the risk of trading
them all here. Will I get a fair price? Will he turn me in to
this lord of Ennor, or worse, the watch?

"You have something you wish to trade?"

I shrug, casting my eyes over the other items littering the
room. Ink bottles holding silver ink, miniatures of fine-
featured people. Jewelry, some glinting, some dulled by age,
one with a winking jewel, pink as a blush. Blades with han-
dles of bone, some so sharp they look thirsty for a cut. I turn
to the display in the window, deceptively dusty and nonde-
script. A selection of pearls too yellow to be precious. A hat
that moths have attacked, stealing the violet glamour of it.
This shop isn't meant to be noticed, I realize. Not by people
who don't deliberately seek it out.

Movement out of the window draws my eye and with a
jolt, I see a head of brown curls. Seth is crossing the market
square, shoulders hunched, hands thrust into his pockets. He

stops by the girl playing the fiddle, whispers something in her ear. She arches her neck and laughs. I pinch my lips together, wondering what Seth is up to and how he knows that girl. As I watch, she bends down to pack away her instrument, snaps the case shut, and hauls it up with a hand. And all the while, Seth is talking, frowning. The girl shakes her head and he trails after her, trying to grab her shoulder.

Perhaps he is trying to find a crew to join, like he told me. Or perhaps…perhaps he knows this isle and its people better than he let on.

A cold creeps over me, shivering along my skin.

I should get on my way as soon as possible.

"I do have something I wish to trade." I rip my gaze away from Seth and the girl, focusing on the shopkeeper. I smile, crossing the wooden floor, and open the pouch a little onto the counter. The trickle of glass rings through the shop as I allow a few of them to cascade like jewels, glittering. Like they've been scooped from the sea's treasure trove.

The man says nothing for a moment. Then he lays both palms flat on either side of the beads. "Interesting."

I shrug one shoulder.

"Name your price."

We haggle back and forth, my blood heating with the hunt for the price I want. Enough to cover safe passage to the coordinates in my mother's illustration and some provisions. A smile curls up his mouth as we settle and I spit in my palm as I always do, holding it out to him. He hesitates for a second before gripping my hand in his. Then he places the coin on the counter beside the glass beads. I silently thank Kai and Agnes for giving me their share. The coin I have now is enough; I'm sure of it.

"Keep your head down in this town, girl," he says softly. "And if you wreck any more ships, find your way back to my door. Not many brave enough to land on Ennor to barter."

I look at him sharply but he only shrugs. "I don't ask where the things that make their way here come from. And I don't tell either."

"Not even if the watch come knocking?"

"Especially not if the watch come knocking. Not that they dare set foot on Ennor," he says, flint in his eyes. "But a word of advice, girl. Don't linger here. It's not the watch that control these waters."

I nod and leave the shop, the two warnings from Seth and now this shopkeeper chiming in my ears.

CHAPTER NINE

AS I BUY PROVISIONS, I FEEL EYES UPON ME. Cutting into my back. There is something watchful about the Isle of Ennor that I didn't notice at first. I wonder if I stand out, if they know every face, every visiting trader.

I swallow down my fear and approach a group of women, baskets balanced in their arms and gossip on their tongues. They all narrow their eyes, turning quiet as I ask about onward passage and any seafarers who might be passing through. I try my luck with a stallholder instead, trickling coins into his outstretched palm for information. But he's tight-lipped too, his gaze narrowing just like the women.

It's only when I skirt the market square that I realize I am being followed. A tall stranger with dark hair is tracking me, stopping as I pause to grab an apple from a stall or exchange words with a trader. He's broad with the kind of casual stroll of someone trained to be lethal. I try to lose him before giving up.

I wait just around a corner, Agnes's blade pulsing at my thigh. When he appears, all ease, I block his path. "Are you following me for a reason?"

He laughs, eyes flashing in surprise, and thrusts his hands in his pockets. I gulp, suddenly wrong-footed. His eyes are rimmed with soot-dark lashes, his skin olive toned, like he lives for the sunlight and sea. His jaw is strong with just a shadow of stubble and as he moves closer, I taste his scent, like midnight and the whisper of wild things. He's the most beautiful boy I have ever seen.

"Not for any particular reason," he says, his voice low and alluring. I find myself leaning in, catching the soft lilt of an accent I can't quite place. "Are you visiting someone?"

"If I was, would you know who they were?"

He laughs again, shrugging one shoulder, and my heart does a little swoop. "Maybe. I was born here."

I look away, feeling the first signs of a blush mar my cheeks. "I'm just passing through."

"You'll need a ship then."

"I have my own boat."

"That little skiff tied up alongside the quay?"

My eyes snap to his. "How did you—"

"If you're traveling farther than Penscalo, then you'll need a bigger vessel. Even a crew. Did the shopkeeper give you a good price for those beads you carried?" He leans against the wall, crossing his arms, and raises his eyebrows, just a fraction. His jacket bunches and tightens across his chest, outlining the muscles underneath. His shirt, unbuttoned to just below his clavicle, gives a hint of the way his torso looks, of the glow of his skin. When I look back at his face, he's grinning, as though he can read my thoughts.

My blush deepens and I curse under my breath. He's beautiful, but he knows it. And he's using it as a weapon. I bite my lip, my gaze sliding past him, to the people hurrying past. This boy who can't be much older than me has been tailing me since I arrived on Ennor. And I was too caught up in my own head to notice.

"I want no trouble."

"Of course not," he says, his voice disarmingly gentle. He smiles, his mouth slightly lopsided, a dimple appearing in his left cheek. "You'll want the Mermaid. It's the pub just off the quay. You'll find the best crews and captains to take you on your journey in there."

"Why should I follow your advice?"

He chuckles. "It's up to you. You could try your luck elsewhere, but that's the only place you'll find a crew on this island. Unless, of course, you want to tarry with me a little longer."

"I... I'm in a hurry—"

I catch the flare of triumph in his eyes. He's tormenting me. Pressing ever so carefully against my defenses to see how I react. I bunch my hands into fists at my back, willing the crimson hue of my cheeks to cool. He laughs throatily, then steps away, giving me the space to turn and leave.

The Mermaid is the best lead I've got to find onward passage, and all I want to do now is get off this isle. It's too watchful, too full of eyes. At least when I'm on the sea, I'm in familiar territory. And it's very clear that this stranger is not all he appears. There is a lethal edge to the way he moves, the way he is sizing me up. I do not want to find out what would happen should this stranger turn on me. Whereas I feel I could square up to Seth and have a fair chance, with this boy, I'm not so sure. His gaze sends a prickle down my spine, every inch of me alert.

I clear my throat, summoning my most stony stare. "Are you planning on following me there too?"

His eyes narrow, a wicked grin curving his features. "Are you asking me to follow you?"

"I— *No*. No, that's not—"

"This has been most enlightening. I do hope our paths cross again. Best of luck on your journey."

The blush on my face doesn't die down for a good five minutes as I pick my way back through town. When I glance to check, the beautiful stranger is no longer following me. I decide to try the pub, and keep my fingers closed around Agnes's blade—just in case this turns out to be a trap.

The Mermaid has deep-set windows, carved into granite walls and a sign that swings over the thick oak door. The sign has a painting on it of the kind of mermaid the sailors lust after. She has a pale blue tail, a nipped-in waist and curling dark hair that covers her chest. Her eyes are half-lidded, watching me as I cross to the door.

Stepping over the threshold is like stepping on board a stately ship. The chairs are heavy wood with green velvet cushions, the tables perfectly polished. The bar glints with a hundred bottles and glasses, the colors of the liquids inside ranging from molten gold to neon green. People cluster around the tables, holding pipes pluming with delicately scented smoke—nothing like the rough tobacco Old Jonie chugs on. The bar is perfumed with herbal notes, woven through with something sweeter. I inhale and rake my gaze across the gathered groups. I walk silently around the tables, where everyone seems to be either in deep discussions or playing cards. Coin is heaped in careless piles in the center of the tables, so much wealth it makes my mouth turn dry. One woman looks up at me, her eyes crinkling with mirth. She has a tattoo on her left cheekbone of a compass. It's so discreet, I almost mistake it for a birthmark.

"Do you play?" she asks in a smoky voice. I shake my head before moving on.

Then through the haze of pipe smoke, I spy a familiar face. He doesn't see me at first. He's sitting with the girl I saw playing the fiddle earlier. To her right is a girl with short white-blond hair holding a tiny glass full to the brim with blue liquid. And on the other side of Seth is a boy with broad shoulders and sharp cheekbones, his hair a chestnut mop that he shakes out of his eyes.

I know the moment Seth sees me that whatever he says next may be untrue. Our eyes lock, a shadow passing over his features, before he stands up and pushes back his chair. He walks over to greet me, his features reassembled into the perfect picture of ease.

"I found a crew to take me on," he says.

"Congratulations."

"If you're in here, I guess you're looking for a captain?" He cocks his head to the side, assessing me. "I know it wasn't part of our deal, but this crew might actually be able to help you too."

"How so?"

"The captain has a fine vessel. The perfect size for onward travel, cuts fast and quick to avoid the watch."

I sigh. It's clear that Ennor wants me off the isle and on my way as soon as possible. And this is what I desire too. If this is the only place where I can hire a crew and ship, then this pub holds my only options. Looking around at the card players and the drinkers, those options are slim at best. I take a proper look at the crew Seth points at and don't find anything out of the ordinary. They look weather-beaten and hard, all around my age, which isn't necessarily unusual for the crew of a smaller vessel. They don't seem like they're hiding any more than their fair share of secrets. I trace the shape of my mother's notebook in my pocket, and the coin I have left to bargain with. Maybe it will be an advantage to have Seth on board. After all, I already know who he is and what he is. At least, I think I do.

I shrug nonchalantly, and let him lead me to their table. He pulls back a vacant seat for me to sit in.

"Mira, let me introduce you."

The fiddle player with the eye patch lounges back in her chair, casting her gaze up and down me. The other two do the same and I wonder if they've marked me as an easy target.

"You can't afford us," the girl directly across from me says bluntly before I can even speak. She juts out her chin. "You're an islander."

I relax back, measuring them in turn, trying to hide the fact that my heart is thudding wildly. I have to navigate this meeting carefully. I pick out my next words, opening my mouth ready to protest, but Seth just rolls his eyes at the girl.

"Pearl, you wouldn't know good money if it jangled in your own pocket."

She glances at him before looking back at me. "Where did you find her?"

"*I* found *him* on my island," I say pointedly, folding my

arms on the table. "Yes, I'm an islander. But that hardly matters if I can pay, does it?"

"True," the boy rumbles at my side, reaching forward for his drink. It's a china cup of amber tea, the leaves drifting gently in the bottom of the cup as he lifts it.

I notice Seth quietly eyeing the fiddle player and I turn my attention to her too. She has dark curly hair falling to her elbows, partly tied back to reveal her light brown skin. She smiles at me with teeth a little foxy and sharp, like Seth's, and I note how everyone shifts slightly in deference to her, waiting for her to speak. She must be their captain.

"We might be able to come to an…arrangement," she says.

I accept a glass of rose-colored liquid in a crystal tumbler from the barman, taking my time to answer. The trouble is, I have no idea what they want. Or whether their final offer will be a fair price. All I know is that I need this if I am to save my father and Bryn in time, and now I only have eight days.

"Are you familiar with the area I need to get to?" I ask, reeling off the set of coordinates before taking a sip of the rose drink. It tastes of spring, delicate and floral with a freshness that tingles on my tongue. "I'm only interested in passage on a vessel that can take me there and back swiftly."

"How swiftly?"

I level my gaze at her, figuring I might need some leeway. "Seven days."

She nods, her eyes shifting to the broad boy sitting next to me. Is he her second? Seth leans back, watching them, and I do the same. As though they are not my only option.

"We can do it," she says suddenly. "All up front."

"Half now, half on my safe return to Penscalo in seven days' time."

She smiles, twisting her drink around and around on the table. Pearl, the girl with white-blond hair, clicks her tongue. It's as though a secret current passes between them, an unspoken conversation playing out before me. Then the captain leans forward, holding her hand out. "Half now, half on your safe return."

I shake her hand briefly, establishing that point, and we move on to the price. As we haggle, I watch Seth from the corner of my eye, trying to gauge his reaction to the final figure we narrow down on. Sweat prickles my skin as we move closer and closer to the only coin I have. If any extra expenses crop up, if anything goes wrong, I will be eating into the second payment that I have promised on arrival in Penscalo. I will have to bluff my way through the next week, keeping them convinced I can pay.

"One more thing, the skiff you arrived on…it remains as insurance," the captain says.

I hesitate, picturing Kai's face. His disappointment if I do not return with it straightaway. But two lives are worth more than a boat, and I know he would sacrifice far more to see my father and Bryn released. We can collect it when we're all home, and safe.

Finally, we spit and shake, twin grins snaking their way across our features. I catch Seth's frown and decide to ignore it. There's no way now but onward. I have gambled a hefty chunk of the glass bead haul on the hopes that my mother's coordinates will come good.

"Join us at the far end of the quay in fifteen minutes," the captain says, pushing back her chair to stand. "And by the way, I'm Merryam. This is Pearl and that's Joby."

Joby and Pearl both nod at me, rising as Merryam does.

"Delighted," I say. They all look so different, and yet they have the same way about them. As though they are all cut from the same cloth, born of sea and salt and wind.

Merryam signals for the bill, tipping her chin at me when the barmaid walks over, rubbing her hands on her apron. "She'll pay. Seth? You've got fifteen minutes too. Don't make me regret this."

I swallow down the worry that wriggles up my throat as I watch the crew walk out of the door. A deal is a deal and I've made it now. There's no turning back.

"That went well," Seth says as I pay the barmaid with a handful of small coins.

"Did it?" I ask lightly.

He smiles as we head for the main door. "No one got knifed and she agreed to your terms. I'd say that's a success."

CHAPTER TEN

THE QUAY HOLDS MORE LIFE NOW THAN WHEN
we arrived. As I step onto it, the sun-washed stone casting
warmth up my calves, I have to weave my way with Seth
through the crowd of fisherfolk and merchants selling hot
buns and fresh fish. I brush them off, shouldering my pack
of provisions and hoping the coin I still carry on me doesn't
clink as I walk.

A smattering of posters and advertisements nailed to the
seawall snags my gaze, luring me closer. I drift toward them,
wondering if I'll find an old Wanted poster with Bryn's face
on it. Bryn wasn't born on Rosevear. He washed up with a
band of smugglers when I was a young girl and never left.
We only found out later that he was wanted by the watch for
some petty crime, not that it bothered any of us. Especially
not when he began using his contacts at Port Trenn for information on when the merchant ships would pass close by.
The thought of Bryn now sitting in the watch's prison after
evading them all these years leaves me cold.

I shiver a little and bite my lip, scanning the pieces of salty parchment, my finger tapping a restless pattern against my leg. Bryn has been like a second father to me. He was the one who shaped the seven of us that swim out on the rope into one. I trust him with my life and in turn, he trusts me with his. I can't let him down.

There are new Wanted posters layered over old ones. Captain Renshaw, the fabled smuggler and cutthroat rumored to have many vessels in her grip, peers at me from under dark eyebrows. This poster says she is wanted by the watch for a sum that makes me whistle. We all know of her, at least the rumors of her. The whispers and stories the sailors and smugglers tell. Even Bryn has a tale or two from his time before Rosevear. Agnes rolls her eyes every time she hears the tales, disinterested in smugglers and their hidden loot. But I always lean in, glean as much as I can, and wonder what it would be like to sail forever through the wide expanse of sea and sky.

We don't have any dealings with her directly; Bryn says she's too ruthless. The smugglers we allow to land their haul in our cove have a long-standing friendship with us, some going back generations. It's a fine balance, and a risk. We stay loyal to the crews that have kept our secrets. Renshaw has never made the cut. She's the type that makes us uneasy, like the promise of a knife in the back.

I keep scanning, moving to look at the newer posters. They feature ships lost, rewards promised, more wanted outlaws—

I stutter to a halt. There's a poster there, white and crisp, telling the tale of a ship lost off the Fortunate Isles. *My* isles. The *Fair Maiden* with a cargo of precious glass beads, belonging to a rich merchant, bound for a port town off the west coast of Leicena. I glance left and right, suddenly wary, raking the nearest faces, seeing if any of them are looking my way, if that shopkeeper has sent them after me.

A hand reaches over my shoulder, tearing down the poster, along with several others. I whip around to find Seth standing there. His eyes are flint, flicking from the poster of Captain Renshaw to the torn ones in his hands. Gone is the warmth I'm growing used to seeing, his jaw set and tense. He scrunches up the posters in his fist. His eyes settle on me, all traces of good humor gone. Maybe he's as rattled as I am. That poster about the *Fair Maiden* must have been freshly pressed and delivered just this morning. Even now, the watch could be circling the waters just off Ennor, searching for answers. Searching for islanders like me that might be trading the glitter for coin.

"Best get out of here," Seth says quietly. "You got everything you need?"

"But what if they saw me? What if someone knows?"

He scrunches up his eyes. "Who did you trade with?"

I picture the dusty shop, the inky key sitting alone on a shelf among the ropes of pearls and all the other forgotten treasures. "A man with white hair and spectacles in a shop full of oddities."

A ghost of a smile lingers on Seth's lips. It's so quick, so fleeting, I blink and it's gone. He shrugs, turning to walk toward the edge of the quay. "Sounds harmless enough."

"You know him?"

"This isn't my island. Ennor is owned by Lord Tresillian and he's particular about who stays longer than a few hours. There are…stories told about him. He has a dark reputation. I don't know anyone here, Mira."

I taste the lie in his words. It's bitter, like the healer's best tonic. "Could have fooled me."

He stops abruptly, facing me. "What does that mean?"

I square up to him, pull back my shoulders. "It means, I think you're lying to me, Seth. I think you know this crew that just so happens to have taken you on far better than you're pretending."

He says nothing for a moment, staring steadily at me. I daren't look away. Daren't blink and miss the moment when he shuffles his thoughts, deciding which lie to tell next. My heart quickens under his gaze. I lower my shoulders, getting ready to drop the pack of provisions and clothes if I need to reach for Agnes's blade.

But he surprises me. He deflates.

"You're right. I did lie to you." He sighs, dropping his eyes to the ground. "I do know someone here. Someone I trust with my life."

I wait to see where this tale leads.

"Merryam, the captain of the crew. I've known her for a while. She told me before I signed on with the crew of *Fair Maiden* that if I ever needed to jump ship, I could work for her. So Ennor seemed a good isle to get to from yours."

Squinting up at him, I turn over his words. I fumble over the conversation in the Mermaid, the words I exchanged to make the deal. How I saw him talking to Merryam in the market square, then his ease around the crew in the Mermaid. "So you know all of them."

"When you've worked at sea your whole life, you do see the same faces turning up again and again."

"Makes sense, I guess."

His eyes take on that foxy slant, humor spilling out of him, and I swallow, raising my shoulders again. I still feel that I'm missing something, but nothing he's told me seems untrue.

"There's something you should know though."

My eyes dart to his.

"I'm telling you this because I want you to trust me. Merryam—" his gaze shifts up the quay and back "—has no intention of giving that skiff back."

"What?"

He shrugs, looking at his feet. "I thought you would have figured that part out. If you leave the skiff here, it will van—"

I step toward him, poking a finger into his chest. "Get her back and I'll make a new trade. She's not having the skiff as well."

"It doesn't work like that."

"*Make* it work like that," I hiss, temper flaring quick and hot up my throat.

He throws up his hands. "Whatever. That's the price— either you take it or stay here. Do you *want* to stay here and find someone else to take you? Personally, I don't like your chances. Ennor is not the kind of isle you stay on uninvited."

I frown.

"Didn't think so." A smile curls over his lips. "Your friend, Kai, is it? He won't miss it."

"You don't know that."

"I know enough."

He sets off down the quay before I can get another word out. In only a short morning, I've lost everything I came with. The skiff and the glass beads and I've exchanged them for what? Thin air. A deal I can't entirely trust. I contemplate turning back, jumping on the skiff by myself and navigating my way back to Rosevear to make a new plan.

I nearly leave. So very nearly. But as Seth disappears past a cluster of loudmouthed sailors with ruddy cheeks, I realize how stuck I truly am. Because if I turn back now, I may not get another chance to trade the glass beads. I won't be able to gather enough coin to release both Bryn and my father and I will be back at the beginning again, no plan, no hope.

I have to go.

I grip my pack, pushing my way past the sailors. Blood runs cold in my chest as I turn over the events since I left my island. Somehow, I've lost. I've allowed Merryam, this captain, to get the upper hand, and I'm not sure how to take back the power I had on Rosevear. This world is all new to me, but I would bet every coin I have left that it isn't new to Seth. That I'm stepping into something bigger.

A gull cries overhead, lingering by a woman selling sticky buns. They are studded with apple pieces, just as Agnes makes them. I slow, watching the woman with her navy blue dress, her apron smeared with apples and flour. And I remember who I'm doing this all for. What's at stake if I don't succeed. This whole crew might be liars, but they hold the only way forward so I can claim whatever my mother left behind, and use it to save Bryn and my father. My people. And maybe even myself.

I take a breath, walking past the woman, the scent of baked apples following me down the quay. Merryam might have gotten the upper hand with this trade, but she underestimates me. I am an islander and I am made of salt and granite. And once we are out there on the open ocean, pretty lies and untruths won't hold any sway. The sea can be calm, but she can also be ruthless. She will strip anyone down to the marrow before she ever turns on me.

I will see what's beneath these lies.

Seth whistles up ahead, drawing my attention. But it's not at me; it's at Joby, standing on the deck of a schooner. She's a tidy vessel, perfect for coastal trade and sailing. She isn't built for long voyages across the ocean with her two masts and shallow draft. I glance at Seth, wondering if he realizes that this is a clue. That I've spent hours with Kai, helping him and his brother over the years, and can spot a smuggling vessel a mile off. We aren't going far offshore to follow the coordinates. And this ship doesn't belong to a mainland merchant, which only confirms my suspicions about this crew. I decide to keep this knowledge to myself; I don't want any of them realizing that I know what they are. What this kind of schooner is used for.

"What a beauty," I say, eyeing her name painted on the side. *Phantom*.

A chill creeps across the back of my neck as Seth ushers me on board and I smile at him, as if nothing is wrong. I walk the gangplank up to the deck, ignoring the way my skin prickles. Two sets of eyes greet me, Joby's and Pearl's, silent and watchful.

"I can drop your pack in the cabin belowdecks if you like," Seth says, reaching for the strap. "They're giving us that space as our quarters."

I step back and his fingers catch on thin air. "One cabin? For both of us? Surely you're crew and sleep where the others sleep. I'm paying."

He shrugs. "Those are the arrangements. Unless you'd prefer to sleep under the stars."

A whistle not unlike Seth's slices across the deck and the

gangplank is hastily pulled up. Pearl, short hair tufting around her shoulders, unloops the rope tying us to the quay.

And then it's too late to turn back.

The Isle of Ennor, with its wall of Wanted posters, unseen young lord, watchful people, and shop full of mysteries falls away. And I'm unsure if I've made the right decision stepping aboard *Phantom*. I watch as the star-shaped castle, the town, everything disappears, consumed by sea mist.

A voice, soft and smoky, reaches down from the rigging and I look up to find Merryam tangled in the rope and sails. She carries on singing, a sea shanty about fair winds and smooth journeys. Pearl and Joby take it up, the singing swelling around me. Merryam's eye falls on me, and she winks. I stiffen, wanting to jump over the side into the waves.

Phantom feels like it shares a secret with all but me. I have always been the hunter of treasures, the wreck swimmer, the one who lures the ships in. But now, I stand on the other side.

As though *I* am the ship they have lured and trapped.

CHAPTER
ELEVEN

"A CABIN WITH ONE BED," I SNORT, DUMPING MY pack by the door. I can barely move around the space. It holds a narrow bed and a small cupboard and shelves set into the creaking sides.

"You can sleep in one of the bunks in the main galley if you wish," says Seth, leaning against the door frame with a sly smile. "Only, you'll have to share with one of the crew."

I scowl at him, sitting on the end of the bed. It isn't even as wide as a single. "*I* will sleep here. *You* can find a bunk."

His smile widens into a grin, his eyes glittering with mirth. "What, you thought we'd be sharing the bed at the same time?"

"I—"

"We'll take shifts."

I nod. An image crosses behind my eyes, of Seth lying beside me, his body shifting closer, fingers trailing, ever so slowly up my arm...

I cough, looking away, and pin my gaze to the floor. "All right."

"Good. There are no other bunks available, so that would have gotten a little too cozy. You can have the cabin now. It was a long night on that skiff. I'm sure you need some rest."

Before I can respond, he disappears, closing the door behind him. Leaving me once again wrong-footed.

I try to get comfortable, but sleep is lost on me. I curl up in the far corner of the bed, turning irritably as the schooner makes her way through the waves. It should lull me, this cradle of tide, but instead it unnerves me. I've never spent this much time aboard a ship before; the trips to trade are always on a skiff or a vessel smaller than this. I don't know where we're going or if I trust we'll be following the coordinates I gave. Or what discussions are happening on the other side of the cabin door. So after a fitful snatched few hours of sleep, I get up and scrub my face. Then I go in search of Seth.

The door from the cabin leads directly into the main galley, and as I pull it open, three sets of eyes lift to mine. The crew are sitting together around the long table, empty bowls in front of them. Seth gestures to a spare seat.

"Sit. Eat."

I make my way to the seat and Pearl swiftly fills a bowl with fish broth for me. She tears a hunk of bread off the loaf in the center of the table and pushes both carefully toward my place at the table. I pull them the last few inches into my chest and catch her eye. I didn't notice before, but she has a scar running down her left cheekbone. It's a narrow line, cutting through the faint sun freckles dusting her pale white face. When she tilts her chin up, the flickering light from a couple of lamps casting her features in soft shadow, the scar is no longer visible.

"Thanks."

She shrugs and the rough-spun pale blue tunic she's wearing slips off one shoulder. She quickly adjusts it, flashing me a set of pointed little teeth. "You're welcome."

I begin spooning the broth into my mouth, the creamy sauce perfectly salted, offset by a combination of herbs that taste almost floral on my tongue, and slowly they all start talking. Hesitantly at first, but I keep my eyes low and focus on the spoon and the food in front of me. Let them see me as anything but a threat.

It's clear very quickly how at ease Seth is around them and how little of himself he showed us on my island. At the healer's cottage he was compliant, making himself seem smaller and less of a threat. Now, he leans forward, intense and gesturing as Joby, sitting to my right, throws up a hand, waving him off. They're talking about the route. About their cargo.

"Joby, we have to be there on time. There's no way around that," Seth says, accepting a cup of tea. "Thanks, Pearl. Merryam agreed to Mira's time frame."

Joby clears his throat, crossing his arms. His chestnut hair catches at the candlelight, threaded with golds and reds. His nose is upturned at the end, set between eyes that have an almost startled quality, they're so big. It makes him seem younger than me, but watching him now, so assured among this crew, I can see it would be a mistake to underestimate him. He can hold his own. "You forget we had a plan *before* Mer struck that deal."

My ears prick and I glance between them. Seth is still looking cool and unfazed. But Joby is leaning in, tapping a knuckle on the table as though to drive the point home.

"Surely you can do the drop in a week, even a couple of weeks," Seth begins.

"What, and haul it all halfway to the Far Isles and back? *No*," Joby says, taking a cup of tea from Pearl as well with a nod. I catch the look between the boys just before Joby's chestnut hair flops forward, hiding his features. It's a warning look, sharp and clear. I'm just not sure what it means. Joby leans back, taking a sip from the cup and sighs. "Just drink your tea, Seth. Leave the route to Mer."

Seth shakes his head. "You know I can't do that. Not this time. Mira made a deal."

I look up to find Seth's eyes on me. But they aren't angry like I expected. They're glazed, as though his thoughts have wandered far from here. I frown, unsure why he's fighting for me on this. Perhaps it's just that he feels he still owes me, after I saved his life on Rosevear. I blink and he shifts in his seat, focusing again on Joby.

"Do you want tea?" Pearl says to me. She offers a cup, the fragrant steam curling up, all lavender and milk with a hint of honey. The scent reminds me of Agnes's blend.

"Yes. Please," I say, closing my fingers around the ceramic sides. It's aromatic and rich in a way that Agnes's isn't. I taste the whisper of fennel, but there's also a hint of bitterness, as though touched by something more potent than leaves. Perhaps this is an apothecary-made blend.

"Bratha root. Helps with seasickness if it gets lumpy out here," Pearl says with a wink, noting that I've tasted the edge of bitterness. I smile at her, not mentioning that I've never been seasick a day in my life.

I take another sip as Joby grabs my empty bowl, getting up to move around the galley. He passes it to Pearl and they work quickly together, tidying up. There's not much space with the bunks set into the walls, dark gray, heavy curtains pulled around them, the long table in the center. Every nook has a purpose. Every space is utilized.

Seth and Joby keep talking as they clear up, about the cargo, about the coordinates. Joby's frame is tall and angular, the shirt he wears bunching across his collarbone as he moves agilely around the galley. Pearl barely seems to inhabit any space at all and it's not until she whisks my empty cup from my fingers that I know she is standing behind me.

"Look, all I'm saying is we've got to be at those coordinates at that time and we've got to be *fast*. We made a deal," Seth says, leaning back in his chair.

"You mean, *I* made a deal," I say quietly.

Joby shrugs, placing his hand on the back of the chair across from Seth. There's a ring on his middle finger, a simple band of silver that taps against the wood of the chair as he grasps it. A faint compass is etched into it, a symbol I'm sure I've seen somewhere before. "She won't like it."

"She won't like what?"

That soft, smoky voice chimes from the ladder steps leading up to the deck. Merryam dances down, lingering on the bottom step as she eyes us all. Pearl and Joby exchange a look and Seth's fingers curl into a fist. He sees me watching and moves his hand under the table, as though trying to hide his unease from me.

"Seth wants us to follow the coordinates first, Mer," Pearl offers up, ducking into a lower bunk and drawing her knees against her chest. "Which Joby has pointed out isn't part of the plan."

"Joby's right," Merryam says, moving toward Seth. She pulls out the chair at the head of the table, a bowl of broth appearing in front of her. Joby pushes the whole loaf toward her and she thanks him, tearing off pieces and dropping them into her bowl. Her long fingers are elegant, a musician's hands. But the brown skin is riddled with tiny scars, as though earned from a lifetime of wielding a blade. "We've got a full hold."

"And what exactly does that mean?" I ask, finding my voice. Merryam pauses, a piece of bread hovering in her fingertips. The focus of the galley narrows on me. But I stare back steadily, refusing to back down. "What is the plan?"

Merryam smiles, dunking the piece of bread into her broth before bringing her fingers up to her mouth. She licks them like a cat, her gaze never leaving my face. I can feel the heat rising up my chest, threatening to rise farther. She's playing with me, waiting for a reaction, or for me to look away first. "I guess we haven't got to know each other properly yet."

"I guess not," I say. I can feel Seth's eyes burning into my skin but I refuse to play this game. This may be her schooner and I may not be on my island, but the rules are the same anywhere.

If you look away, you've lost.

She laughs softly. "All right. There's something you should know about me. I'm fair. If I make a deal, I stick to it. We will get you to the coordinates you gave me and we will return you safely in the time frame we agreed on. But…"

"But?"

"*But*, Pearl and Joby are correct. We have a full hold and we'll lag in the water if we don't make the drop. Aside from

the fact that we had an agreement before we took you on…
we can't not make this stop."

"You kept that from us, it wasn't part of the—" Seth starts.

Merryam holds up a hand. "You know how it is. Can't lug
a full hold halfway to the Far Isles without losing pace. Not
even for you, sweet boy."

Seth snorts and I finally look away from Merryam's eyes
and straight into his. He's angry, furious even. But I don't
understand why. If she's still promising to stick to her word
and get me there and back, then this is just a minor incon-
venience. He's got a new crew; he'll be paid either way by
Merryam. Unless I'm missing something.

"Will it take long, this stop?" I ask carefully, tasting the
atmosphere down here in the belly of *Phantom*. Judging how
many steps it would be to the ladder steps and whether Seth
would be any use in a fight. I don't trust any of them, especially Pearl, dancing so silently on those delicate little feet
around me.

"One night. That's all," Merryam says, raising her eyebrows
at Seth. "You know where."

Seth shakes his head, cursing quietly. "Mer, this *wasn't* part
of the deal."

But Merryam just shrugs and carries on eating.

"Well, I guess if that's all…" I say, pushing my chair back to
stand. I weave around Joby and wonder where they keep their
weapons. If they all carry a blade like I do. "I need some air."

I swing up the ladder steps as casually as I can. But my
heart is jumping, fighting against the cage of my ribs. It's not
until I'm standing with the scent of the sea surrounding me,
the cold air sharp against my skin, that I feel steady. The sails
are full, fair winds carrying us along the coast. I can see the

blink of lights along the land, the flash of a lighthouse marking a deadly set of rocks. I move to the railings, brushing my
fingers along the smooth wood. It's warm and solid, just like
the boats Kai builds. I grasp it, pressing my palms into the
rail. As though I can push my fears out and somehow sum-
mon Kai and Agnes to be here with me.

But it's just me. Me and the ocean and a crew I can barely
trust not to dump me over the side. I close my eyes and take
a full, shuddering breath.

"I'm sorry," Seth says, coming to stand next to me. "Mer
is adamant. They have to make the drop first."

"It shouldn't set me back," I say, finding a level of calm in
my voice.

"It's not that," Seth says, staring over the waves. "It's *where*
they're making the drop."

"Well, it won't take us much out of the way. Surely, we—"

"It's Finnikin's Way."

I pause midsentence. Finnikin's Way is a barely uttered secret. It's a place woven through sailor's stories, a place even
the watch can't find. It's not on any map except the ones held
in people's heads. And the few who hold the knowledge are
too afraid to part with it. It's a place of ghosts. A smuggler
once told me that his brother had left for a drop on Finnikin's
Way. He expected good coin for his haul; he was a chancer.
But he never returned.

"We...we can't go there. I'm an outsider. I haven't been
invited. The people there won't like it."

Seth's eyes land on me, softening. He reaches his hand toward me and for a second, I think he will close his fingers
around mine. But he stops, leaving his knuckles just grazing
my own. A current passes under my skin, something deli-

cious. Something that makes my heart skip. I move my hand away, severing the closeness between us. There's something about Seth, his charm, his way of talking. I don't trust him and I don't trust myself around him. I don't trust my own eyes, my heating skin, and I can't allow myself to be tricked. But… I can't stop myself from wondering what it would be like if his hands grasped my waist, if his thumbs skimmed the top of my hips, if he pulled my body to his…

"Promise me one thing. When we're there," he says, turning his whole body to me.

I snap from my reverie, annoyed with myself. Now more than ever, I cannot lose focus. Seth is a distraction that I can ill afford. "What?"

"You won't wander off. You'll stay by *Phantom* and not engage with anyone. Don't even *look* at anyone. They won't know you're not part of Merryam's crew that way. You're right—they won't trust you. They don't like anyone new knowing how to get there, and how to leave."

I laugh, shaking my head. Father has coddled me for years, bending his life around mine to keep me safe. The last thing I want now I'm away from Rosevear is Seth taking the same role. There's a reason why I'm one of the seven. And if Seth thinks I know nothing of the wider world, he's a fool.

"Worried I won't survive a smuggler's drop? Yes, I know what they are. I know what this ship is."

"This drop isn't just any drop," he says, turning back to the sea, a frown etched into his forehead. Maybe he believed I would be compliant? That I would lean on him on this journey? "If I had known… Anyway, just do as I ask. Please."

I can taste the truth in his words. It's the opposite of the bitter Bratha root. It's sweet like Agnes's apple buns. I don't know what to make of it. Is he seeking to be my protector, to trick me into trusting him? Perhaps Finnikin's Way truly is a place where I am out of my depth. "Why? I'm no stranger to smugglers. Why is it so important?"

He grasps my shoulder, turning me so our faces are close. Nearly as close as when I found him on the beach, his clothes clawed at by the tide. My breath hitches.

"The people of Finnikin's Way aren't just any smugglers, Mira. And yes, maybe I do care. Maybe I'm grateful you saved me from the wreck." He shakes the curls from his face, impatience marking his features. But there's more underneath. More beneath the surface of his eyes. "Promise me you won't interfere with the drop."

I catch the glint of fear, true fear, as his gaze bores into mine. It's the kind that Bryn gets if we're swimming out to a particularly beaten-up wreck. Maybe Seth feels like he owes me still. Maybe that's all this is and I'm imagining the connection between us. But I can't be sure.

"Why, Seth?"

"Because the stories are all true. They loathe strangers. If you don't look like you fit with Merryam's crew, they will kill you."

CHAPTER TWELVE

FINNIKIN'S WAY IS SHROUDED IN MORNING MIST. After a calm night on the water there's a bite to the air, but the sea is watchful. Waiting. As though not even she dares fling her wrath upon this secret pass. In the hours overnight I traded places with Seth and found a blanket to huddle under on deck. Leaning against the mainmast, I traced the shooting stars as they burned brilliantly, tiny lines flaring briefly in the bowl of wide sky. I wondered if my father could see them. If he even has a window on Penscalo where the watch hold him.

I have seven days.

Just seven short days and nights now to reach the coordinates, find whatever my mother has left there and persuade the watch captain to make a deal with me. With every passing moment, I'm surer that she is leading me there, that she has left something there that will help me. But so much could go wrong. And every hour that ticks away, every detour, prickles under my skin like nettle leaves.

The damp in the air belies my restlessness. I can barely see a few feet beyond the ship, and what I do see leaves me cold. A sheer cliff face, a small gap between two hulking giants. Rocks that have seen many centuries and will see many more. A castle, round and built of shaped granite, perched atop the cliff face on one side of the pass and covered with narrow openings for nocking an arrow or, if they have them, aiming a rifle. It's different to the star-shaped castle on Ennor. These walls are smooth and rounded, impossible to breach. I shiver, clutching the blanket tight to my chest. Everything is painted gray. The sky, the sea, the land. I wonder how many ghosts linger. How many people weren't welcomed here and didn't survive the pass.

Pearl comes to stand beside me, handing me a round of bread with some mackerel slipped inside it. I nod in thanks, biting into it. The fish has a charred taste, balanced by tiny layers of pickled beetroot that color the fish purple. I glance at Pearl as I chew, realizing she is so much more than she appears. An excellent cook, for one, if she is able to pull together meals like this from the scantest of ingredients. She sighs, her eyes trained on the castle at the top of the cliff with its many narrow windows. Its dark secrets.

"I hate this place."

I swallow my mouthful. "Why do you make the drop here then?"

"Because it's not up to me," she says, leaning her forearms on the rail. "It's up to…someone else."

"Merryam?"

She shrugs, pushing off from the rail, smiling a slightly crooked smile. Her hair fans out around her cheeks in a pale, cloudy haze. "Sure. Merryam."

I turn back to the pass, finishing my breakfast, and it sinks like a stone inside me, despite how tasty it was. But it's better to be full. I wonder guiltily if my father and Bryn have managed to share a meal today. A flurry of commands issues behind me and I glance around, finding the crew all on deck. They look like a pack, like the werewolves that roam the northern wilds of Arnhem and the nearly uninhabitable regions of the Spines that the sailors tell tales about. Even Seth moves as they do, tying down sails, moving silently over the deck. I catch Merryam watching me and she does not look away. Not immediately. I taste unease radiating from her and the dark churn of many, many secrets.

She releases a breath, her eyes tracking past me. Obviously spotting a signal she has been waiting for. "All right, Joby. Ease her in."

Joby stands at the helm, holding the great wheel steady. With small movements, he guides *Phantom* toward the cliffs. I grip the rail in my fists, the grooves in the wood nipping at my palms. As we draw closer to the castle, I see it has an exposed platform at the top with three cannons pointing out to sea. There are people standing there, still and watchful. I shiver, removing one hand from the rails to tighten my shawl around my shoulders.

This place whispers of death.

"Remember what I said. Don't talk to anyone. Don't even *look* at anyone."

I glance at Seth, his eyes fixed on the castle as mine were. They're narrowed, his face closed off and distant, all traces of his natural good humor and warmth drained away. How does he fit in to all this? If he's lived his whole life on the ocean, he must have visited this place before. Another thought occurs to me. My mother arrived on our island on a smuggler ship. Was she part of this shadowed world before she arrived on Rosevear?

"You know, you haven't told me anything about yourself," I say quietly.

He says nothing for a moment, not until we're through the pass. The sheer rock faces close around us and I hold my breath. Then we're through. I breathe out as Seth does, sagging against the rail. Joby puts more distance between us and the castle with its cannons and silent guardians and I feel the tension unspool from the ship.

Seth hands me something small and cold, made of metal. "I grew up knowing that every word comes with a cost," he says. I find sadness in him, buried beneath the warmth that has spilled back into his voice now we've made it through the pass. I wonder what it means. He has handed me a blade. So now I have two: one to fight with and this one, to throw.

"Keep that hidden. If you need it, you'll know."

"Have you been here before?" I ask, keeping his face in my peripheral vision.

He smirks. "Full of questions this morning."

"Maybe I'm trying to work you out," I say, sharpening my gaze. His smirk disappears as he clears his throat, avoiding my eyes.

"All you need to know is that I know how the people here operate. Yes, I've been here before and I've seen how vicious they can turn in an argument. My mother—" He stops short.

"Your mother?"

It takes a moment for him to reply and I wait, wondering how many untruths he can slip into his next words. He frowns, searching my face. As though unsure how much to tell me. "My mother lost her sister here. She's never forgotten and nor have I."

A shiver rises up my spine. Seth's eyes stutter into darkness, as though reliving some moment from his past. I can taste no lies in what he has said. It seems he did truly lose his kin here.

"Just mind what I've said. Be careful."

The cliffs guard a cove of shells and white sand. Beyond that are buildings, a whole town secreted behind the curtain of rock. I blink, hiding my shock. This isn't just a smuggler's drop point, hidden from the gaze of the watch. This is a whole way of life, born of the need to remain a secret. If secrets are a way of life for Seth, then he must be hiding more truths from me than I can possibly uncover. Maybe Kai and Agnes were right. Maybe I shouldn't have trusted him. Even though I feel he has shown me a sliver of himself, he could be anyone.

Merryam whistles low, calling her crew to her. They work as one, just as we seven do on the rope. They drop the anchor, haul up the sails, secure the lines. And keep a careful watch on the silent cove.

"To me," Merryam says softly, signaling as a small rowboat is lowered over the side. She glances at Joby and nods. He nods back, leaning up against the mainmast and crossing his arms. I take it he's staying to guard the ship.

I follow Seth down the rope ladder, finding my feet on the boards of the small rowboat, and hunker down next to Pearl. Merryam takes up the oars, rowing us in with slow, deft strokes. Seth's hand strays to an inner pocket, as though checking something is there. I wonder if it's a weapon.

We hit the shallows just as a group make their way onto the beach. It's a wide cove, but with a narrow strip of sand, even at low tide. They are only a few feet from us when we pull the boat up above the tide line. My boots crunch on the shells, white and yellow, all tinged with green. I feel the ghosts of this place press closer. Watching us.

A man with flecks of gray in his beard steps forward, clasping his hands behind his back. He looks us over, lingering for a second on Seth before coming back to Merryam. Then he nods. "Well met. I trust no trouble this time?"

"None we can't handle," Merryam says. "She's full. Same rate?"

The man chews on the inside of his mouth. "Gone down."

"By how much?"

"Halved."

Merryam laughs far too casually. Pearl takes a step closer. "He won't be happy, Jev."

The man shrugs, gestures to the people behind him. "They need feeding. It's been a harsh winter. The buyers aren't so fast with their coin. Watch is everywhere. Hard to shift it in Leicena and Skylan."

"It's been harsh on us all. And the watch is always everywhere. Nothing new in that," Merryam says, licking her lips. "Perhaps we can discuss this some more?"

Jev's eyes turn into sharp little beads and I feel the turn of the tide in this cove. His people step back, none of them speaking, just watching us. Pearl's gaze darts back and forth, Seth stiffens at my side. Agnes's blade beats like a pulse and I want to reach for it, feel the comforting weight in my hand.

"As you say," Jev barks.

The tension seeps away.

Jev turns, following his people up the beach, and Seth signals for me to hang back. I watch as Pearl and Merryam disappear behind the first line of buildings.

"They'll be a while negotiating," Seth says, sitting down on the sand. He brings his knees up. "We may as well relax."

"You're not going with them? What if they don't agree?"

"Then we'll have to get out of here sharpish."

I frown. "You're not worried for them?"

He grins up at me. "Those two don't need a nursemaid, trust me. Besides, it's not my negotiation. I wouldn't be welcome."

"How do you know they don't need help?"

"None of us do out here. Not unless we ask for it."

I flop down next to him, wondering how he can be so calm. Jev looked set to murder one of them and feed them to his people. And with the guardians in that castle by the pass, I doubt we would make it away unharmed.

"We'll give it an hour," he says. "If you hear shouting, swim back to the ship."

"What about you?"

He says nothing.

I ignore the prickle of unanswered questions building inside me. Instead, I push my hands into the sand and shells, the cold grounding me. Reminding me why I'm here. I realize it would be all too easy with Seth to get caught up in the ebb and flow of his world. And that this is only the surface, the depths of it still beyond my understanding. But all I need is a way to rescue my father. All I need is what my mother has hidden at those coordinates, and then I can leave this world behind.

I don't need any more than that. Not the sea and the tide and this whole ocean ready for me to explore.

I *can't* want that, can I? There is no space for it in my life on Rosevear. I have to keep that door firmly closed. For my father.

In moments I'm restless again. I stride down to the sea. I

pull off my boots and socks and feel the water flow over my feet. It sends warmth across my skin, delicious and inviting. She is calm in this bay with the cliffs surrounding her. I wonder if she ever unleashes her full fury on these people. If they've ever seen the sea's rage.

A whistle pierces the air and I freeze.

"Was that...?"

Again. Then silence.

I run back to Seth, who is alert, scanning the beach. With a jolt, I notice the knife glinting in his hand. "Get back to the ship, Mira. Get ready to move."

"But you, and the others—"

"The ship, Mira." He shoves me, hard. "Go!"

I watch as he runs toward the buildings, disappearing from sight. A shot rips through the quiet and I stumble back. Scanning the buildings back and forth, blood beating hot in my ears, I search for anything, anyone, but there's nothing, no sign.

Then I hear it. A scream.

I shove on my boots, pull Agnes's blade into my fist, leaving the one Seth gave me concealed for when I truly have need of it. I could do as Seth says and swim back to the ship. Turn tail and run. I don't owe these people anything. I'm not a smuggler, this world isn't mine, and I have a purpose already. And time is running out with each minute we spend in this place.

But I am one of the seven and I have never turned tail. It's drummed into me to save as many as I can. To work together as one.

I never leave a beating heart behind.

CHAPTER
THIRTEEN

THE BUILDINGS LOOM UP AS A CROOKED MAZE around me. I hug the walls, checking each winding street before dashing to the next. It's oddly quiet, not a soul in sight. The silence presses down on this eerie, gray town and I half imagine faces at the darkened windows marking my path beneath them. A tangle of curses pricks my ears and I turn in their direction, heading farther inland. Into the belly of this place.

I pause at a corner, throwing my back against a building. It's cut granite, just like every wall here, all uneven and awash with creeping lichen. I press my fingertips into the rough stone, gathering my courage. I know that around this next bend, I will find them. I take a breath, in, out, steeling myself for a fight.

Then I push off, rounding the corner—

And find nothing.

I blink, scanning the small square, the squat buildings all hunched together, the fishing nets coiled in a pile.

The sound of voices echoes off the walls. A sign painted in pale blues and sea greens swings above one of the buildings. Of course. It's a pub, a meeting place, the sign painted with a ship at sea. The Albion.

I dart for the windows, launching myself beneath them. The door is right next to me and if it opens, I'm too exposed to run. Especially if they have rifles. The voices rise and fall in a pattern growing more heated by the second, the occasional growl from the man, Jev, punctuating the steady stream from Merryam. She's trying to negotiate. But I'm not sure if it's for the drop, or for her life.

A noise, soft and throaty as birdsong, sounds to my left and I start. It's Joby, hugging the shadows on the other side of the square. I nod, imitating his whistle, keeping it gentle and low. Merryam keeps talking inside, apparently oblivious. I crane my neck to listen for the sounds of any others as Joby slinks from wall to wall, finally sinking down next to me.

"I thought you were staying on the ship," I whisper.

"Mer thought this might go sideways," he whispers back, the dagger in his hand catching my eye. "It's what we wanted them to think. Let's just say there's history."

"What do you mean?"

Joby's eyes narrow. "Merryam has a score to settle here, back when she was working for someone else, and Jev's never forgotten it."

I nod when Joby falls silent, realizing he isn't going to elaborate further. I look back around the square. It's still so silent.

"Seth's at the back, I'm going in the front on his signal."

"What about me?"

Joby eyes the blade in my own hand, then looks up to search my face. For a beat, he doesn't respond, as though weighing me up. Perhaps working out if I would be a help or a hindrance, or maybe if he can trust me at all. I square my shoulders, waiting for his judgment. He gives the briefest nod. "You're with me."

A shrill gull cry splits the air around us and I glance up and around. But the gray clouds are empty. It's the signal. Joby stands, fire igniting his face as he kicks down the door. I rise, gritting my teeth. Readying myself for blood.

And I follow.

There's a bar at the back crowded with rows of dull-looking bottles, nothing like the glinting, jewel-like ones clustered in the Mermaid on Ennor. Rough-cut wooden tables and chairs are grouped in corners and scattered in the center of the wooden floorboards. On a table by one of the windows, four people sit. Merryam, Pearl, Jev, and a woman. Jev and the woman leap up, rounding on us as Seth barrels in from a doorway behind the bar. I hesitate, searching the shadows and the corners, all empty. There is no one else in this room. Who fired the rifle? Where are the others that were crowded around Jev on the beach?

"Get out. It's a trap!" Pearl shouts, getting to her feet as another door, one I hadn't noticed at first, flies open on the other side of the bar and people begin pouring in. Joby runs for Jev, slicing up with his blade and spinning to tackle the woman at his back. Seth goes for the people storming in, smashing a fist into the face of a man carrying a rifle. The man loses his balance with a gasp, the rifle sliding across the floorboards. I weigh up the room in less than a second, just like on a wreck. And I go for the people I can save.

I jump over a chair, pushing past a woman with her fists flying at Joby's side. I brace my feet, bringing my knee up to her ribs, and she doubles over with a gasp, hands clutching her side. In a blink, I'm at the table with Pearl and Merryam, pushing Pearl toward the window.

"Mer!" she shouts, her hand reaching out. Merryam pauses, clutching her fingers briefly and Pearl's face shatters as she turns away.

"Run!" Merryam cries, pulling two knives from her belt as she joins the fray.

I grab Pearl, hauling her slight frame to the window, shoving at the catch until it opens wide. "Climb now, go!"

"But Mer, Joby—"

"I can tell you're not a fighter," I say desperately as a glass sails past our heads, smashing against the wall. I duck, cursing as fragments rain over our shoulders, and shove her out.

Pearl hits the ground, leaping up like a cat as I drop down beside her. "Do you know the way back to the ship?"

She nods grimly. "I grew up here."

I blink, folding this information away. Now isn't the time.

Shouts snag my attention from across the square and Pearl flinches at my side. "They'll kill us!"

I grab her hand and we run.

She leads me a different way through the web of buildings, flitting around granite walls and corners until we lose the echo of footsteps. I breathe heavily, cursing my boots as they rumble over the rough cobbles and Pearl guides us, tugging me along.

There. *Phantom.* She's still and unruffled where we anchored up in the cove. Just as we left her.

"Think you can swim?" Pearl says, already tugging off her boots, tying the laces to loop them around her neck.

I grin at her. "I think I can."

I yank off my own boots, tying the laces as Pearl does, and we linger at the edge of the sand, under the shadow of the first row of buildings. Just long enough to check we are alone. A shout from the town at our backs startles me and I push Pearl toward the sea.

"I don't think there's going to be a good time. We just have to make a dash for it."

We sprint across the exposed, cold sand. My blood heats as we wade into the water, as it rushes across my skin. It's like flame, reaching up my legs, and I dive in, cutting swiftly toward *Phantom*.

I move quickly, slip over to the rope ladder, and pull myself out of the water. Pearl pushes back her hair, shivering as I help her up onto the deck. "You've done that before," she says as I quickly hustle her belowdecks. "You should be f-freezing."

"I'm an islander, remember?" I say, brushing off her suspicion.

Pearl chuckles softly as I wrap a blanket around her and pour tea from the kettle into a mug. "You need to bring your body temperature back up. Stay down here, I'll watch for the others."

I don't wait for her answer as I climb back on deck. The wind is picking up, but only slightly. I bite my lip, tracing the shape of the sails, and curse. With a full hold, *Phantom* will only limp out of this cove. And even then, we have those sheer cliff faces and the manned castle waiting to pick us off. We're trapped.

I grit my teeth and shove my wet hair from my face. No. Not trapped. This ship is sound. There *has* to be another way.

I make my way back belowdecks, swinging off the ladder to land by the table. "Pearl, you grew up here?"

Her teeth chatter as she answers, her lips tinged blue. "I did."

"Is there another way out? A secret way?"

On Rosevear we have our hiding places, our routes around cliffs and coves that are seemingly impassable. We know the ways through the rocks with their hidden jaws. We know how to escape if we need to. How to survive. And even though there is a harshness to this place and these people that I don't recognize in my own, I can see the will to survive written in every heartbeat. There has to be another way out.

Pearl blinks and sighs. I watch her inner battle as her eyes tangle with mine. She doesn't want to reveal it. It was probably drummed into her all her life, never to betray the secret. Never to betray her people. But I catch her flinch and wonder if she's thinking of the others. Her crew. Of Mer and Joby...maybe even Seth. If they are her people now, more than the kin she grew up with, then she has to decide who she will save and which secrets she is willing to betray. Her eyes turn to flint.

"There is another way. But it's risky. Hard to navigate—easy to get wrong and blow a hole in a ship's side. But it'll mean we won't get picked off by the watchers on the cliffs."

I nod. I was right. In a place like this, there's always an escape route. A secret way. "Can you navigate it?"

She opens her mouth, then closes it again. A thousand thoughts and memories flit over her face before she says, "I can."

"Good." I turn on my heel, already leaping back up the steps. "I'm going to pull up the anchor. Get ready. The minute they appear on that beach, we have to move. And, Pearl?"

"Yes?"

"We have to get rid of the cargo. Tip it overboard and cut your losses. Or *Phantom* could be too slow."

"We...we can't do that," she says, swallowing, not meeting my eyes.

I pause on the steps, eyeing her carefully. "What's in the hold, Pearl?"

"I can't tell you."

"Bullshit," I hiss. "We both know that cargo has to go."

I leap back down the steps, crossing to the hold.

"Wait, don't!"

Wrenching the door open, I steel myself for riches. For stolen jewels or perhaps even a catch of rifles. Something valuable that the crew would be in hot water for losing.

But what I find leaves me cold.

Blood.

Vials and vials of blood. Tiny glass tubes in an unusual shade of red, a vibrant, screaming crimson. I stand on the threshold, eyeing the myriad rows of them, all sealed with corks, labels hanging around the necks.

"I told you not to look," Pearl says quietly at my shoulder.

My stomach churns, the boards tilting beneath my feet. "Are you— Did you kill for this?"

"No," Pearl says quickly, moving back toward the table in the galley. I glance back at her and she seems suddenly tired.

"Then who?"

"The witches," she says, voice as soft as a needle slipped between two ribs. "Their hunters track the wild creatures and kill them for their blood. Then we collect what they don't want and it's shipped to the apothecaries for their potions. Easier if we make the drop here. Jev takes a cut, he distributes to the territories on the continent, and everyone is happy. Usually."

Nausea curls like a knot in my stomach. I knew witches were magical. I knew that somehow the apothecaries got the magic for their potions from the witches. But this... I swallow. Is this what the witches' magic is born from?

"What kind of creatures?"

"Whatever their hunters can slay," Pearl says. "Narwhal, wyvern, firedrake, phoenix...pretty much anything except sirens. Almost impossible to kill and drain. Don't think that I agree with this, Mira. This is just the way our world works. The way *magic* works. The witches use the magic for spells and hexes—they live off the blood of these creatures. It turns their nails black, sometimes their eyes and veins if they imbibe too much. Then whatever is left, like these vials, they sell to the apothecaries. We're just the middlemen. And at least we buy direct from the covens in Arnhem. There's nothing else mixed in."

"It's vile. This is *vile*," I breathe, closing the door to the hold. I can't bear to look at all that blood anymore. Just knowing it has been in there this whole time sends my stomach roiling.

I remember the tales my mother told as I grew up, of firedrakes soaring through the mountains in the north. Of phoenix burning and people trying to steal just one feather from their nests. Of the gentle narwhals with their powder-white horns, shifting time around them to slow or speed up.

She told me the true magic of the world lay in the corners. That the witches would drain our world dry, stealing the raw beauty of it. That the apothecaries were no better, even if they did cure people. She believed that they shouldn't. That some people were meant to die. That it was part of being human, being mortal. I didn't really understand what she meant until now. I didn't know that what the witches were draining was the blood of these wild creatures. That this is where true magic comes from.

I turn back to Pearl and walk past her, up on deck. Somehow in my desperate hunt for something that will save my father, I have stumbled onto a path that goes against everything my mother believed in. Is the blood in those vials on my hands now too?

Gunshot splits the sky. I hasten my steps, scanning the beach and the buildings, fingers digging into the railings. Pearl joins me on deck, shivering as she rakes her gaze across the town.

"I'm going to pull up the anchor," I say, already striding for the capstan. "We have to leave."

CHAPTER FOURTEEN

A SECOND GUNSHOT RINGS OUT. I PACE RESTLESSLY to and fro as Pearl chews on her lip, still as stone, hands steadying the helm. I've pulled up the anchor, but kept the sails down. It's all we can do to hold the wheel steady, to drum our restless fingers. We're drifting slightly, but on this eerily still day, not by much.

"Where are they?" Pearl breathes beside me, anxiety bleeding into her voice. We don't say it. That Merryam, Joby, and Seth might not come out of there. That those people, *her* people, are ruthless. That we might have to navigate a way out of this cove without them.

"Five more minutes…" I say, gritting my teeth. From what I know so far of Seth, he'll slip from this place with a grin and pockets filled with loot. He's cunning and far too quick to turn on the charm. But the others… I don't know how far they're willing to go to escape. What they will sacrifice to survive. Especially if Joby is right and Merryam does have a score to settle.

A rifle shot pierces the silence. Then another. And I am the still, watchful water beneath us. The quiet of the inky deep. The silence wraps around me, sharpening me. I scan the houses, searching for signs of them.

"There!"

I draw a breath as they burst onto the beach.

"Pearl, hoist the mainsail, we have to go *now*!"

She leaps for the ropes, pulling them with her whole body, her heels digging into the deck as I throw my weight against the helm. I watch as Merryam, Seth, and Joby all crash into the water, not even bothering to remove their boots.

Then I see them. The people of Finnikin's Way. They're not chasing them into the sea. They're taking aim from the shadows. I gasp as a shot fires. And I'm back on that beach on Rosevear again. Watching the red coats swarm the beach, powerless to stop them and save my father.

Seth sinks like a stone.

I swallow, leaning over the wheel, searching for him in the water as Merryam and Joby reach the rope ladder, the swirl of dark sea rippling below.

"They got Seth!" Joby shouts as he hits the deck. Merryam thumps on the boards right behind him, coughing and wheezing, trying to draw breath.

"Take the helm! Pearl will direct you," I call to Joby.

I can't leave Seth. I can't lose him in the water, not again. I feel that tug, hear the sound of the song that lured me to my mother's notebook. But it's not leading me anywhere. It's almost as if it's telling me to turn within, to the strength I have inside me. I steady myself, scanning the water. Feeling rather than looking for signs of his body, his breath. Then I spot it. A hand, his fingers, uncurling and retracting just above the surface, bending the water for less than the breadth of a heartbeat. I focus on that point, marking it. Then I turn, running for the side of the ship—

And dive into the deep.

My blood ignites. I open my eyes, pushing through the quiet to find him. The water undulates around me, threading over and across my chest as I rip through it. I dive deeper, my fingertips touching the seabed, and try to slow my heart. I cast around, tracing the patterns of life, searching for the place I marked.

Blood. A whisper of it, clouding out above me. It's just like that day my mother died. The whisper of red. It's not the exact shade, but it fills me with dread all the same. I call his name, bubbles streaming from my throat, and follow the trail of his blood, heart pounding urgently, too fast and too hard.

Then I see him.

He's falling slowly, too slowly, his eyes closed, blood blooming from a wound near his collarbone. Even from here I can see the marks on his face which will turn to bruises. He's been fighting for his life.

I swim faster, arcing through the water, and finally I reach him. I circle my body around his, that tug in my chest deepening to an ache. I blink from the force of it and grip him tighter. I don't know what this is, why flames course through me when I am near him. It's a feeling I should ignore. *Have* to ignore. But I can't lose him, not now. Not like this.

I kick off from the seabed, expecting to rise like an arrow. But pain, jagged and sharp, lances along my foot and I crumple in the water. I roar into the quiet, my foot pulsing as blood

pours from it. I've caught it on a rock, sliced my heel wide-
open. I whimper underwater, losing myself for a moment.
It throbs, my insides pinched with the shock of it, and I feel
Seth slipping from my grasp…

No.

I can't fail. I grip him tighter, pushing with only my left
foot, kicking out against the current. Fire flows through my
veins, forcing back the pain. I follow the shadow of the ship
above, tracking *Phantom* through the water. The voices echo
eerily, softened to a pounding sound as I move under the
body of the ship. And I see where Pearl is heading. A narrow
opening in the cliff, littered with rocks, only just wider than
Phantom. I hope Merryam and her crew are skilled enough.
I hope Pearl truly does know the shape of the path through
those rocks.

I surface, pulling in a deep, soothing breath, and kick toward the rope ladder. Seth is a deadweight in my arms, dragging me down, but I need his head above the waves.

I need him to breathe.

"I've got him!" I choke out and see Pearl appear above me.

She gasps, eyes wide in a pinched, white face, and Joby
quickly joins her. I grab the rope ladder, wrapping it around
my arm and draw my whole body around Seth. His head falls
back against my chest, his body too relaxed. I can't feel his
lungs filling beneath my hands as I watch our blood mingle
on the surface of the water.

"Pull us up. Now!"

They pull on the rope ladder, my back scraping against
the side of the ship, leaving a trail of pain down my spine.
I grit my teeth and cling to Seth, my legs and arms gripped
around him. His curls stick to my neck and I try to see past

them to his face. I can't feel the warmth of his breath. This moment unspools, just like after the shot cracked open the beach on Rosevear. Like an eternity to reach the sand, like seconds. As I grasp Seth's limp body, I am suspended in time, on the tip of a knife. And we could fall either way into the abyss awaiting him.

They get us over the side just as we pass the first submerged rocks.

"Is he breathing?" Merryam calls over, eyes fixed on the opening between the cliffs. The white of her eyes show her true fear. She jerks the helm and I note the bloodied state of her; the shallow gash from elbow to shoulder, the mess of her knuckles. "Is he alive?"

I'm on my knees next to him, bringing my face down to his, feeling for the hush of air, for any sign that his lungs are unfurling. I pull the rope of my wet hair away from my neck so it doesn't fall into his face, my sodden clothes clinging to my skin as I lean over him. The pain in my foot flares sharply but I ignore it.

"Is he alive?" Merryam roars and I note the desperation. The way her panicked eyes flit between Seth and the passage between the cliffs. And I realize in that moment, everything about the two of them clicking into place. How their mannerisms are similar, how they bicker in such an old, familiar way. He means something to her, more than just some boy she's seen around and picked up for her crew. They've known each other a long time.

They have history.

I look back down at Seth, the tug in my chest tying into a knot so tangled and sharp, it steals my breath. I lower my mouth to his, just as I did on the beach on Rosevear and I hope more than anything that today will end how it began: with us both alive and well. I lean in, so close I can taste his skin. I pinch his nose, bringing my mouth to his, and breathe. His lungs fill like wings beneath my chest and I breathe again, knowing that he's not dead. He hasn't left, not yet anyway. That whatever is tying us together hasn't snapped or severed.

His body convulses.

I move away, wiping my mouth with the back of my hand as a stream of sea gushes from his lips. I have an eerie sense of that first moment repeating, only this time, it's so much worse. He rolls onto his side and Joby sinks to the deck beside us, a wad of bandages in one hand, a smoky green bottle in the other.

"Stay still," he says urgently to Seth, nodding at Pearl then at me. "Hold him steady. Take this, Mira." He hands me the bottle and bandages and I watch as he gets to work. Joby pulls open Seth's jacket, exposing the bloody bloom beneath his shirt. I grit my teeth as Joby assesses the bullet wound, turning him carefully to check his back.

"It's still inside," he says softly as he probes Seth's collarbone.

He looks up, eyes locking with Merryam's. Something passes between them; a question and an answer. Joby sighs, and takes the bottle from my hand.

"Drink this," he orders Seth, uncorking it. "Don't give me any shit. We have to get you to port."

"What does that mean?" I ask, looking from Joby to Pearl. Anywhere but at Seth's pale features as he sips the liquid inside the smoky bottle.

"We have to get him to the apothecary," Pearl says quietly, not meeting my eyes.

She presses her fingers to her heart, then to Seth's and stands. I turn to look at Merryam, seeing her make the same gesture, touching her fingers to her heart as she stares past me at the horizon. A bell tolls at the back of my mind, a low chime echoing through my thoughts, weaving the events of the past few days together in a different pattern. They don't only know one another, Seth and the members of this crew. There is a common understanding between them, a code. A familiarity that speaks of kin. Seth *knows* these people. He has a history with all of them, not just Merryam.

I'm sure of it.

I stare down at Seth and he meets my gaze. It's as though everything is stripped away, as though I can see right through him, to the beating heart at his center. And it pounds with a rhythm I should have noticed earlier.

It pounds with the same rhythm as theirs.

I get up, clumsily stepping back, putting distance between us. He frowns, gulps more of the contents in the bottle and mutters something I don't catch. Merryam turns to him sharply and growls. Whatever they're concealing, they still don't want me to know.

"Hold steady, I've got to bandage you up," Joby says. Then his gaze lands on my heel, eyes widening as he takes in the slick of blood I've left behind on the deck. "Mira, sit down. Let Pearl wrap that."

I take another step, finding the railings at my back. Pearl reaches for my foot, props it up against her thigh and sucks in a breath. "If this had gone any deeper, you would have grazed the bone."

Pearl carries on talking as she presses herbs into my heel, bandaging it carefully, as though to distract me. Seth's eyes

search for mine as Joby gets to work, agony breaking as a
storm across his features. I never look away, never let my gaze
slip. Even when he cries out, even when he nearly faints with
the pain, I pin my eyes to his, staying with him.

We clear the pass between the cliffs and collectively breathe
a sigh of relief. With Finnikin's Way behind us, my shoulders
drop an inch, the unease cramping my stomach subsiding a
little. Merryam hands over control of the helm to Pearl, her
features suddenly drawn and exhausted as she brushes a brief
kiss along Pearl's cheekbone, their eyes locking. Then together, she and Joby help Seth belowdecks. Suspicion nips at
me as I hobble to the railings on the starboard side, leaning
my forearms against the old wood to stare out at the waves.

My foot will heal. Left untreated, it could fester, but I was
lucky there were herbs and bandages on board. It throbs with
a dull ache, but I can handle it. It's not the worst the sea has
done to me.

But Seth could die. On Rosevear, we've seen wounds like
his before. A deep enough gash in the water can be fatal,
even in a shoulder or arm. And with a bullet lodged inside
him… I shudder, pulling my still-damp sleeves down over
my wrists. There's something Seth isn't telling me—or many
somethings—but I need him to be all right for my sake. And
that's what I don't understand. That thread, trailing between
us. That sharp tug, binding us, sending waves of fire through
me. That's what scares me the most. I don't understand it,
and I can't make sense of it. Every time he's in danger, I have
to save him.

Staying with this crew is a risk. I can see that now. Especially after that gesture they all shared, touching their own
hearts, then his. A shared blessing, a known expression passed

between them. A bond. I wrap my arms around myself, feeling the stiffness of the sea settle in the folds of the fabric as it
dries. The sea is whipping into sharp peaks as the wind picks
up, swinging around to bring a touch of ice from the north.
It's already nearing twilight. I've lost a whole day to the drop
on Finnikin's Way. I shiver as the sea dries on my skin, the
cold finally burrowing its way into my bones.

"You should change. Warm up. You were in the sea for
some time," Merryam says, back on deck and striding toward
me. There's a bandage wrapped around her arm and as she
tosses me a blanket, I notice her knuckles have been cleaned
up and carefully treated. I nod in thanks, draping it around
myself. I don't want her to know that I could have stayed underwater for so much longer, and never felt more than the
fire raging inside me.

It's only now, as I stand on deck in this icy wind, that I
feel it. If I dove into the ocean surrounding us now, I would
warm again. I think about those vials of blood in the hold. Of
magic and wild creatures…and my mother. I feel for her notebook resting against my heart and want more than anything
to reach the coordinates. And I want to reach them with him.

With Seth.

"How is he?" I ask, my voice quiet and cracked. It exposes
what I can barely admit to myself. That I care. I care if he
lives or dies.

"If we can get to the apothecary in time, he should live."
She takes a shuddering breath, casting her gaze out to sea.
"It'll take a good few hours to make port if this bloody wind
doesn't swing back around. We'll be fighting our way to the
harbor."

I open my mouth to ask her more questions, to offer her

help. But she's already moved away to check the ropes and the sails. Her shuddering breath and the shadows at the corner of her eye prickle under my skin. I hope I get the chance to ask Seth who he really is. And what this crew means to him. I hope we reach these coordinates together, after he argued so fiercely with Merryam against doing the drop, wanting to carry on without detouring to Finnikin's Way.

I hope this isn't the last time I see him alive.

CHAPTER
FIFTEEN

"IT'S A RISK IS ALL I'M SAYING," JOBY MURMURS. He's speaking to Merryam as they crouch over Seth's still form in the cabin we were sharing. *Are* sharing. He's not dead yet. I hover on the threshold, moving to listen through the crack in the door. There's no one in the galley but me. Pearl is at the helm, but if I'm belowdecks for too long, she might grow suspicious.

"He won't like it."

"He won't know."

Joby blows out a breath. "Look, I would do the same in your position. I would. But what about the girl? Seth's got eyes for her. You have to see it—"

"Seth's business is Seth's business."

"What if he finds out?"

"Leave that to me," Merryam says. "We'll be at the apothecary for one night at most. We'll drop the goods with him and I'll square it with Eli later."

"He'll owe you."

Merryam chuckles darkly. "Seth? You know he already does."

The boards creak overhead and I scurry across the galley on silent feet, climbing the ladder steps before Pearl reaches the hatch. For the next two hours I stay on deck, picking up each puzzle piece, each fragment of information they've given me. I know that their drop went wrong, and that they have a kinship with Seth that runs deep. I know that they're carrying cargo far more deadly and costly than the goods we find on merchant ships and that there's someone called Eli involved.

I know that Seth is lying to me.

It all adds up to one certain truth. I hired the wrong crew. With every hour, every minute that ticks away, I'm drifting further from saving the lives that matter most. Father, Bryn, and in a way, even myself.

Port Trenn rises from the sea, climbing up from the docks in layers of rooftops. It's a town clinging to the cliff side, alleyways snaking through it like a maze, twisting and turning between the buildings. This is a mainland port, a stop on a bustling trading route. Ships tower around *Phantom* as we pass them, a steady mist swirling atop the water. We anchor in a space to the west, the oily waters slapping against the bow. Twilight is creeping across the gathered crowds, the lamplighters carrying their torches to light the candles.

I stand at the railing, taking it all in. It's everything the sailors told us about. Everything I imagined, down to the scent of ash and fish, the grime coating every surface in a fine film. But underneath all that is anonymity. Like you could be anyone in Arnhem, anyone on the mainland and simply disappear into the crowds.

"We need to get him through the streets after dark," Joby says to Merryam as they both stride for the hatch leading belowdecks. "He can't be seen like this if the watch are about."

They disappear and I turn to find Pearl watching me. I can hear her mind ticking over. Trying to work me out. I know I should go belowdecks and see how Seth is. But I can't bring myself to. To see the blood. To wait and watch as he slowly dies. I haven't felt that tether between us since he was hurt and I worry that it means this is his end. I'm not sure I am brave enough to face that.

"Is this apothecary far?" I ask Pearl.

"Not far," she says softly. "He's tougher than you think. Everyone living on the ocean is."

I look over at her, this tiny slip of a person with white-blond hair framing her cheekbones. It seems impossible that she was forged in a place like Finnikin's Way. I must be missing something about her, a hidden steel that she chooses to keep out of sight.

"How long have you known Seth?"

She opens her mouth then closes it again. Frowning, she shrugs nonchalantly. "I'm not certain."

"Not certain you can tell me, or it's been so long you've lost count of all the fond memories?"

"Just not certain." She cuts across the deck to check on the knots. I watch her, deciding not to pursue my questioning. I can feel the edges of the truth they're hiding from me, the curling at the corners, and I know I'm close to discovering what truly lies between this crew and Seth if I just keep peeling away. I look back out toward the docks. They can keep their secrets a little longer. But I do intend to uncover them.

Night darkens across Port Trenn, the moon brimming with

silver light as we start to disembark. Merryam and Joby lower
Seth carefully into the punt, the only vessel we have now
to reach the quayside after the other one was abandoned on
the shore of Finnikin's Way. It's much smaller and we crowd
around him. I sit at the far end of the punt from Seth as Merryam rows us into the quay. He is watching the stars, his head
tipped up to the skies. I can't look at him. Every time I do, I
feel that knot in my chest. He's a distraction, and every stop,
every day that turns, is bringing my father and Bryn closer
to the noose. The very thought of it tightens my chest, leaving me breathless.

We make our way quietly past groups of sailors standing
outside pubs in huddled groups. There are whispers, snatched
conversations that I only hear fragments of. The word *Rosevear* snags me and I turn sharply. But I don't recognize any
of these sailors. And when I hear the word *watch* in the next
breath, I wonder if the people I left behind are all safe. Or if
the watch are tightening their grip. A few pickpockets weave
slowly, circling us like they're picking out their prey. I'm still
hobbling, the bandage on my foot sticky with blood. I would
be too slow in a fight tonight and they know it. I smile boldly
at a couple of their dirt-caked faces, their eyes gleaming in
the dark as they fade back into the gloaming. But I feel their
stares pinned on me all the way to the apothecary.

Merryam and Joby are holding Seth up between them,
his head lolling as they shuffle toward a door. It's set deep in
granite walls, illuminated by a flickering streetlamp. Merryam steadies Seth against Joby before knocking three times.

I hold my breath as the quiet wraps around us. For a beat, I
wonder if anyone will answer. I open my mouth to ask Merryam to knock again when the door swings inward, framing a

gray-haired man standing on the threshold. He wipes his hands on a cloth stained purple, his eyes taking in Merryam, then Seth. His wrinkled, closed-off face doesn't reveal what he's thinking.

"One for your table, Howden. Taken a bullet," Merryam says gruffly, stepping forward so her face is bathed in the lamplight from inside. "And another with a cut foot. Only minor, but she can't walk well."

He raises an eyebrow and tuts, but without a word he moves back, beckoning us inside. His eyes drift down to my foot, already assessing, as though he can see right through the bandage to the jagged cut beneath. I am all too aware of how exposed I am, how vulnerable. So when he looks at me, I stare back, unflinching. Hiding my fear behind a wall.

We follow him through a shop lined with pearly glass bottles containing tinctures and brews. He pulls up the wooden counter and walks through a doorway hidden behind shelves of large glass jars. Each one has a wooden scoop and an ingredient. There are no labels. Only things that look like eyes and needle teeth, bats' wings and ground red blood.

I swallow, averting my gaze, and focus on my footsteps. But I can't help wondering what nature of creature these things in jars came from, human or something else. And now I know how the magic works and where it comes from, it turns my stomach.

The narrow corridor behind the shop leads to a space set with worktables and a fireplace. It's not unlike the healer's front room in her cottage on our island. The windows are small, set high at the back, and the only light is from the glow of the fire and the lamps fixed into the walls.

Joby and Merryam lower Seth on to the worktable in the center and I catch his expression. The shadows highlight his tight features, the pain lacing his jaw. There is blood leaking through the bandage on his collarbone. I linger at the back of the room as the apothecary gestures silently to his assistant, a slight girl with brown skin and hair. He gives her a little jar, pointing at me. She nods, keeping her eyes cast down and walks to me, gesturing that I follow her.

"I'm not to stay?" I whisper as the apothecary speaks for the first time, issuing orders in cracked, deep tones. His voice reminds me of Bryn's and I stop still, the cadence taking me straight back to the meeting house and staring at all that glitter. The last time I felt a surge of real hope lift my bones.

The girl shakes her head and I catch a glint of something at her throat, half-hidden beneath her shirt. A necklace, with a pendant shaped like a compass. I've seen that symbol on Ennor, and on the ring Joby wears. "You're not one of us."

I frown as she leads me away from the workroom, away from the gathered crew. Does she mean I'm not a true member of the crew...or something else? Before the door closes, I hear Seth hiss through his teeth, the apothecary asking him how it happened. But his answer, along with the secrets they're all keeping, is sealed away behind the door.

The girl takes me to a room at the end of a corridor, offering me the jar from the apothecary. "I will bring you tea. Rub this into the cut and let it breathe. Stay here."

When she leaves, I hear the sound of a lock clicking. And when I try the door handle, it won't budge. I pinch my lips together, breathing out a string of curses, and turn back to face the room I've been left in. A window at the far end overlooks the docks, the ships and boats crowded together on the inky water.

There's a bed in the corner, a chest and two armchairs. I unbandage my foot, sniffing at the jar from the apothecary.

It smells like chamomile and a metallic tang I can't place. It's most likely apothecary made, which means it's laced with blood like in the vials aboard *Phantom*. The blood of wild creatures, steeped in magic. I don't want to use it. But I have to be able to move, and fight if it comes to it. Right now, hobbling, even the pickpockets are marking me.

After a moment's hesitation I rub the paste into my heel and wince as it itches. The itching soon subsides, cooling to a line of frost, and I limp over to the window, trying to keep my foot off the floor. When I test the window, I find that it's locked as well. I pace the room in frustration. There are two things that have become clear since I joined the crew on board *Phantom*.

I am being kept very purposefully in the dark.

I can't trust any of them.

The moonlight silvers the room as she rises over the docks outside. I stand perfectly still, counting out my options like coins. They are few. As I move my hand to smooth back my hair, the crackle underneath my jacket reminds me of what I am carrying next to my heart.

The notebook.

I turn to the door, but not a whisper of sound comes from behind it. Carefully, I draw my mother's notebook from my jacket, unfolding it on the window ledge. By the light of the moon, I trace the pattern of the eight-pointed star, tapping my finger on every number of the coordinates woven along the points. Maybe when I free my father, we could return here to Port Trenn then onward, through the snaking alleyways and beyond, into the heart of the mainland. Maybe all the way to the wilds of the north, we could just keep running until we reach a place where the Wanted posters are not printed and hung. Until the watch cannot reach him.

The ink on the illustration isn't smudged. In fact, it's completely unmarked by the sea it was submerged in. I bite my lip, smoothing my palms over the paper. It's bone-dry. I snatch back my hands, wondering what ink was used to create it. Or what kind of parchment this is.

Magic is found in the wild places of the world, in the blood of the creatures that dwell there. So why do my fingertips prickle as I touch the star that marks where my mother is leading me?

I have a memory of an evening in front of the fire with Mother and Father, her sketching his likeness in one of her bound books. Him chasing her around the room, all of us laughing as he tried to get a peek of the drawing. It makes my sides ache now to think of it, but not with mirth—with a needling pain that I would do anything to remove. I grew up too fast on that rope, swimming out to wrecks. I forgot all those moments that stitched together my happiness. Maybe I can reclaim some of them yet, and make new ones with my father. Maybe finding what my mother left me will soothe that pain. But only if I keep going, keep fighting to find a way to free him.

I should run. I should close this notebook, hide it against my heart, and find another ship to take me. From tomorrow, I only have six days. Is it even long enough? I place my hand on the windowpane, feeling the chill of night, and I shiver. It's a raw cold that sweeps into this port. But the coordinates surely aren't far…maybe I could swim there? My bones warm at the very thought of lowering myself into the waves. Perhaps that's the only option now. I can't afford to pay another crew. At this point, maybe I can only count on myself.

I place the notebook back inside my jacket and look up

as I hear voices from outside the door, a low muffled cry. My stomach twists and I hold my breath, listening for more sounds. Was it Seth? Is he in pain?

"He's nothing to you. Nothing," I say softly, moving toward the door. A cry comes again, sharper than before, then suddenly cut off. Another door slams and a set of quick footsteps trails into silence. I lean my forehead against the door and close my eyes. But there's only ringing, jarring quiet.

"He would not do the same for you," I whisper, trying to convince myself.

That knot ties tighter inside me. I listen for the sounds of life. Anything to know his heart still beats.

"You are wasting time."

I step back from the door.

"He could cost you everything."

I sink down into an armchair.

"You are imagining that thread between you."

I press my hand into my chest. Into the notebook, into that steady tug on my heart. And I decide to stay. I stay and watch as the moon trails silver through the night. And I hate myself for it, this division inside me. Between my father, Seth, and myself.

I care for Seth like a candle that never should have been lit, but now it's blazing steadily every time he looks at me. And I can't seem to put that dancing flame out. It's spreading through me, muddling my thoughts, aggravating me with its persistence. He's hiding something from me. Something secret, something with weight. And if I don't stamp these embers out, this flame for Seth that's burning inside me, I am afraid I will perish.

CHAPTER
SIXTEEN

"YOU CAN JOIN THE OTHERS NOW."

I jerk awake, uncurling from the armchair. I was dreaming of flying. Of the night all around me, filled with blazing stars, a hand in mine, just like I dreamed on Rosevear. I blink, pulling myself from the dream, wondering as I always do on waking, who that hand belongs to.

The apothecary's assistant is standing in the doorway, arms folded across her chest. A small smile plays across her mouth. Hastily, I smooth down my clothes and discreetly check the notebook is still tucked into my jacket. When I stand, my foot is completely healed. As I suspected, the apothecary must have laced the little jar of paste with magic. I suppress a shudder, picturing the vials of blood, and try not to guess whether I've been healed by a phoenix, a narwhal, a wyvern. I follow the girl out into the corridor, wondering what I'll find in the workroom.

As we walk past open doors, I catch a glimpse of Merryam

and Pearl standing together by a window. Pearl has her head on Mer's shoulder, her arm around her waist. My heart claws up my throat, and I hope Seth is all right. That the apothecary could dig the bullet out and fix him.

"Is he…?" I begin, but the words stick to the roof of my mouth.

In the dark workroom, the fire is still smoldering, casting flickering shapes over the bottles and equipment. The apothecary is gone, but Joby stands next to the table. And there, sitting on the edge of it, hands braced against the sides, is Seth.

"You're alive," I gasp, before I can reel my relief back in. "I thought…"

Seth shrugs, a lazy smile playing on his lips. His shirt has been cut away completely, leaving only his trousers and boots. I gulp as he lowers his feet to the floor, stepping toward me. He's broader than I realized under his clothes. A flush creeps up my chest, warming my cheeks, and I look away, focusing on the wall. The floor. Anywhere but his smile, his bare skin. His hair casually tousled, as though he has just awoken from a sound sleep. And I curse myself for caring.

"You sound worried," he grates out, tipping a finger under my chin so I look up at him. My heart rattles against my ribs and I tell myself it's just the relief of seeing him alive. My eyes trail down his chest, then up to the neat silver scar curving along his collarbone. Without thinking, I brush my fingertips over it. It's smooth and ice-cold, as though it is years old.

"That's not possible. It shouldn't be… It can't have healed already."

Seth chuckles. "The apothecary does his job well."

His eyes soften, capturing mine, holding them. For a handful of heartbeats, I allow my fingertips to rest against his skin.

I can hardly breathe. Then I pull in a lungful of air and break away, moving toward the fire.

"Admit you were concerned about me," Seth says at my back. "It's all right—it's only me and Joby here. He won't tell."

Heat flares in my throat as I choke out a laugh. "I was only concerned about getting on with our journey."

"Of course."

"You dying would have…held me up."

"Undoubtedly."

I tug the sleeves of my jacket over my hands, just like I always do when I'm nervous or wrong-footed. I can't comprehend how he can be healed and whole.

Is this what magic can do? If anyone on Rosevear had lost that much blood, Kai would have been carving their coffin by now. I don't know what to think of this world I have stumbled into. How cutthroat it is, how wild. And how full of fierce secrets, whispering truths just beyond my reach.

I swallow, keeping all my questions inside. But they're stacking up by the day, just waiting to spill out. I wonder if I begin asking them, if I will find myself shot, with no one in sight to bring me to an apothecary who can do more than mix strange ingredients.

I tilt my head to the side with a sniff. "But apparently, you're fine. So we should get going."

Seth and Joby share a look and I catch Joby's grin before he ducks his head, moving through the doorway I just walked through, leaving me and Seth alone.

"Were you really worried?" Seth asks softly, reaching for a fresh shirt that's been left for him. There's a hint of vulnerability, all the swagger of a moment ago abandoned. He sounds uncertain, as though he is not used to true concern. Like he didn't expect it from me at all.

He buttons the shirt up slowly and I have to look away, focusing on the row of surgeon's implements on a tray. "I was."

"Good," he says, pulling on his jacket. "I guess that makes two of us."

Heat flares along my veins, warming every inch of me. "You were worried for me too?"

"Perhaps."

He leans against the worktable, grinning. I scour my mind for a retort, anything to break this tension. I want to go to him, I realize suddenly. I want to wind my arms around his neck and feel the pressure of his warm body against mine. But the door opens before I can get any words out and Joby, Merryam, and Pearl all pile back into the room. Pearl passes me a bread roll and an apple as Mer strides straight for the door that leads to the shop front. I take a bite of the apple, tart and crunchy with a hint of loam, and follow the others to the front of the shop.

The apothecary is waiting for Merryam, strangely awake after a whole night of work. She turns to Joby, raising her eyebrows, and he draws a vial from his pocket. With a careful tap, he places it on the counter, leaving it to roll back and forth until it stills.

My stomach churns, but the apothecary smiles, running a single fingernail over the glass. After a pause, he fixes his eyes on Merryam. "What grade?"

"The finest," she says. "We've got four crates. You would be doing Eli a favor."

The apothecary picks up the vial between thumb and forefinger, inspecting the blood within. I shudder, but don't take my eyes off them. There's that name again, Eli.

"I'll shift them for you to my contacts on the continent. For a cut, of course. But...you'll have to move carefully. The watch are about this morning. Now the ruling council want more control of magic, I don't know how long it'll be before they begin insisting on paperwork. Taking *their* cut."

The crew mutter uneasily, the atmosphere in the shop thickening. "Don't worry about us. We know how to avoid them. You can have half our cut. No more."

He shrugs, pocketing the vial, and holds out his hand. Merryam grasps it, never breaking eye contact. "Just a friendly warning," he says. "You've heard about Rosevear? Bad for business. Bad all round. Harder to shift the wares, and the watch pocket more and more of my profit. The bribes I have to pay... Well. Fetch the crates now. My assistant will sort them and start contacting interested parties."

"Wait," I say without thinking, pushing my way to the counter. "What do you mean about Rosevear?"

He blinks. "The watch carried out a raid. They're after anyone who knows about the wrecking of that ship with all the glitter in the hold. They're sure there's a group that swim out to the wrecks, and they want names. They took a few personal items, roughed the islanders up a bit. The usual scare tactics, some say. But they're growing in power. Getting bolder. Like I said, bad for business. The last thing we want is them taking too many liberties. Folk spend less and won't risk as much." He narrows his eyes, considering me. "Why, do you know someone from there?"

I shrug, even as my veins turn to ice. Picturing the people I've left behind. "Just curious."

★ ★ ★

Joby and Merryam ferry the crates back from *Phantom* while we keep watch on the docks. We have to turn our collars up, shifting our gaze to our feet when two of the watch walk past. My fear thumps in time with my heart, but they only glance our way. I see them pushing some of the street kids around, demanding they hand over coin, and my hatred of them grows. They're everywhere. And if what the apothecary says is true, they've crossed a line on my island. They've always questioned us, but never taken anything personal. Or anyone. I clench and unclench my fists, over and over, picturing Kai and Agnes. All I can do is keep going and hope this journey will save us all.

I drift over to a wall of Wanted posters much like the ones on the Isle of Ennor and the words *wanted* and *reward* bleed black down curling parchment. One poster catches my eye: an illustration of a boy peering out, moody and stern, the very image of rebellion. The curve of his jaw is strangely familiar, along with the dark eyelashes ringing his eyes. There's no name, but the reward turns my mouth dry. It's obscene. I trace the shape of the illustrated features, shaking out my memories to try to work out where I have seen him before. He's beautiful yet deadly, the kind of boy who would slit your throat, even as he's stealing a kiss.

A whistle, much like the one used on Finnikin's Way, splits the eerie stillness of the docks and I take that as the signal to depart. But the boy's likeness on the poster, along with the news of the watch harrying the people of my island, haunts me as we depart Port Trenn, the docks and the life teeming behind its walls soon swallowed up by the ocean.

* * *

As the morning drifts into the afternoon I stand at the rails, watching the iron-gray sea, the white horses riding the tips of the waves. It's rougher today. The wind fills the sails, and icy fingers search through my clothes. I shiver, wishing I was swimming through those gray depths. Then I would know if she's simply impatient or hungry. If the threat of a storm looms close or if we have time to find what my mother left behind.

"It's your turn for the cabin," Seth says to me, leaning against the rails at my side. "Better get some rest if you need it. Tomorrow we'll be there."

"And what can I expect? Is it open ocean?"

Seth shrugs. "You supplied the coordinates. I know as much as you do. It's in a stretch of sea most merchants avoid with the deeper draft on their vessels. A few rocks, but no land mass. Beyond that... I guess we'll find out what your mother left there."

I nod, weighing up his words. Picturing a place much like the stretch of water surrounding Rosevear with rocky out-crops waiting just beneath the surface. Seth grows quiet and I dig my hands into the rail, deciding to ask. Needing to know if I can truly trust him.

"Look, before tomorrow, I need to know. What are you keeping from me? I can tell you know this crew better than you let on. I can feel all the secrets you're holding. It's like you're brimming with them. It's like—"

"Mira, I—" He shakes his head, turning to me. "There are some things that are best left alone. But you can trust me. Honest, you can. I... I don't want anything bad to happen to you. I want to get you to those coordinates."

I bite my lip. So he admits to hiding things. "Perhaps you

can tell me after I find what my mother left? I want to trust you, I do…"

He smiles, taking my hand quickly, then drops it. As if my very skin scalds him. "Thank you. For saving me," he says quietly. The wind around us dies down, *Phantom* gliding silently. Seth's eyes seek mine and I find the gleam of truth, of a vulnerability I have only seen when he's toe-to-toe with death. The questions shrivel up on my tongue and I swallow them back down. I will learn his secrets. But for today, I am sure of him. I know that he does not intend to hurt me.

As I make my way to the cabin and curl up in the bed, I can't help picturing my father. And Bryn. How hopeless they must be feeling. And for the first time, my fear wins. What if there is nothing at the end of this journey but a handful of aged sand and stone? I toss and turn, trying to cling to my hope. That sureness I had when I left Rosevear with Seth to find what was beyond the horizon. It has to be something I can bargain with for their lives. It *has* to be. Fate would not have led me here at this very moment if it was all for nothing.

I wrap my hope around all that fear as I fall asleep, smothering it. I breathe in the scent of pine trees on the pillow. And I dream of the boy I found in the sea.

When I wake, it's full night. The ship creaks and mutters as it cradles me, but the sea doesn't pummel. There is no murderous snarl of wind. I sigh in relief, gathering wakefulness to me slowly. I sip the air, tasting tea and the lingering scent of supper. Pulling a blanket around me, I walk out into the galley. Pearl and Joby are sound asleep in their bunks. I step past them and up the ladder steps, the chill of night raw on my skin as my head and shoulders emerge from belowdecks.

The sky is a bowl brimming with starlight. I gasp in wonder, tilting my head up, and breathe in the quiet and the cold. There are stars layered over stars. So many, I can hardly pick out the constellations. The night blazes silver, navy pockets of true dark rippling like velvet between. I have never seen so much brilliance.

"Look at the ocean," a voice says and I whirl, finding Seth leaning against the rails. I go to him, my breath pluming like smoke, and find the inky dark like a mirror beneath us.

"Beautiful," I breathe. The water is a crisp reflection of the sky above. We are floating through a sea of starlight. I laugh softly, watching as the trail of a shooting star blazes over the still water.

"This place isn't on any map," Seth says quietly. "It's the one patch of ocean that is kept a secret by those that have sailed over it. You see how this reflective bowl has edges?"

I look where he points, finding the ripples of sea far away, where waves are forming. "Yes."

"I don't know why. But this small circle of ocean is always mirrorlike. Even in a storm, the sea is calm. And strangely warm. As though in this bowl of sea it is forever summer."

"She rests," I whisper. I lean closer to the sea and trace the patterns of starlight. "Can I…?"

"I'll come with you."

I smile, dropping the blanket to the deck. I strip off my breeches and shirt, leaving only the thin camisole beneath. Seth does the same and I glance over to see the crescent moon of a scar rippling over his skin. Seth waves at Merryam, who nods from the helm. I grin, stepping over the rail and draw in a deep, heady breath.

Then I dive.

I come alive as I hit the water. Fiery kisses shiver over me as I plummet down, down, deep beneath the stars. I open my eyes and feel the silk of the water. Its heat moves over and around me and I laugh, bubbles streaming from my nose. There is no end to it. Only ocean shot through with molten starlight.

I rise up gradually, letting the ocean carry me back to the surface. Seth is lying on the water, arms outstretched, staring at the stars overhead. I join him, spreading my limbs out, my chest expanding as I fill my lungs with air. For a moment, I let everything slip away. My fear, my worries. The ticking clock that plagues my every thought. The restless tumble of questions I carry in my heart. His knuckles graze mine, edging closer until our fingers are tangled in the water. A small current passes between us and I daren't move in case it shatters this fragile thing. I know in this moment that I have tipped over the edge with him. That I want to do more than just tangle my fingers through his.

"Seth…"

He turns and pulls me toward him. We tread water, eyes only for each other, and close the distance between our two bodies. I bite my lip and his eyes track the movement, his thumb reaching for my mouth to trace a soft pattern around it. I shut my eyes, my whole being melting at his touch. His closeness.

"Mira…" he whispers, bringing his hand to the back of my neck. Then carefully, softly, he brushes a kiss along my jaw. I sigh as my body unspools, his kisses trailing slowly to my mouth. My hands travel up his back under the water, running over the shape of him. He murmurs against my mouth and

I tip my head back, wanting to feel him everywhere. Never wanting this moment, this kiss, to end.

I could stay here forever. The night blazing above, Seth dusting soft kisses along my skin. The deep, wide ocean beneath us.

Cradled by a bowl of starlight.

CHAPTER
SEVENTEEN

ONLY FIVE DAYS LEFT. I HAVE LESS THAN A WEEK
to reach Penscalo and negotiate for my father's and Bryn's release. It doesn't seem long enough. Not when I still have to
find my mother's legacy. The notebook presses against my
chest as I heave a breath, eyeing the sweep of rocks and islets
before us. We arrived all at once as though dragged here by
an invisible hand, surrounded by a fog so thick, I felt certain
I could reach out and grasp it. It gave me little time to prepare for this moment.

We anchor as close to the coordinates as possible, but Merryam won't move any farther. Half-submerged rocks wait like
fangs between the islets. There is only gray here. No life, no
gull cry. Only endless, watchful ocean, as though we are the
only living things for miles.

"I can see why she chose this place," I say to Seth. It whispers with hidden secrets, just beyond my fingertips. I lean
forward, wanting to feel her presence. Wanting to reach back

in time and see this place as she saw it when she was here. My mother, I realize, was made up of so many layers. And I wonder now if I ever knew her at all.

"She chose it because it's a graveyard. No one lives here—no wreckers and yet countless merchant vessels have disappeared in these waters," Seth says, assessing the sea critically before offering me a tentative smile. "No one can navigate a vessel through here. The only way is to swim. Or more likely...drown."

I narrow my gaze, picturing her going out on the rope that day. Her defiance of my father, how she burned for the sea. Of course. She hid something here so only she, or someone like her, could find it. Someone who could stay submerged in the water without freezing to death or drowning. A smile quirks my lips despite the task ahead of me. It's as though I have peeled back a layer of her and shone a candle flame on my memories. Everything twists, exposing each of those moments in a new light. Maybe we were not so different. This is exactly the kind of place where I would hide something secret too. It means she was like me, able to warm herself in the sea. I turn over the stories she told of the deep. Of the kraken devouring ships whole, and of other creatures. Creatures that dwell in the depths.

Who were you?

I look over at Seth, then the gathered crew in turn. Their faces are grim in the thin morning light. I need to do this alone. Whatever is hidden down there is for me, and me alone, to discover.

"You can all stay here. It shouldn't take long," I say, already reaching for the buttons of my jacket.

"I could go with you," Seth says, his eyes stormy. Unreadable. Is he conflicted because he wants me to be safe? I feel the

ghost of his mouth on mine, the kisses he trailed down my
throat in the water last night. As though he is thinking of it
too, his face softens into concern. "Or just don't go at all. We
can get back to Port Trenn. I'll help you make another plan."

I place a hand on his arm, silencing him. He frowns, his
plea turning to a mutter, but he doesn't move his arm away.
There was no one on Rosevear who could swim like me.
And although Seth is clearly troubled by the danger of me
searching alone in this place, I know from rescuing him that
he does not have my ability. "I can't leave without knowing,
not now I'm here," I say quietly. "Not just to know if she left
something I can use to free my father, but also because... I can
feel her here. There's an energy." I release his arm, yanking
my jacket off my shoulders. "I won't leave without knowing."

Pearl looks between us, then back at the sea. She clutches
her own jacket tighter to her chest.

"I think this is for me to do," I say to Seth, readying the rope
ladder to climb down into the water. "Only me. I think that's
what she wanted. That's why it's here and not on Rosevear."

Seth nods, ripping his gaze from the stony sea to glance at
me. There is a battle inside him. I can feel it. He can't join
me, but he also knows he can't stop me. I'm eager to dive. I
need to find a way to save my father and Bryn, and uncover
the pieces of myself that I do not fully understand. How I
yearn for more than the roots that bind me to Rosevear. How
I wish to float without an anchor and explore the world.
How I do not feel like I wholly belong on land or in the sea.
Perhaps there are answers here. Now that I understand more
about magic's danger and wonder, I need to understand why
I come alive in the sea. Why my body can do what no one

else's can in the water. What was my mother trying to tell me, that my father never could?

Once I've rescued Father and brought him back home, the watch will still loom as a shadow over us. Darkening and consuming all that lies in their path. If I am to protect Rosevear, I may not get another chance to return to this place to answer these questions that burn within my soul.

"I'll be fine," I say, stripping down to my camisole once again before swinging myself over the rails. I hesitate, but look up, conceding that I need, at least, to trust that *Phantom* will still be anchored here when I return. "I may be some time under the water. There's no need to worry though. Truly."

Seth sighs, running a hand across the back of his neck. He gazes out to the west, tracing the steady grace of the waves with the flicker of his eyes. Finally, reluctantly, he says, "All right."

I grin, and climb down into the ocean's depths. My waist drops beneath the water, then my chest, my shoulders. It welcomes me and I close my eyes as fire licks along my veins. I look up at Seth and something fleeting crosses his expression. Something close to sorrow. But as I blink, he smiles at me reassuringly, bracing his arms on the rails. I wave, disappearing into the ocean, sure I imagined the sadness breaking over his features.

The eddying water swirls around jagged rocks and deep, inky pools under the surface. There is little light down here. Little to mark the wending way of the waves. I swim through the waterways between the rocks and islets which tower like cliffs around me as though they are watching me. Waiting to see which way I will turn.

A thin voice, something I feel rather than hear, echoes

through the water. I pause, winding my body around a slice of granite, and peer around. There is a presence here. Something lingering nearby, and it echoes the song that lured me to the notebook. I will my heart to calm as my chest becomes pinched and tight. It can't be her. It can't be her hiding in this barren place. I saw her body washed up on the shoreline that day.

I buried her.

But as I wait, the midnight shades of sea undulating around me, I feel it again. A beckoning. Something overwhelmingly familiar is calling to me.

I slide away from the granite, following the sorrowful sound. There is no threat; I'm sure of it. It's like a secret or a memory buried within me that I am only now remembering. I graze my fingertips over lichen-clad rock, skimming toward an islet that glows luminous. The echo of sound vibrates through me again, and I cling to it like a thread. It's almost my mother's voice, or a whisper of it. It trails forward toward this islet, and back, so far back inside me, a memory of a song she used to sing.

I know now that she would not have left something hidden above the water. I swim around the islet and suddenly, my mother's song chimes as a bell in my mind. I stop, closing my eyes. I am five again and she is taking my hand. Leading me into the sea. My heart is burning; I am alive for the first time. I follow her song, the sound of her voice as she leads me under. It's the song she always sang just for me, never with my father or the other islanders. I learned how to swim and how to understand the changing moods of the sea with the cadence of this song echoing through my blood.

And I never want to leave. I want to swim with her forever. And somehow, in this place, I do not feel the burning need for air. It's as though this place is freeing me, allowing my body to move with only the air trapped inside my lungs. Before, I would always seek the surface, taking a breath out of habit. But perhaps…perhaps I don't need as much air in my lungs as I thought. I open my eyes, the song stuttering to a halt. And there, in the silence, nestled between two rocks in front of me, is a chest.

My heart pounds against my ribs as I swim down to it, the pressure change making my ears pop. The chest is lying on the seabed, made of wood and, I can see even in the gloom, glints of gold. There are twisting words carved into its lid in gold letters. I run my finger over them, an echo of a memory tugging at me. These words are not in the written language that my people use. They are ancient, from a time before the mainland swept in with its influence over our tongues. But the memory eludes me.

Gradually, I pry the chest from the rocks. It's almost welded to the stone, sunk deep within it as though the rock has grown around it. I wonder if I should have brought tools with me, some way of chipping it out. I use the tips of my fingers, crumbling away the edges, levering it bit by bit.

I plant my feet on either side once it begins to move more freely. Angling my body, I straighten my legs, using my weight to displace the chest. The rock seems to groan, shifting beneath me, and in a sudden rush, I pull it free. It's heavy, but not impossible to carry, and I cradle it in wonder. It's the width of my rib cage, so I can wrap my arms around it. But there's no keyhole set in the lid. I try shaking it to hear what might be inside, but under the water, I can't tell if it's empty or full. Reluctantly, I realize I'll have to take it back to *Phantom*, back to the others on the surface to work out how it opens.

I hesitate, casting a wide, sweeping glance around this place. What led my mother here? Why did she leave this chest behind? I mark the islet, the shape and feel of it, in case I want to return. Now that I can no longer hear my mother's song I wonder if she lured me here at all, or whether it was the echoing beat of my own heart in the sea. I have peeled back a layer of her and the memory of our first swim has tumbled out. I hope that means something. I hope that the contents of this chest will help me free my father.

I start to swim back to the surface and my heart stops. There, in the water, is something I have seen before.

Red eyes.

Eyes burning with hunger, swaying unnaturally a few feet away. Out of the darkness, shapes form around me. Female shapes. Slender and gray, perfectly camouflaged in this place. My eyes dart left and right, counting swiftly. There are at least five of them. Five sets of needle-sharp teeth, five sets of blazing scarlet eyes.

Fear, true fear, pounds against my ribs as one of them moves a little closer. These are not gentle narwhals or the firedrakes of distant mountains—but these creatures hold the same kind of blood, magic and wild, twisting within them.

I gasp as a voice scrapes like a claw in my mind.

At long last, sisters. A fresh heart that still beats…

Sirens.

The creatures that dwell in the deep, that lure and sing and thirst for human hearts. Suddenly, I remember one of my father's tales. When my mother had gone, he warned me to never swim after something that sounded like her. Even if I was sure it was her voice in the waves.

I throw myself backward and my mother's chest sinks to the

seabed. The rigid granite bites into my back and in a moment of clarity, I see my own death. I pull out Agnes's blade. Memories of stories, of magic and blood and warnings all come crashing in, screaming in my mind. The creatures smile, circling me, the red in their eyes turning a vivid crimson. Their fingers are claws, sharp as their teeth. Meant for shredding.

Designed to kill.

I grip the blade handle, my gaze darting between them, one by one. Trying to work out who will pounce first.

Don't sour your blood with all this panic, the same siren as before says, voice flaring in my mind as though she spoke directly into my ear. Her hair mists out around her in a silver cloud, catching the glimmers of soft light from above. If it wasn't for her eyes, claws, and teeth she would be beautiful. An ethereal thing made of sea and pearl. But as it is, her bloodlust transforms her into something else. Something inhuman. Monstrous to behold. I catch the glint of a blade in her claws, something sharp and spiny, a knife similar to one I have seen before—

She darts forward, faster than I can trace. Her fingers grip my side, shoving me back against the rock. I cough, air flowing from my lungs as my ribs scrape the granite. She's found the bruises that haven't fully healed yet, the place I caught on the swim out to the wreck. My vision blurs and for a second, I am weightless, stomach roiling with the pain in my side. Then I blink, fighting to stay conscious.

Even as the siren presses her claws into me.

We only want a taste, she murmurs, sniffing my throat, bringing her jagged blade up to angle at my heart. As though she will carve it out. *Just a bite. We promise we'll be quick. You won't feel a thing.*

I choke on a gasp, bubbles streaming from my lips, my lungs near empty, burning in my chest. "Is that what you told my mother before you killed her?"

Memories engulf me. I am twelve again, searching the sea for her. Searching the storm-swollen waters for an echo of her song.

The next day, her body washed up on the shore. I am crouched down beside her, desperate and alone, too afraid to pull the hair from her eyes and find them lifeless. To find that she is truly gone.

Then we are burying her on the cliffs, cracking the frosted earth. Everything is silent; even the ocean is still. I am clinging to my father's hand, but he loosens his grip, falling to his knees as she's lowered into the ground. A keening sound shatters me as he breaks down, as he weeps for the woman he loved when his heart was whole and full.

That sound burns in me now, seared into my mind, replacing my fear with something else. With my rage. I eye that vicious blade, mere inches from my chest. Then I stare into the blooded eyes of this creature.

This siren.

"Is *this* what you did to *her*?"

They stop still, all five of them.

Watching me.

"I was there," I say bitterly, the sea slithering down my throat as I speak. I remember her. I remember her ravenous eyes. Maybe they can't hear me. But as the water chokes me, the air nearly wrung from my lungs, I say it.

"You murdered my mother."

CHAPTER EIGHTEEN

TIME STOPS. I LOOK AT EACH OF THE SIRENS, waiting for the one pinning me to strike. My chest is on fire, lungs almost empty, and the world around me begins to fade. Knowing these are my final moments, I feel regret that I never found out where I belong. Who I am. That I only tasted freedom oh, so briefly. That I didn't save my father from his fate. I ready myself, waiting for the dart of that vicious knife. I will take one of them with me if I can. I clutch Agnes's blade tighter, even as my body shakes and sways. I will avenge my mother and make them pay for her death.

But the one pinning me to the rock lets me go, drifting backward to the others. I falter, finding my mind filling with the cadence of sorrow. With a siren song that echoes my own grief and rage. The creatures are singing. In shock, I recognize the familiar notes, the way the sounds weave around and through each other. It haunts my dreams. It's the song that came from my mother's locked chest all these years.

"That's my mother's song," I splutter with the final pocket of air held in my chest. And even though I should be drowning, even though all the air is spent, I find myself relaxing. As I listen to the melody, the notes weaving in and out, I find my body does not need that sip of air. Being down here, I suddenly wonder if I am capable of more than I ever imagined. If this is another reason why my mother left this chest here for me to find.

The singing stops abruptly. For a moment, the creatures waver, faces turning to one another as though a silent conversation is taking place. Then four of the five sirens leave, disappearing between the folds of rock. One stays behind.

She sweeps closer, reaching out a hand. Again, her voice echoes inside my head. Her voice is sweeter now, softer as it washes through me.

Is it you? Mira? We didn't recognize you. You are so unlike her, yet...

I blink, taking in the creature's transformed features. Her eyes no longer flash an unearthly crimson, but instead smolder like embers. Her face assumes a more human shape; her fingers no longer end in claws. She touches my arm lightly and I flinch, all the pain that I locked away so long ago resurfacing. I wonder if we can communicate without speaking. If I can somehow speak as a thought, and she will hear me.

Were you there that day when she died? I say in my mind.

I turn accusing eyes on her and she withdraws her hand. She understands. Somehow, in this place, she can hear what I'm shouting in my head.

Yes, I was there. But we didn't kill your mother. How could we turn on one of our own?

Her words explode in my mind.

I tried to save her. Tried to warn her. But…

One of our own. I reel backward.

We didn't get there in time. We were so close, but by the time we got there, she was already gone… We would never harm a sister.

The blade clutched in my fist drops away. Each word she says pulls me closer to the truth. The truth I've been looking for. The truth I *knew* existed inside me all along. And now, now I know; in my final moments, I have the answer.

We would never harm a sister.

Sister…

She was hunted, Mira. As we sirens are. For blood. For magic.

Siren.

My mother was a siren.

I gasp, water pouring down my throat, my vision turning black as I choke, trying to rid it from my lungs. Arms, strong and supple, close around me, guiding me down, down, farther into this graveyard world. I tense, fighting back, then feel my limbs float and soften. The siren's voice warms me, comforting me.

Then we surface.

I take in deep, shuddering gulps of air, coughing and choking as the sea rushes out of me. I pull myself up onto my hands and knees, feeling rough rock scrape against my skin. But the siren is there, helping me expel the water from my lungs, helping me come back to myself. We've come up in an underwater cave, a pocket of air buried deep under the water. I sit up, watching her as she watches me.

There are storm lamps burning in the corners, the kind you carry on deck at night, and in their light, I can see that out of the water she is no longer gray. Her skin is almost translucent, delicate as tissue, the palest blue I've ever seen. Her hair hangs in ribbons of silver around her face, streaming down to her elbows. It shimmers like captured moonlight. I frown, blinking at her, then take in the cave she's brought me to. It's lined with shelves. And on all of them, in every crevice, clustered together in jewel-bright tangles, is an ocean's worth of treasure.

Beaded necklaces coil around framed artwork, shuffling up against fans and feathers and gilded shoes in a tumble of color. There are miniatures of loved ones, the kind Agnes covets, the glass jagged and cracked, splintering stern features. I stand carefully, walking over to a shelf set into a crooked corner. It holds a cluster of vases painted in blues and whites, the patterns suited to the kind of fancy houses I only hear about in stories. Then there are the books. Haphazardly stacked piles of them with ragged pages and faded covers.

I look over at the siren and she smiles at me. "It's how we learn your languages," she says in a lisping, high-pitched voice. "We read the books we find on your ships."

"Before you drown everyone on board?"

She shrugs. "We are hunted, by humans, by witches. In our world, you have to make a choice. Kill and survive, or be killed."

I measure her words, balancing them against my own life. How we lure ships to the rocks. How we take what we can on Rosevear to fill our empty bellies. The sea gives. The sea takes.

"I understand survival," I say. "But we do try and save people. Whenever we can. We don't murder them."

"That's where we are different," she says with a smile, running her fingers along a shelf brimming with brooches. "We accept what we are. We don't try to hide our true nature. But you humans...you would kiss a lover with a dagger pressed to their throat and call it love."

I watch her as she moves around the cave.

"How do you know my name?"

"She named you long before you were born," the siren says with a sigh. "She wanted you so badly, she longed to be with him, your father, and when she found a way to live as she did, half on land and half in the sea, she took her chance. She couldn't bear to be separated from you. Or him. But she couldn't live fully on your island. And eventually that became her undoing."

I freeze, waiting for her to continue. Needing to know what happened that day. Needing to know who hunted her.

"She had been on land for too long. Every part of her was in torment, needing to be with you and your father and yet longing for the sea. She trusted someone she shouldn't have. And that's how she paid the blood price for having everything she ever wanted. For being able to belong as she did, between two worlds. A hunter took her life." The siren smiled sadly. "Her fate is our reminder that we cannot have it all. That if we choose to live as she did, on land, then we have to say goodbye to our underwater kin. We have to leave the deep ocean forever. And very few will sacrifice so great a piece of themselves for that."

"Is that why...why I can stay underwater for so long? Why I feel as I do in the sea?"

"Yes. The ocean is in your blood. But you also have your father in you. So maybe you'll find a way to exist between two worlds. Or maybe it will tear you apart, as it did her."

I take a breath, feeling the weight of that day pressing on me. The desperation as I searched for her, longing for her to be alive. Then the next day, how it destroyed us to find her broken body. How it changed my father. How it changed the way he looked at me.

"Did she grow up here? In this place?"

"She did. She hoped you would find your way here. That it would mean something if you did."

I nod, moving to the shimmering pool of water in the center of the cave. I picture my mother swimming there. Picture her young and free and full of curiosity about the land and the people who lived there. How it led to her trusting too much.

"Do you know who killed her? Who hunted her?"

The siren shakes her head. "I do not see them as you do. To me, they are all beating hearts or dead hearts. But I must warn you, whoever killed her may have wanted the things she left behind for you. They may know about you, what you are. If you open the chest, you will find what you're looking for. But...there may be a cost."

I turn back to the siren as she places the chest on a table. Then she places Agnes's blade next to it. I realize she is showing that she trusts me. She is choosing to trust me with a blade, and with whatever is inside this chest.

"Our sister brought these here for you."

The inlaid metal of the chest gleams in swirling patterns, almost as though liquid fire moves through it. It lures me as my mother's illustration did. With a beckoning finger. I lift my hand, touching the wood on the lid, and it warms to my touch.

"Is this your language? My mother's?"

"Yes. It says your name in our tongue. She carved it herself."

I swallow, a lump forming in my throat as I imagine her

down here in this place, carving my name in her language for me to find one day. "How do I...?"

"Blood," the siren whispers. "It opens with a drop of your blood, and only yours."

I nod, fumbling for Agnes's blade, and hold my index finger over the lid. "Just one drop?"

"She had the witches craft it from the blood she gave them. From the magic that ran through her veins. It requires the human blood that pumps through your heart."

Her words shiver over me, the reference to what keeps her alive. What must have kept my mother alive. Human blood, beating within human hearts. I cut the length of my finger, avoiding the soft pad on the end, and let it bead on my skin. The siren sniffs, taking a purposeful step back. Then another. I glance at her, but her features betray nothing. Not hunger, not thirst.

"Touch your finger to the chest."

I do as she says, pressing my finger to the cold metal. And when my blood touches it, the metal catches fire. I draw my hand away quickly, stumbling back as pale flames engulf the chest.

"What? I don't understand. No!" I watch as the chest disintegrates, the metal dripping off the edge of the table. I step forward, heart leaping in panic. But the siren's hand clamps over my wrist, fingers far stronger than they look.

"Trust the legacy."

In moments, all that is left of the chest is char and cooling metal, fusing to the table in feathery veins. But in its center are two folded pieces of parchment, one fitting within the folds of the other. I reach out, holding the parchment delicately, reverently. And unfold the smaller of the two.

"It's a letter," I say, "addressed to me."

When I look up, I find the siren has gone. She has slipped back into the water and left me in this cavern to discover my legacy alone. I curl up on the ground, blinking down at the letter, at my mother's careful penmanship, her beautiful, lilting script.

My Dearest Mira,

If you're reading this, then you have found the chest. And it means I am no longer with you. I should be telling you this now, when I can hold your hand in mine and lead you down to the shore where it will all make sense. But you have to prove yourself worthy. And fate has to play a part too.

I was never meant to live on land for so long. I am a daughter of the sea, a siren, just as you are. That feeling, deep within you, that sense of coming home you feel when in the ocean? That is your truth. It is your home, Mira. And even though your father is human, and you may be able to live on land and in the water, your soul will always long for the sea.

I give you this gift knowing it is also a curse. There are those that will hunt you. That will want you to calm the ocean for them, or create a tempest. There are those that will call you a monster. Be careful who you show your true self to. Guard your heart. Be the storm the world needs to right itself.

I hope you find the balance between the sea and the land that I never could. I hope you find the place you are most at home without sacrificing pieces of yourself. I hope you find love. The true kind. The unwavering, steady kind that does not seek to hold you down, but anchors you. Your compass point to return to.

Do not blame your father for keeping this from you. He only ever wanted to protect us. But you were never meant to stay on Rosevear, Mira, however much he wished for that. Now you must find your own path in this world.

You will find a map enclosed with this letter. It hides nothing. You will see the world as we sirens see it—every hidden waterway, island and sharp set of rocks. This knowledge is part of our memories, passed down from mother to daughter, but because you are human, you weren't born with it already planted in your mind. This was the only way I could pass it down to you, mother to daughter. Guard it with care. This knowledge is a weapon in the wrong hands.

I love you.

A single tear splashes on the letter. Then another. I clutch the letter in my trembling fingers and let the tears slide down my cheeks. She left this for me in a place that I would have to find for myself. Perhaps to help me accept what I am, what I have always been. Perhaps, given the knowledge within the map, to prove I am worthy.

In a way, I have always known it. That my mother was different, that she wasn't meant to live on land for so long. And maybe that was her undoing in the end.

Maybe a hunter found her in the one place she kept returning to. To our island. To Rosevear.

To the human man and child that she loved.

CHAPTER NINETEEN

"SO NOW YOU KNOW," THE SIREN SAYS AS SHE slips back into the cavern from the water. "How we know where to find the beating hearts we need. How we navigate the water so swiftly."

"It's imprinted in your mind," I say with a sniff, unfolding the map. It's beautiful and intricate. More detailed than any map of the Fortunate Isles I have ever laid eyes on, and it charts beyond our waters, to the Far Isles and farther, around the curve of the mainland to the north and the coast of Leicena to the south.

There are isles here I've never seen on any map, whole archipelagos tucked into the folds of the ocean. And creatures of the waves, the telltale tentacle of a kraken slithering below the surface, lurking in the waters to the north. I blink, seeing the currents shift, the faint lines of the tide as it moves. It's a living, breathing map. There are so many secrets hidden here. So many places the watch do not know about.

I trace a fingertip around Rosevear, every line of jagged rocks marked with precision. This is a gift. All this knowledge is power. It's the key not only to our survival on Rosevear, but to us *thriving*. Yet, I can see what my mother meant in her letter. In the hands of the watch or someone else, it would destroy us all.

"How did she look human?" I ask the siren. "She didn't look like any of you."

"She made a bargain with a witch. Two vials of her blood. One to create that map for you—the daughter she longed for—and one to make her appear human. Then a vial of blood every year after that, sent to a coven in Arnhem. Of course, every witch's spell comes with a cost. Your mother appeared human, but she never lost her thirst."

My hands tremble as I fold the map away with the letter, slipping them inside her notebook. I place them right where they all belong, pressed against my heart. "That's…"

"Repulsive?" The siren chuckles, crouching down by the pool to stare at her own reflection. "It's nature. It's what we are. And she should have known that all witches' spells come with a curse attached. She hungered for your father's heart every day. Enough to drive her back into the water to kill when her hunger grew too great to resist. Only then was she sated."

I shudder, crossing my arms over my body. "But I don't have that hunger."

"No," the siren sighs. "You're far too human."

I let the silence steal over us. There are so many memories I have to reexamine and trick new meanings out of, because I misunderstood so much. I always wondered why she left Father and I, and where she would go. Did he wonder too? Or did he know what she had to leave for? He would tuck me in each night with a story in her absence. But he never whispered tales of sirens. I heard about them from sailors, and even then I didn't really believe. Perhaps he was just leaving that knowledge for her to share. But then, after her death, he was too afraid that if I knew, I would leave him too and never return.

"I have to get back. My father—"

"We know. The watch have him."

I nod, turning my gaze away from hers. "He's all I have left."

Before I know what is happening, the siren is beside me. She takes my hands in hers, the smooth, slippery skin wrapping around my warm palms. Her eyes are brimming with sorrow and something else. Something that could almost be love. But it's so fierce, so harsh, it's not the kind of love I am used to. I have only ever seen it in my mother's eyes, I realize with a jolt, whenever I swam with her through the sea.

"If you need us, we will come. It is my greatest regret that we could not save your mother," she says, her voice like crushed glass, like the ocean in a tempest. "You are not alone. You never will be. And this map…guard it. It will appear blank to humans and witches, but they may know what it could become."

Twin tears track down my face and I shudder. My heart, my vulnerable, human heart cracks apart as the siren squeezes my hands. I take a deep breath, shutting my eyes and allowing it all to seep in. This whole other side of myself.

When I open my eyes, my heart has mended, reshaped itself around this new knowledge. And somehow, I don't feel so adrift anymore. "Thank you," I say. "Thank you for everything."

★ ★ ★

I leave the siren and follow the waterways back to the schooner. My side still aches, the wound I sustained on the swim to the wreck burnished afresh. I feel her sorrowful eyes on me, perhaps looking for all the ways I am like her. Her sister. My mother. I cannot yet comprehend how I am like them, at least a part of me. They don't feel like human kin do; they don't love in the same way. I am not one of them. I can never be. Just as my mother left this quiet, watchful place, feeling as though she belonged elsewhere, wanting to walk on land. And yet, I know I can count on them. The truth echoes deep within me until I start to accept it. When this is all over, when my father and Bryn are free, I will slowly begin to make sense of it. To untangle the two parts of myself until they fuse back together in a shape that feels whole.

My fingertips flutter to my chest, to the map and the letter tucked away there, hoping it brings me what I sought here. That I can glean some kind of bargaining chip from the map she left me. A way to save the kin I have left and carve out a future between him and the wide ocean. My mother tried to find that balance within herself. But in the end, she didn't belong on land. She didn't belong with us. Even if her heart sang a different song, even if she made a deal with a witch to appear human, she was always tethered to the ocean. But although she could not divide herself between two worlds, I have hope. Now I understand why my soul longs for the sea, I can find a way to bridge these two worlds. Perhaps I can carve out my own space to belong.

With every kick, I climb toward the surface. My heart beats faster, feverish with the knowledge clutched against my chest. I will free my father and Bryn. I will find a way. When

I get back on board, I will tell the crew there was nothing but weed and rock and silence in the depths. I steel myself to lie to Seth, to hide away in the cabin and pore over the map. There is so little time left, but now I am armed with the knowledge of the sirens. I have to find *some* way that won't betray them, or their secrets. Before, all I had was desperation. But now, I have real hope.

As I emerge under *Phantom*, I find the rope ladder hanging over the side, swaying slightly in the breeze. The scent of a storm lingers in the air, all temper and frost.

"Seth! Merryam!" I shout up, hoping one of them will appear. The wind whirls through the sails, a sign that a storm is approaching. We need to leave this place with its treacherous rocks. The sirens may resist the temptation of my beating heart, but if a tempest does come for us, I'm not sure they would be able to resist Seth's, or the rest of the crew of *Phantom*. And with an ocean alive and boiling in the clutches of a tempest, we'll make slow progress through the waves.

I pull myself up gradually, pain needling my side as I cling to the ropes. With a final heave, I haul myself over the side of the railing, thumping onto the deck a second later. I draw in deep breaths, my ribs bruised from the effort of holding the air inside my lungs for so long. It reminds me of my very human limitations. I sit back, placing my hands behind me, and peer around. I need some of Pearl's healing herbs and a brace around my chest. I fear that this time a rib is fractured. Each breath I pull in bathes me in flame and I suck in short, sharp gasps, shifting myself carefully. I call out again. But the deck is silent. Only the slap of the water against the bow and the cry of a lone cormorant pierce the quiet.

None of them are here.

"Seth?" I push up slowly from the deck, make my way to the hatch and scale the ladder steps belowdecks, wincing with every footfall. "Pearl? Joby?" I thrust back the blankets on their bunks, then stride through to the cabin I share with Seth and throw open the door. But it's empty. Dread pools in my stomach, swirling bitterly up my throat. I hug my arms around my body, feeling the quiet too keenly now. They're not here. None of them are on board.

I change as quickly as I can, stripping off my sea-sodden clothes, and scrape my hair back into a quick plait, all the while longing for Seth to appear in the doorway. To see his grin and his freckles and feel the warmth I felt as he trailed kisses down my throat in the starlight. I probe my side, feeling along the length of my bones, and hiss when I find the tender place. I imagine Seth rubbing his thumb in slow, gentle circles over it, tipping back my head to brush his mouth with mine.

I force him from my mind and try to focus. Theories tumble in of why *Phantom* is a ghost ship. Did they all leave? Did they go in search of something? Or worse…were they ambushed?

A thump sounds overhead and I freeze. Perhaps they grew concerned and followed me into the graveyard of rocks. Are they only now returning? I don't like to think of the alternative. That while I was with the siren in the underwater cave, the others lured the crew into the sea. That the beating hearts they sensed on board sent them into a thirsting frenzy. Another thump has me making for the ladder steps. My fingers tremble with all this silence, too eerie to be nothing. They should have been waiting for me. Something's wrong.

When I reach the deck, I find the rope ladder gone. Someone has pulled it up, cutting off anyone trying to climb aboard. In a panic, I whirl, searching for them, looking up to the masts then back to the ocean. And there, under the threatening clouds is a vessel. Flying a sail that would blend with the night.

Another ship.

I gasp, stumbling back, and feel a hand on my shoulder.

I turn to find a woman, taller than me with dark red hair falling around her shoulders, smiling. She holds the coils of the rope ladder.

"I see you paid a little visit to the sirens. How interesting." She nods to someone behind me, and before I can move or speak or bunch my hands into fists, a hood blots out everything.

I breathe in quick gasps, tasting smoke, tasting poison. My limbs ache with sudden weariness and my knees give way beneath me. I try to scream, try to fight, but the sharp tang fills my lungs.

Then nothing.

CHAPTER TWENTY

I WAKE WITH ASH ON MY TONGUE. THE SLIP OF ocean against the sides of a ship rocks me from side to side. For a moment, I'm confused. Is this *Phantom*? Are we still traveling? Then the fractured flurry of events hit me. The silent, eerie underwater world where my mother hid that chest. The sirens and the knowledge that I have their blood in my veins. The map and letter, those secrets left for me. Then the ghostly silence of *Phantom* as I pulled myself back on board, searching for the crew, for Seth, for anyone—

Then a woman.

I gasp, filling my lungs as I remember the world turning dark, the sharp tang of poison as it tugged consciousness from me and left me to drift. How long have I been out? Where am I?

I blink, tracking my eyes back and forth, trying to adjust to the cloying darkness surrounding me. My hands are numb and tingling, wrists bound at my back. When I try to move my feet, I find my ankles are pinned the same way. I'm sprawled against a heap of barrels, the wood at my back making my bones ache where I was slumped against them. When I try to twist, my side barks with pain.

I twist the other way, even as the pain spikes and sparks crowd my vision. But the cords won't give. I stare up at the ceiling, trying not to cry. Bitterness coils in my stomach from whatever they drugged me with. My mind is still blurred at the edges, the woman's features, her voice as elusive as a ghost. In a panic, I realize I cannot feel the notebook pressing against my chest. Which means that woman, or someone with her, has taken it and the map and the letter. I curse, struggling again against the bonds, tears of desperation welling in my eyes.

I listen for footsteps, or the low rumble of conversation. Anything to signal where I am and who else is here with me. A shanty, ancient and favored by chancers, drifts in through the crack under the door. I hear the caller, then the crew of this ship answering him. The lyrics spin on with a ceaseless rhythm, the same three lines over and over, sung in a round to rally a crew. It's a work song. One I've heard smugglers sing as they pulled their haul into the secret cove on our island.

Smugglers...

They can be ruthless. More likely to dump a body overboard than to let them walk away with the secrets of their ships. I gulp, trying to pull at the cords again, casting around for anything I can use. I'm in some kind of storeroom with only the narrow door at my side and the heap of barrels at my back. There's nothing sharp, and I doubt they will have left me my blade.

I stare without seeing into the shadows surrounding me. And then after a moment…they seem to stare back.

"Looks like you're in quite the predicament," a voice says, curling around me like smoke. I frown, peering into the gloaming as the shadows in the corner intensify, rippling and deepening. A chill creeps across the back of my neck, down my spine and everything inside me, everything I *am*, screams a single message.

Run.

I pull at the bonds again, fighting the ropes as a boy—a tall, very human boy—steps into the room. But…he hasn't come through the door. He seems to step from the shadows themselves.

"Who…? How?"

He chuckles and the sound sends skittering fear right through me. "*How* is a question for another day." He steps forward, his boots soft on the planks of worn wood. I can barely make out his face, but I can discern enough from his height, how he holds himself. Casually, watching me. Like a wolf circling its prey. "I would rather hear more about you."

I swallow, giving the ropes binding my wrists one final, desperate tug. He really did step from the shadows, from the maw of darkness surrounding me. But he's no witch—they're all female. And an apothecary would not have such power from the potions they brew, as far as I know. This is no magic I've ever heard of.

"I'm no one. Just a captive. Wrong place, wrong time."

He smiles, his teeth flashing, then leans back against the wall opposite me. "You like to hide secrets inside truths."

"I like to know who I'm talking to before I tell them any-thing," I hiss, fear making way for panic as I pull my knees in close to my chest, putting as much distance as I can between us in this small, enclosed space. Where are the others? Where is Seth? Where is that woman I saw before the world turned black?

"Let's say I'm an interested party." He puts his hands in his pockets and I scan his clothes, the shadows lining his face. Searching for any clue as to who he is, why he's in here. And how he could have walked through a wall to reach me. "How did you find that chest?"

I blink. Somehow he knows what was left for me down there in the ocean. "Luck."

"No help?"

"I was born lucky."

"All right. I see we won't get anywhere without a little... persuasion."

My heart picks up, thrashing against my ribs as he pushes off from the wall and takes a step toward me. For a moment, I can trace the shape of his features. Even half in shadow, they seem familiar. Beautiful, even. I've met this boy before.

"Where are you from?" I try again, inching myself backward. If I could *just* place him, if I could only remember...

"How about you answer my questions and then I'll tell you where I'm from."

I pretend to consider his offer, watching as the shadows deepen around me, crawling up my calves, slithering along my thighs—

"No," I snarl.

"Wrong answer."

The shadows leap higher, pressing upon me, and I draw in a quick breath as velvet dark surrounds me, choking me—

"Tell me."

I cough as the dark claws down my throat, pouring like poison into my lungs, flooding my veins—

These shadows, the way he stepped out of them. This is true magic. Raw, *wild* magic. The kind I felt on the Isle of Ennor, whispering all around.

Ennor.

The boy...the mysterious boy who was following me. Who toyed with me, with his dark lashes and wicked grin, with his lethal swagger, who told me where to find the crew...

It's *him.*

The rattle of a key chimes quietly outside the door. Then a whistle, the lock clicking open.

And the shadows evaporate.

I gasp, pulling in deep, soothing breaths, coughing as though drowning. I look up, scanning the room for the boy, for the shadows deeper than velvet...but he's gone.

A light swings in my face, held by a rounded hand. Two ordinary gray eyes stare into mine.

"She's awake," he calls to someone in the doorway before turning back to me. "Cap wants a word with you, girl."

"The boy who was in here..."

"Ain't no one here but you," he says before angling a blade at my ankles and slashing away the ties.

I barely have a chance to get my feet under me as I'm dragged from the storeroom and those staring shadows.

The man with the lamp jabs me in the back, hastening my steps through the ship. I try to mark anything I can as we walk. But all I see is a low corridor, running like a snake through the belly of a ship, doors closed and bolted in the swinging lantern light. We stop at the only door at the end of the corridor, in front of a brass plaque gleaming with etched lettering.

Captain's Cabin.

The man reaches past my shoulder to knock on the door. "Enter."

My wrists are roughly untied and I'm shoved over the threshold, the door closing in my wake. I spin, taking in the captain's cabin as I rub my wrists, pins and needles prickling in my fingertips. There is a wall of diamond-paned, pearly windows, with a navy swirling sky beyond. Cluttered shelves line one wall, filled with dusky red books and sheaves of parchment shoved into every gap. The polished meeting table dominating the center of the cabin shimmers as a mirror, as though it could be wet to the touch. My gaze falls on the desk in front of the window, where the red-haired woman is sitting. She leans back in her chair; the desk before her is scattered with maps and ink pots. In the center of all of it, there is a piece of parchment.

The map.

"What do you want with me?" I say, trying to keep my gaze from straying to her desk when all I want to do is snatch the map from her and leap into the waiting sea. To her, I imagine it appears as an unmarked sheet of parchment, just as the siren said. The fact that she hasn't just discarded it means she knows it isn't exactly what it looks like.

As though sensing my thoughts, the woman leans forward, a small smile flickering over her lips, and places one hand possessively on the parchment. Her nails are painted the same color as her hair.

"Mira. In another life, we would have known each other

very well by now. We would have been friends. *Allies*, even. Such a shame."

I step forward, drawn in despite myself. "What do you mean?"

"It hurts me that you don't know who I am. That your mother chose to take you away from this life." She casts a hand around the cabin before bringing her fist to rest against her heart. "That she chose to hide away on that sad little island."

I frown, taking another step to place my hands on the back of the chair at the head of the meeting table.

"Your mother was very dear to me." Her fingers tap against the parchment. "She wanted me to find this. She left it there for me, in that underwater graveyard she came from."

"How...?" I swallow, pushing back the fragments of my own memories of my mother. Pushing everything away until all that is left is my father. The beach. His eyes. He is the reason I am here, standing before this captain. The reason I need that map and the secrets it contains. "Why would you think that? It's just a piece of parchment. Nothing special."

"We both know that's not true because, dear Mira—" the woman smiles, her eyes narrowing as she points to the wall behind me "—she left me that."

I turn, a creeping dread feathering down my spine. And there is the evidence. A map, huge and wide, depicting the Fortunate Isles and Arnhem coastline. But it's not as detailed as the map my mother left for me. And it's still, unmoving, no predictions of the tide and weather. No suggestion of tempests forming. It seems perfectly ordinary, like any map we have found aboard the ships we wrecked. There is a compass, wreathed in shadows and waves in the top right corner. But in the place where I dove down, the place Seth led me to, there is a star.

"She painted that star for *me*," the captain says.

I walk toward it, heart thumping louder and louder in my ears.

"She meant for me to follow. She meant this map for *me*."

I place my fingertips on the star, navy and flecked with gold. It's an eight-pointed star, exactly the same as the one in my mother's notebook. A roaring begins in my chest, in my head, and I close my eyes, tasting ash.

Tasting lies.

"It's not yours. This map. It can't be yours. She wouldn't have drawn that," I whisper, tracing the lines of the star. The roaring in my head builds and builds, crackling with lightning, thumping like a storm is breaking inside me. And I realize in that moment, standing before this map, who this captain is. She is the woman on Wanted posters from here to the Far Isles. Who even Bryn won't speak of. A captain so ruthless, so infamous, that she has commandeered trade routes, slitting throats and burning ships until they are nothing but ghosts on the water.

Captain Renshaw.

"It is mine, Mira. And now all I need is a drop of your siren blood."

I stiffen as the door creaks open at my back. My eyes dart to the right just as two hands come down on my shoulders.

I am shoved toward the desk. I blink rapidly, heart thrashing in the cage of my chest.

"Cut her finger."

I wince as my hand is wrenched forward, a silver blade slicing through my skin. The blood wells quickly, already dripping down my palm.

"Hold it over the parchment."

Two drops, then a third soak into the ivory paper. My heartbeat drums in my ears, the shock of the cut making my eyes water. I look at her and find a hunger in her eyes that fills me with dread. My mother may have trusted her once; perhaps, it may have even been this smuggler ship she arrived in on Rosevear all those years ago.

But I'm sure she was no friend.

The woman hisses, bending closer to the map, searching the creases as my blood soaks into it. "It's not enough, not *enough…*"

The siren said it would appear blank to humans and witches. She didn't say my blood would change that.

But this woman doesn't know that. And she doesn't know that I can read the map. For some reason she believes it will reveal its secrets with a mere drop of siren blood.

My blood.

"Cut her throat. Drain every drop."

I gasp, thrashing against the arms that clamp around me, drawing in a breath to scream.

"Let her go."

The arms that hold me slacken and I wriggle out, turning to stumble back. And there, holding a blade to the man's throat, eyes pinched and full of flint, is Seth. I freeze, blood cooling to ice, sure her men will leap on him, that he is about to be killed before my very eyes.

But Captain Renshaw laughs. I watch in disbelief as she sighs, sinking farther down into the chair behind her desk. She flicks her wrist at Seth, as though bored. "Fine, slit his throat. Show me you're more capable than I thought."

The man struggles against Seth, his throat bobbing as he

swallows. Fear sharpens his eyes to nothing but darkness as the blade nicks his skin, crimson welling in a shiny bead.

"Seth?" I say. "What's going on?"

Seth blinks, as though he forgot I was still standing here. Sorrow crashes over his features, just like on *Phantom* the last time I saw him, before I dropped below the waves into the siren's graveyard. He withdraws the blade from the man's throat, pushing him roughly aside.

"Mira..." he says, his voice raw, beseeching. "Mira, I..."

Then it all becomes clear. I look from him to the woman, realizing his wrists are not bound. That they never have been. He isn't a prisoner as I am.

"What have you done, Seth?" I choke out, shock searing a path up my throat.

"Meet my son," the captain says. "The one I sent to go find you on that wretched little island. Such a bonus, you leading us straight to where your mother hid the map." She smiles, her lips a red gash across her face. "To *my* map, I should say."

"Is it true? She's your *mother*?"

But Seth has no answers. Nothing to say to the facts thrust before me. He pales, gaze sliding to the floor, shoulders shrugging inward, as though his whole being has crumbled.

"Seth?" I say again, my voice cracking around his name.

I remember when he tore down that poster about the *Fair Maiden*, her Wanted poster near it. How his eyes strayed to hers, peering out from the ink. He distracted me, reassured me. Not, I realize now, to protect me and stop my worries. It was so I wouldn't realize the truth. So I wouldn't spot the likeness between them that I see now, how their eyes are the same, how the sharp jut of his cheekbones matches hers. This boy, with salt tangled in his hair, who held my hand below the stars, dusted kisses over my skin, who I rescued not once but *twice* from the clutches of death.

I take a stumbling step back, reeling from it all. Realizing how deep his lies have run. How dangerous it is just to know him. And now, *now...*

"It's just business, Mira," he says softly, eyes still trained on the floorboards. "Nothing personal."

"Nothing...*personal*?" Heat flares through me. Hurt and fear and something darker.

Fury.

"Don't take it too badly," Renshaw says, and I turn to look at her. I mark the twist of her smirk, the cold glint of triumph in her eyes. She wanted her son to do this. She wanted him to bring me here, to dive down to the sirens. I realize, as I stare at her, what it is to truly hate.

The cabin door swings open once more and I feel a gust of cold, the scent of the ocean carrying across the threshold. "We all have to make a living, after all," she says. "Did you really think we would let you wander off with the treasure the sirens keep down there? This map is mine, along with *all* its secrets."

I look around, finding Seth's eyes have finally risen to meet mine. I search hopelessly for any hint of the boy I've grown to care for. The boy I rescued from the sea, freckles so vivid I could map the stars with his features. The boy I trusted. Who I thought was helping me. But there's nothing there I recognize. Nothing in those silent eyes but inky depths and endless cold. All I see is Renshaw's son.

"You betrayed me," I whisper.

Then I lunge for his throat.

CHAPTER
TWENTY-ONE

HE CATCHES MY HAND. I GROWL IN FRUSTRATION as his fingers clamp around my wrist and I grit my teeth, turning my other hand into a fist. I thump him, hard. He folds in the middle, coughing and choking out my name.

"Don't," I hiss as more of the captain's men crash into the cabin. "Don't you *dare* say you're sorry."

They grab me, pulling me from Seth as the captain stays behind her desk, watching us thoughtfully. Their fists grip my side, fingers twisting into my ribs, and I gasp with the pain. Seth straightens, breathing hard, hurt contorting his features. I don't know if it's from my fist, or from regret. Regret that he has betrayed me. *Used* me. Or regret that he was caught.

Suddenly, the fury spiking in my veins slips away. A sob threatens in my throat as Renshaw's men push me toward the doorway.

"Wait—" I hear Seth say. "Wait, Mira, please, I can explain."

But I don't want to hear it. I've lost the only chance I had of saving my father. The last piece of my mother. The answers I've been searching for all my life.

And it's all his fault.

I'm left alone again. I pace the small storeroom, rattling the door handle. Searching for a way out. But as the ship glides through the vast ocean, the walls creaking and groaning as she cuts against the salt and cold, I know there is no way out of this place. I'm trapped. I picture my father and Bryn, the last of their hope draining from them as the day draws closer for their execution. By my count, I have just five days left. I cover my face with my hands, bitterness curling in my stomach.

I have failed them.

"I don't think you're trying hard enough," a voice says from across the room.

I stumble back, knocking into the barrels. And there, leaning against the wall, face shrouded in shadows, is the boy again. The boy I first met on the Isle of Ennor. I should be terrified after the last time I saw him, when he doused me in shadows and velvet dark. But I'm still reeling from everything I have learned about Seth, and how I may have lost everything.

I scrub at my face, sniffing back the bile coating my throat. "I know where I've seen you before. You told me where to find the crew. Are you working with her? The captain?"

The boy sighs and I catch a flash of teeth in the gloaming. "Captain Renshaw is the last person across the *entire* continent I would work with."

"You're just as underhanded. You're all the same. *You* tried to suffocate me for my secrets—*she* tried to cut them from me." I swallow hard, running a hand over my throat.

His voice softens. "Perhaps I was a little hasty. I assure you, I am nothing like that woman."

"And *Seth*... I can't believe—"

"That he's her son?"

I nod, the truth of it settling in. Every moment, every time his knuckles grazed mine, his eyes darkening as they swept over me...the bowl of stars, his hands wrapped around mine in the water, our kiss. Was it all a lie?

Fresh fear that I will never see my father again rattles through me.

Suddenly the room is too small, the ceiling too low, constricting me, squeezing me. My breath turns rapid, fire burning in my lungs, my head softening and spinning dizzily. The missing puzzle pieces click into place and I can see Seth for what he really is. A liar. A trickster. He avoided so many questions, I never learned the real connections among the crew. Smugglers and murderers the lot of them. Probably paid to keep quiet and offered a reward for their silence. He never wanted to help me. He never...

"Easy," the boy says, catching me under my elbow. His grip is firm and strong as he guides me down to the floor. "Try to take deeper breaths."

Sparks cluster at the corners of my vision, spilling over everything as I close my eyes and dip my forehead down to my knees.

A strong arm comes around me. A cool hand on my forehead. I lean into him, into his broad chest, his steady heartbeat, searching for an anchor in this endless despair. Shadows wrap around me, darkness swallowing each of my shallow breaths. A coolness, much like the ocean at night washes over me.

And somehow in that velvet nothing, I find space.

I empty my mind, wringing out every thought, every memory. Of Seth, of my purpose, of the journey we've taken together. I leave only myself. Only the soft patter of my heart, the warmth of my breath. And gradually, I begin to calm. With that arm around me, strong and sure, I can feel myself unwinding.

"That's it, Mira. Slow and steady."

His voice is the calm command of the sea. The smooth darkness of deep waters. I follow it, letting it soothe me. Allowing it to calm the thunder in my heart and in my head. Until all that is left is clear, cold certainty.

I open my eyes to find him staring down at me and I'm reminded with a jolt how very beautiful he is. His serious face is framed with dark brown hair, so dark it's almost black. His eyes are two dark stars, piercing mine. Somehow, they hold so much. As if he has lived a lifetime of experiences already.

He smiles, his lips quirking, a thought flaring in those two dark stars before he blinks it away. I can feel his heart beating steadily in his chest. And something twists inside me, something old. Something I've never felt before. Almost as if my heart knows him from before I met him on Ennor. As if it has always known him.

His arm holds me closer, as if he doesn't want to let go.

"I didn't think I would find you here. Someone…different. Someone…not entirely human," he murmurs, before gently, reluctantly, removing his arm and standing up. "I am sorry for how I treated you before. Truly. I have grown too used to resorting to those tactics. Forgive me."

I swallow. The imprint of his body is still warm against my side but fading fast like a ghost. When I look up at him, all I see is a face wreathed in shadows. Hands tucked into his pockets, as though he's on some casual stroll. I want his arm around me again, to feel that steady, certain calm. Where Seth seems to bring out a tempest inside me, this stranger is like the harbor I didn't realize I needed. "I suppose you want to use me like they have."

"I do," he says with a small, teasing smile. "I could find many uses for you."

I sniff. "At least you're honest about it."

He chuckles, moving farther away to lean against the wall opposite me. Now I am used to the dark of the room, I can make out his features far more easily. The teasing tilt to his smile is gone, replaced by a cool seriousness. I pull in a breath, flicking my gaze up and down him, seeing the casual way he pulls his hands from his pockets to cross his arms, the bulge of his muscles bunching under his black jacket. Now he looks every bit the lethal predator I believed him to be when we met on Ennor. "You know what I want. I want what you fetched from the siren's graveyard. I certainly don't want it in Renshaw's grubby hands, *especially* if it's what I think it is. If it's knowledge the sirens guard with their lives."

I narrow my eyes, focusing on the way his mouth moves when he speaks, picking apart all that he's saying. "You can't have it. It would be useless to you anyway."

"How so?"

I consider my answer. How I could turn this to my advantage. "It *is* knowledge from the sirens. But...only I can read it. To you, it would appear as it does to anyone else, to Renshaw, to Seth, to anyone who happens to pick it up. A blank piece of parchment."

His eyes bore into mine, his entire being focused on me. And I find it oddly thrilling and unnerving in equal measures. "Go on."

"But I see it differently." I choose my next words carefully. "Help me escape Renshaw and get off this ship, and all that knowledge will come with me. It won't be in your hands, but it won't be in *hers* either."

He grows quiet, turning this over. "A bargain then."

"A bargain."

He smiles in the dark, his face turning wicked. "You are learning fast, Mira. But you should know that if you make a bargain with me, it will leave a mark."

"What do you mean?"

He spreads out his hands. "It's what I trade in. Bargains. Secrets. Whispers. Were you never warned about making a deal with someone like me?"

"I don't— Someone like you?"

"I take that as a no." He closes the small distance between us and I wonder for the first time if he is not quite human. "But I am willing to agree to this bargain. To saving you along with that *apparent* blank piece of parchment in exchange for help escaping this ship, so neither you, nor the secrets you've brought back from the sirens, are in Renshaw's hands."

I consider his words. Would it be so terrible to make this bargain with him? I could escape this ship, get back to my father and Bryn in time, and hopefully whatever secrets I can glean from the map will be worth enough to free them both.

But doubt glints like the reflection of the moon on the sea. Catching at me, reminding me. My mother warned me of what lurks just beyond our understanding. She never warned me not to make bargains, but maybe she would have if she had lived. She might have warned me that a bargain, especially the magical kind, comes at a cost. And even if this boy with a predator's ease and grace is no witch, I am sure any bargain with him will have a price. What if I do not learn of it before it's too late?

I look up into his eyes, this boy who seems steeped in shadow, able to walk through locked doors and step through the darkness itself. Is he one of those mysterious monsters? One of the creatures I was warned never to trust? Or...am I? Am I the kind of creature the sailors tell tales about, able to do more than any human can? Am *I* the monster in this bargain? I blink, wrapping my mind around that question. Wondering if we are two monsters making a bargain, or maybe I am indeed the unsuspecting victim, about to meet a cruel, dark fate.

But...his arm when it was wrapped around me. His warmth. The steady beat of his heart in his chest... I take a deep breath, trying to straighten out the snarl of my thoughts. They are all real. Human. Just as my heart is a human heart, despite what I am capable of. When I was in that place, searching for what my mother had left for me, I found I could hold that breath in my lungs and stay underwater longer than I ever thought possible. She mentioned other abilities in her letter...things that would set me apart even further from any of my human kin.

But that doesn't make me monstrous. It's what we choose to do in this world that turns us into monsters.

I consider him, this boy with dark stars for eyes. With the beautiful, perfect features that make my breath catch, just a little. His dark lashes, the strong shape of his jaw. The way his hair falls into his eyes as he watches me, wetting his lips. How he seems so very deadly and yet when his body was next to mine, I felt calm and at peace. Like he quenched the fire in my blood.

Like I had come home.

Maybe I can trust him. Maybe I can't. But if I don't make this bargain now, despite what it may cost me later, then there is no chance of me *ever* seeing my father alive again.

"All right," I say quietly, rising up to stand before him. His eyes flash in the wreath of shadows. "I agree to your wording. I want to make the bargain with you."

I hold out my hand, expecting to shake on it. My heart thumps wildly as he steps from the shadows and grasps my fingers in his warm palm, pulling me close. But then he inches his hold up to my wrist, turning my palm upward to expose delicate, white skin. He places his thumb there, over the blue vein where my hand and arm meet, and I feel a jolt, like a spark, or a sliver of lightning.

I wince, pulling my arm back, and catch the steady flair of a marking, silver against my flesh, the shape of an arrow, a compass point, before it fades to nothing. I look up at him, frowning.

"What did you do?"

He shrugs, putting his hands back in his pockets. "I did warn you. It's a bargain mark."

I frown, looking down at my wrist, then back at him. I wonder if there is more to this bargain than the words. If now I am tied to the kind of person that is whispered about. A boy who hides a monster within.

"When will you fulfil your side of the bargain?"

He licks his lips, eyeing me like a wolf. "Soon. Very soon. Now tell me what you found down there with the sirens."

I rub my thumb in slow circles over my wrist. "That wasn't part of the bargain."

"I only want to protect you. Haven't I proved that?"

"You have proved nothing."

"Then maybe I will take my time saving you. Maybe it will take longer than I thought…"

"That's not fair."

"We didn't agree on a time frame."

I sigh in frustration. He's right. I wasn't careful enough. But if I tell him about the map, will that leave me more vulnerable? Will he save me only to steal me away?

"Fine," I snap, rubbing my temples. I choose a story that nudges up to the truth, so close that it doesn't contain any lies. Just small omissions. "My mother left me a notebook with an illustration inside of an eight-pointed star. And around that star were coordinates. That's why I needed a crew. I needed to get there and quickly to find whatever she left me in the hopes that it would…" I swallow, looking away.

"Go on," he says. He reaches for me, his fingertips grazing my jaw with a featherlight touch. I feel it all the way down my body, that touch. It chills my blood as much as it warms it.

I catch his fingertips in my fist and pin him with my gaze. "In the hopes that it would save my father and a dear friend from the gallows."

He frowns, withdrawing his hand from my grasp as I lock my eyes with his.

"But the object I found in the depths won't save them. It isn't a knife or a rifle or some poison to feed to the watch. As you know, it's a piece of parchment. It's something only I can use, as I've told you. Which makes it a curse, not a gift. And in a way, it makes it worthless. I can't use it to bargain for their lives. I could sell its secrets, the ones Renshaw couldn't reveal with my blood, but now I'm trapped on this ship, my father is miles away, and I only have days before he... Before it's too late."

The stranger is quiet for a moment, watching me. Then he sighs, taking a step back so he is half in shadow. "If it's a gift from the sirens, this *piece of parchment*, it isn't a curse. It's more valuable than you can possibly imagine." He shakes his head, a small smile playing on his lips. "Stay vigilant. Do not give away anything to Captain Renshaw or her son."

Before I can ask him any more, before I can pin him down on when he will help me escape, he steps back across the threshold of shadows, and is gone.

I slump against the barrels, rubbing my wrist, and I realize something. He never gave me his name. Not on the Isle of Ennor, and not now aboard this ship. And although he called me Mira, saying it softly, gently, using it to lure me in, to learn more about the map, to print that bargain mark on my skin—

I never told him mine either.

CHAPTER
TWENTY-TWO

"PUT THESE ON."

I step back as a bundle of clothing is thrown at my feet. Renshaw's men slam the door, leaving me in jarring silence. It's been hours since I was dragged into the captain's cabin and by my reckoning—if I wasn't knocked out for longer than I think—I have just four days now. Four days and nights to save my father and Bryn.

I shiver, running my hands over my shirt. I'm still wearing the clothes Renshaw captured me in. They've melded to my skin, stiff and cold, and as I eye the bundle of clothing at my feet, I realize I'll have to obey. If only to feel cleaner. I pluck the dress they have left for me from the floor, curling my lip in distaste at the gold embroidery, the heavy weight of the beaded fabric. It's a ball gown, meant for mainlanders to wear at fancy gatherings. Not for on board a ship. I'll barely be able to move let alone fight my way out of a corner.

With a sigh, I pick up the narrow evening slippers decorated with tiny seed pearls and the undergarments I'm expected to wear. They're all clean and I wonder if they're stolen. It seems likely. A fist pounds on the door and a muffled grunt indicates that I need to hurry. I change, my stomach groaning as I move. I've barely eaten in two days. They've given me water and a few crusts of stale bread. I believe Renshaw is deliberately starving me out. Waiting until I cave and help her with that damn map.

Just as I finish shuffling into the ridiculous slippers, the door opens and two of Renshaw's men cross the threshold. One is slight with a sneer and thin gray hair, while the other is almost too broad to fit through the doorway. His brow hangs over his pale gray eyes, narrowing them to thin slits. He is the one who Renshaw ordered to cut my throat. I swallow, trying not to show my fear as he grabs at my arm, pinching my skin, and hauls me back along the corridor to Renshaw's cabin.

Music greets me; a thin, whining sound coming from a music box set up on the desk. The grating sound fills the room on an endless loop. I cast a quick glance around, noting that the main table is laid with polished cutlery and candlesticks. There are places set for five and yet, I am the only person here.

"I thought we could have a little dinner party," Renshaw says, striding into the cabin.

I whip around, finding the smile dusting her lips is just shy of a sneer. She flicks an invisible piece of lint from her immaculate black velvet jacket and takes a seat at the head of the dining table. The slight man sidles up to her, showing her a bottle of wine for her inspection. She nods her head and he pours the wine into a goblet in front of her. Leaning back in her chair, she swirls it casually, the liquid catching the candlelight like blood. She's trying to unnerve me. It's like she's tapping a finger against the edges of me, scraping a nail to find a way in, a way to break me down so she can get what she wants out of me.

"Who's joining us?" I ask, keeping my voice cool.

She drinks deep from her goblet, wipes her mouth with the back of her hand, and grins at me. "Sit, drink. They'll be here soon enough."

The other man who dragged me from the storeroom forces me into a chair. My arm pulses in pain where his hands grip my skin, but I don't show it. Renshaw clicks her fingers and the same wine is poured into a goblet in front of me. It glistens, reminding me of the wound blooming along Seth's collarbone in the water. How he turned as pale as moonlight, his life slowly surging out of him. I wonder if he betrayed the rest of the crew, or if they were complicit. I wonder where they are now. I wonder why I saved him.

"Drink."

I set my mouth in a firm line, refusing to budge. She sighs with impatience and I see her wave her hand at the men. I stiffen, waiting for a hand to grip me once more, and I wonder if I should take a small sip, but just then, the door clicks open.

And in walk the three other guests.

It's Pearl I notice first. Her eyes are vacant and her bottom lip is swollen, a bruise forming around her jaw. She's still wearing the blue tunic I last saw her in, paired with breeches and boots. She doesn't look at me as she takes the seat beside mine, but I feel the brush of her knuckles against my own under the table and that brief connection tells me everything I need to know. She's on my side. We have both been betrayed.

Seth sits down directly across from me, leaning back and spreading his elbows out wide. I expect him to look triumphant, but he seems distracted, troubled. Our eyes meet and he quickly drops his expression into a carefully controlled mask, darting a furtive glance at Renshaw. His mother. My blood simmers, but I choose to ignore it, and him, entirely. Instead, I focus on the person who sits down beside him.

"Lord Tresillian, so glad you could join us this evening," says Renshaw, tipping her goblet to the third and final guest. I try not to stare as he pins his gaze to mine. Not a hint of recognition rests in his features, yet in his eyes, I find the smallest ember. I press my lips together, tearing away my gaze. My fingers lace together under the table, twisted tightly to hide the trembling.

This is the fourth time I have met him now, this boy I made a bargain with in the shadows. So he is Lord Tresillian, ruler of the Isle of Ennor. I touch my thumb to my wrist, the mark he left there suddenly flaring with heat. Out of the corner of my eye, I catch him smiling slowly, as if he knows.

I try to recall the details I know of this boy. The real him. He resides in a castle shaped as a star. His empire of apothecaries and smugglers and ships stretches from here to the Far Isles, and beyond. He most likely has influence over Arnhem and the territories that make up the continent to the southeast. And what's more, it was *him* I recognized on a poster at Port Trenn. A young lord, the head of his house, who inherited his family's seat, wealth and power far too young. Seth said *tragically early*.

A boy who has a dangerous magic.

A boy who is wanted by the watch, dead or alive.

He turns to Renshaw as his own goblet is filled with wine. "It's not every day I receive a summons from the queen of the sea herself," he says, sniffing his wine before taking a gulp.

Renshaw's grin exposes her teeth and I feel Pearl tense up next to me. "Invited, my lord. *Never* summoned. You flatter me. Or do you? We both know you hold the routes I desire. I am hardly queen of anything without them."

Lord Tresillian shrugs, balancing his goblet in his fingers, the picture of ease. "Give me something that's worth more than those routes and we'll talk."

Renshaw blinks, a hint of loathing crossing her features before she claps her hands twice. The door opens and a procession of dishes is marched in. Steaming piles of meats and vegetables on exquisite tureens and platters are placed in the middle of the table.

My mouth waters and I swallow, half looking at Seth through the curling steam. He's watching me. Marking my every move, every reaction. I school my features into bland disinterest, even while my heart hammers against my ribs. He can't find out that I know Lord Tresillian, that we've already met. As far as he knows, I was on Ennor for a matter of hours and left without meeting anyone except the crew of *Phantom* and the shopkeeper.

Whatever Renshaw is after from this boy of shadows, whatever her reason for inviting him to her table, I doubt it would benefit me if she knew that he had already found me. That we had already made a deal to get me off this ship and out of her clutches.

"Dig in, please," Renshaw says, indicating the food. "Guests first."

I don't wait to be polite. Using my fork, I spear the food I want, dropping it onto my plate. Pearl does the same beside me and we eat in unison, her small sigh matching mine as we take our first mouthfuls. She must have been held somewhere and fed very little too. From the state of her face, it looks as though Renshaw has been seeking information from her that Pearl has been unwilling to part with.

"What a feast," Lord Tresillian says, eating more slowly than myself and Pearl. "No poison, no strings attached? It's almost as though you want to patch things up." He grins at Renshaw. "Or are you working your way up to it? What is it you want?"

"She'll tell you in good time," one of Renshaw's men rumbles from behind me. A reminder that they are there.

"Anything to do with these two delightful creatures?" Lord Tresillian asks pointedly, staring at Pearl. "I hadn't realized you were expanding your crew."

"Maybe they're mine now," Seth says quietly. "For my new ship."

Pearl snorts, but carries on eating. She's not a fighter, but I wouldn't want to cross her.

"Where are the others? Where's Mer and Joby?" I ask Seth bluntly. He looks at me, then quickly to Renshaw. It's clear who holds all the power on this ship.

"They are…indisposed this evening," Renshaw says softly.

I feel Pearl's leg shift under the table, pressing gently into mine in warning. I nod, taking a big gulp from my goblet and letting the liquid burn all the way down to distract me. I can't let Renshaw see my fear.

I'm sure that none of the crew aboard *Phantom* betrayed me. I'm convinced we were all taken in by Seth. Glancing at him now, I hope to see remorse or at least compassion. I saved him twice and the others, including Pearl, helped him live by getting him to an apothecary. She risked her life for him. But all I find is him staring brazenly back at me, a small smile tugging at his lips. I grip my goblet tight, wondering what would happen if I hurled it at his head.

Renshaw claps again after a few more minutes and the feast is cleared as quickly as it appeared. "Now. Let us discuss why we're all here tonight," she says. She points at Pearl. "You first. I thought you might become more amenable once fed. There is a tiny detail my son does not seem to know. Who do you work for, my dear?"

Pearl sighs, closing her eyes briefly. I watch her, noting the dark smudges under her eyes. The worry, which can only be for Merryam and Joby. "I work for Mer. She's my captain."

"And who does dear Merryam work for?"

"Ask her."

Renshaw chuckles. "You know very well that I have already tried that." She shakes her head. "In that case… Brett?"

Brett, the larger of the two thugs, approaches the table from behind us. He pulls back Pearl's chair, grasps her arm, and tosses her toward the door as if she were nothing but a rag doll. In the seconds before she leaves the table, I feel a note pressed into my fingers. She begins to babble, talking too fast about how she knows nothing, how she only wants to get back to her ship.

And as everyone is neatly distracted by her pleading, I glance at the note and smile: *All in hand. Tell them nothing.*

I look back up as she begins to wail, clawing at the edges of the door frame, and find Lord Tresillian's eyes on me. He winks, then raises his goblet and drinks deeply as Pearl is forced from the cabin. And I realize that Pearl is in on whatever his plan is. That, actually, Pearl is exactly where she is meant to be. I drop my gaze, pretending to freeze in fear and beginning to piece it all together.

I met the crew in the Mermaid, on the Isle of Ennor—Lord Tresillian's isle. They're not some crew for hire…they are *his* crew. Mer, Joby, and Pearl. And he is here to ensure their freedom. Renshaw must suspect they are his crew, and she is trying to provoke him. But he is utterly unruffled.

Renshaw laughs breathlessly, turning on me. "Now, your turn. Tell me how to read the map, or I'll try again to reveal it with your blood."

My gaze darts to Lord Tresillian, our eyes meeting briefly. His flare, in triumph or fury at this new knowledge, I'm unsure. Now he knows it's a map I retrieved from the sirens. But within a heartbeat, his eyes slide to his goblet, and he taps a finger on the side, demanding more wine. As it's poured for him, I scrunch up Pearl's note, pulse thumping in my ears as I run my fingerprints over the ink. Smudging it. Making it illegible before tearing it into tiny pieces to scatter on the floor under the table.

I swallow, deciding to stick with the truth. "I don't know how. It's a blank piece of parchment."

She leans toward me, her grin widening manically. *"Liar."*

"Mother," Seth begins.

"Quiet," Renshaw snaps, holding up a palm. She smooths back her hair, the mass of dark red waves loosening from their pins. I can see she's trying to keep it together, to cap a lid on the storm inside. But her eyes betray her. They're as wild as a February night. I realize with some satisfaction that this wasn't the way she wanted this evening to play out. She invited her biggest rival aboard, intending to break me. To show that she holds all the cards with the map from the sirens, and leverage a deal from him for the routes she wants to control. But she failed to factor in one thing.

I am not under her command.

"If you won't tell me, perhaps you need to be persuaded."

"Now, come on—" Seth tries again, leaning forward. Sweat prickles along his brow, his eyes darting from her to me. He is afraid of her. Afraid of what she will do. But he can't be afraid for my sake. If he was, he wouldn't have betrayed me, would he? Doubt worms its way in as I think I see how fearful he is for me. Truly. Maybe all the tales about Renshaw are true, and I should be afraid too.

"Silence," Renshaw hisses, flashing him a look. She clicks her fingers at the two remaining members of her crew in the cabin. Their heavy footsteps send a shiver down my spine. I flinch, feeling hot breath on my neck just before a hand clamps down on my shoulder. "Take her on deck. She can scrub the boards. Give her lye. Plenty of it."

My chair is thrust back, pushed from under me, and I find myself hustled toward the door. In the split second I have before I'm pushed over the threshold, I catch Lord Tresillian's gaze. He's perfectly relaxed, eyes glittering with menace. And just before the door closes, he nods ever so slightly.

CHAPTER TWENTY-THREE

MY HANDS ARE BURNING. AT FIRST WHEN I WAS shoved on deck with a large bucket and a scrubbing brush, I couldn't feel it. Couldn't feel the building heat under my skin every time I dunked the brush back in the water to drag it across the oily boards. Couldn't feel the lye permeating the water. But I can now.

And it burns.

I'm still in this ridiculous ball gown covered in intricate beadwork and so many layers that I can scarcely move. Now it's ruined, coated in the lye from the bucket, the oil and muck from the deck, and my own cold sweat as it freezes to my skin. The driving rain hasn't helped, casting a vertical slant across the deck. The sailors surrounding me sneer and whisper taunts under their breath, but none approach me. I long to rip off this gown and leap into the sea. But I can't leave the map behind, or my mother's letter and notebook. My legacy.

I have to wait for Lord Tresillian to make good on our

deal, to make sure I can get off this ship in one piece. Alive. And besides, now that I've seen Pearl's face, the split lip, the bruises on her jaw, I won't leave her here—even though I'm sure she can take care of herself. The stars wink furiously in the gathering storm overhead. It's around midnight, I'm sure. Maybe a little later. And no one has said I can stop scrubbing and sleep.

Footsteps on the boards echo up through my fingertips as I scrub. I look up through the haze of rain and sleet to find Seth, shoulders hunched, brown curls in disarray around his temples. I look back at the wooden boards and throw the bucket of water over the deck, ready to scrub the last of the muck away.

"Are you here to bring me more water?" I ask, chucking the empty bucket at his shins. My side aches with every movement, but I don't let it show. "Or are you here to gloat? Either way, you can piss off."

He huffs, wiping the rain from his face before crouching next to me. "I'm here to bring you my jacket. And to talk some bloody sense into you."

I sit facing him on the deck and try to stop the shaking in my bones. I don't want him to know how cold I am, how I would give anything to warm myself in the sea. He drapes his jacket around my shoulders, turning up the collar around my cheekbones. I feel the heat that still lingers from his body in the folds of the fabric. It calms my shivers, leaving me conflicted. I look up at him, this boy I'm supposed to hate. At his wide-set, serious eyes. The mouth I've touched with mine to bring him back to life. The mouth that grazed my skin, leaving a trail of flame in its wake.

I tear my gaze away and sniff. "You betrayed us."

"I had no choice. I'm sorry. You have no idea how sorry I am."

"If you were sorry, you'd let me go now. You'd stop those thugs from hitting Pearl and let us all go."

He sighs, running a damp hand through his hair. Pain and regret war over his features, the foxy playfulness gone. He opens his mouth then closes it again, shaking his head ruefully. "You know I can't do that. You've met her, my mother. I'm doing all I can right now."

"To help her, you mean? You led me into a trap—you led *all* of us into a trap. Did you give her the coordinates on Ennor? Has she been tracking us since then?"

I push my wet hair away from my face, tendrils clinging to my neck. I'm breathing fast and hard, picturing him sneaking away as soon as my back was turned to hand information to one of Renshaw's men.

His mouth folds into a thin line. He can't meet my eyes.

"I knew it," I chuckle darkly, wiping the back of my arm over my forehead. "This was the play all along, wasn't it? She's wanted that map for a long time. And you've dragged Mer's crew, your *friends*, into this mess."

His eyes flash in the dim. "Believe me, if I could wind time back, I would. I would do it all differently. I wish…" He stops, his breath hitching. "I wish I'd never met you."

"Well, you did," I say viciously. "You lured me to Ennor, you *tricked* me, and now my father…now my father will—"

His arms wrap around me, so fast I don't see it coming. For a second, I allow the connection, to believe that he is the boy I met. That we could somehow wind time back and start again. Inside, I am a storm, yearning for his touch, for his lips to graze mine, his hands to move along my skin. But he is a liar and a thief and I do not need his comfort.

I push him off, shoving his warmth and regret far from me. "Don't, Seth. Just *don't*. If you won't help me, then you've as good as tied that noose *yourself*."

"I want to help you," he says in a sudden whispered rush, glancing around as though to check if anyone is listening in. "I want to help *all* of you. I'm being watched too. Every minute of my day is accounted for on this ship. It always has been. It's not as *simple* as just releasing you. There would be consequences. It could go wrong." He takes a breath, staring down at the slippery deck. And there, in that moment I see the conflict. How tortured he's been. "Give me time. I need to work out a plan. Once I have my own ship we can escape, but she can't know, she can't even *suspect*, or—"

"Or what, you'll fall out of favor?"

His eyes shoot to mine, a crushing darkness within them. "Or she'll get rid of me too."

The world stops around us as I take this in. This version of Seth I hadn't seen before. The trapped version. Is it true? More of the puzzle of him seems to click into place. "Seth, if you're afraid she'll…she'll *kill* you…" I swallow, frowning. My voice softens. "Then she's not a mother."

He smiles sadly, the warmth not quite meeting his eyes. "She's the only parent I've ever known."

I let that hang between us. A truth that has governed his whole life, that his mother is ruthless. That if he wants to escape her, he must be just as ruthless as her. "Help us off this ship. Help me recover what she's taken from me and get back to my father. You owe me that, Seth."

"I'll do anything for you, Mira," he says, reaching for my

hand. I glance down at it, wanting to touch his fingers. Wanting to believe this version of him is real. That he regrets the betrayal his mother asked of him. "Anything. Just…just tell her how the map works, would you? Tell her and she won't hurt you. And she'll give me my own ship so we can leave."

I sit back, blinking rapidly, his jacket slipping from my shoulders. I let it fall, feeling the patter of rain against the exposed skin of my chest.

"Wait. Are you asking me to do as she asks?"

He frowns. "You know how to read it, right? I want to help you. Just make it easier for me. You don't know what she's like, what she's capable of."

"What are you saying?"

He reaches his hand closer, but now, I move my own hand away and cross my arms. He frowns then retracts his hand, blinking down at me. "She would have cut your throat. She would have spilled every drop of your blood if I hadn't intervened."

I weigh up everything he's saying. Measuring this Seth against the one who has betrayed me. I want to trust him, desperately. I want to believe that the boy I kissed, the boy I rescued from the sea, feels something for me. Even now, there is something so endearing about him.

"If I wanted to escape, I would be gone by now," I say softly, unwinding my arms and reaching over the space between us to run a hand along Seth's jaw. "But it's not just about my life, is it?"

He catches at my fingers, his eyes turning darker as he watches me. He leans closer, his breath tangling in my hair, his scent of cedar and smoke wrapping around me. I breathe him in, my blood heating. I want to trust all he says. That he is going to help me escape. That he has lived in a state of fear on this ship for the whole of his life. And maybe, he's only realizing now that he can break away from it.

With me.

Seth smiles shyly, hesitantly, glancing at my mouth, then back into my eyes. We're so close now, I could lean in and kiss him. I could pull him to me and choose to trust him. But I stop, waiting. Captured in this moment under the bruised midnight sky.

I know I should hate him. I can't work out where the lies end and the truth begins underneath all his pretty talk. What he says and what he does are two very different things. I'm still not sure I can trust him.

A hideous question seeps into my thoughts. Did Renshaw send him here? He may have stopped her from murdering me, but that doesn't mean he's not still working for her. Does he really want to help me leave, or is this all an act? All just words?

He could be trying to trick me even now.

"Stop making this so difficult, Mira," he breathes. "Just show her how to use the map. Show her and I can get us away. This will all be over."

The moment shatters around us.

I reel back, sucking in a breath. I can't trust a word he says. Not with him still imploring me to help Renshaw. Was it all a lie? Is this just another tactic to try to get me to agree to reveal the map? The fury that is only skin-deep swirls within me, building, crashing. If all he wants is for me to help him with that map, then he's not on my side. If he's not going to help me escape, then he's *against* me.

I should grab his blade and slide it between his ribs, then

continue belowdecks until I find those two thugs who hurt Pearl. My fingers twitch, the anger building inside me. It used to unnerve me, how like the ocean I am. Prone to fury, to twisting tempests, to bouts of rage that can never quite be sated. But now I know how to mold it.

How to unleash it when I need it most.

I pull back my fist and punch him in the jaw. His head snaps back with a groan and I scramble up, shoving the layers of fabric out of my way. I grit my teeth, waiting for his reaction. Waiting for him to pummel me, so I can finally release some of this tension. But he just stands, watching me, testing his jawline with his fingertips.

"I'll take that as a no," he says bitterly. "I can't change the fact that she's my mother, Mira. And I can't take back what I've done." He shakes his head, then stalks toward the hatch that leads belowdecks. Before he disappears back to the warm, dry underbelly of the ship, he glances my way. "I wish you could see that I'm trying to help you. Enjoy the storm. You can keep the jacket."

Lightning splits open the night, the thunder rumbling a few seconds later. The rain worsens, a torrent dumped from the sky, and I huddle down in Seth's jacket. My temper cools, the rage receding like the tide, and it leaves me cold. I close my eyes and lean my head against the mainmast, turning over our conversation. Hating him. Not hating him. Nursing the bloody mess of my fist. Realizing he's in deep too, and I can't save everyone.

I can't save us both.

The next day, I'm swaying on my feet. I haven't slept, haven't eaten. I spent the whole night up on deck in the storm. There's a lump like glass in my throat that I can't quite swallow down and my hands are so raw from the lye they're cracked and bleeding. I feel the first flush of fever as the shivers rattle my rib cage and I wonder dimly how long I can keep going without rest.

As a wedge of sunlight breaks through the clouds midmorning, Renshaw walks up on deck, Seth and her two thugs following close behind. The energy around me is charged and expectant, the crew falling silent as she stalks toward me. She drags her gaze across my body, eyeing the grime coating the gown, the torn hem, my bleeding hands, and smiles gleefully. I lick my cracked lips, blinking slowly through sleep-heavy eyes. I imagine pulling her overboard, then dragging her down, down into the deep.

"My, but you look a little worse for wear," she says, smoothing down the sleeves of her immaculate crimson jacket. "And here was me thinking you just needed some time to cool off. To really consider your incredibly *limited* options."

"If you say so," I croak.

She smiles again, but now it looks a little forced. As though she was expecting me to be a little more broken, a little more amenable. She must have forgotten I grew up on Rosevear. I've had days and nights with no sleep, no rest, no warmth. I can wait out a fever. I can dig deep within myself and find strength. This captain, this woman, will not break me. She doesn't know how.

"I need you in the rigging today. Think you can manage that?" she says with saccharine sweetness, her scarlet lips ending in a pout. "Hope you aren't afraid of heights. Or a little fall."

I swallow, licking my lips again. The taste of blood and

salt mingles with the first tingle of fear that shoots through me. Heights... I have never been one to climb the tall pines on our island or scale the sheer cliff faces on a dare. I do not belong in the sky, so high up that I am level with the calling gulls and currents of wind surrounding us. She has found my fear. The only time I have not been afraid is in my dream, when I am flying. When that unknown hand is holding mine, and it feels as though we are swimming through the night.

I glance at Seth, wondering if I somehow revealed this to him in our time together, and he told her. That somehow, he knows about this reoccurring dream. But his forehead is bunched into a frown, his mouth pressed into a thin line.

"Mother..."

Renshaw holds a hand up, silencing him.

"I won't reveal that map," I say tightly, my body wracked with a sudden wave of fevered shivers. I cough, trying to keep a grip on the world around me. The image of my father and Bryn, nooses around their necks, is the only thing keeping me anchored. I focus on them, on escaping this ship as I force myself to continue. "Don't think you can persuade me otherwise."

"So you *do* know how," she says with a chuckle. "We're making progress already. Hold on tight up there. It's a strong easterly this morn and I don't fancy your chances if you should take a tumble..."

I curse myself for not sticking to my story as I am hustled toward the mainmast and shoved at the rigging, the bloody mess of my hands forced around the rough ropes. Before I begin to scale the rigging with my chapped hands in a gown that has grown twice as heavy from all the rain, I shuck off Seth's jacket, kicking it away. I muster my will, scraping my-

self together. Then I pause, staring defiantly at Renshaw before my gaze slides to Seth. I note with bitter satisfaction the
tortured look in his eyes. And the bruise already blossoming
along his jawline.

CHAPTER TWENTY-FOUR

AS TWILIGHT BATHES THE SHIP IN A GOLDEN HUE, the sea finally calms and I am allowed down from the rigging. I have survived another day aboard this ship with Renshaw's cutthroat crew. I am ragged, worn through from battling with my fears in the rigging and trying not to look down.

There are only three days left now before my father hangs. All I can think about is how weak my fear is.

I caught sight of Joby and Mer in the afternoon as Renshaw marched them on deck, gestured to the horizon then shoved them back through the hatch. Joby looked up at me as she ranted, and I swear I saw him wink.

Renshaw's gray-eyed thug hustles me back belowdecks, and I stumble and trip my way over the wooden boards. He shoves me and my shoulder knocks into the side of the corridor, the whole ship slanting as dizziness seizes my head. I grit my teeth, forming my hand into a fist, and contemplate turning my anger on him. But I'm too weak. Renshaw has made sure of that. He pushes me over the threshold of the storeroom and locks the door in my wake.

I collapse to the ground, my head thudding steadily from thirst. My stomach is hollowed out underneath this wretched gown, my lips dry and cracked. The only luck I've had is that my fever spiked, then plummeted, leaving me cold yet lucid as the day waned to dusk.

"If she thinks she can starve me out..." I say quietly to the walls, my voice little more than a gentle breeze. I laugh, the sound grating along my throat. She will have to try much harder than this. But even so, I hope Lord Tresillian comes for me soon. I need to get off this ship; I need to get to Penscalo, and soon. I banish my father's face, his pleading words from my mind as I knead my temples with my fingers. No good will come of it. It will only make me desperate and reckless if I think of him in that prison.

A barrel on the other side of the storeroom suddenly tips, sprawling on its side. I jump, knocking my elbow against the door with a wince. Blinking into the gloom, I imagine someone there with me. But when I move toward it, there's no one. I step back, my ankle jarring against something made of metal. Something that wasn't there before. I lean down, fumbling in the dark, and find a bottle full to the brim with water beside a bowl containing bread and grilled fish. I laugh breathlessly, gulping the water as I trace the shape of the shadows around me. But I really am alone.

After I've slaked my thirst I pace myself, knowing my stomach could revolt. As I lick my fingertips at the end, I see a message written inside the bowl, underneath the food. It's luminous in the gloaming, and when I check my wrist for the mark that Lord Tresillian left on my skin, I find it glowing in just the same way, the arrow shape like a compass point flaring in the dark. The message in the bowl is a single word. *Midnight.*

I grin, sink to the floor and raise the bottle in a toast. It's been three days and nights since I was knocked out and dragged aboard. At last, I'm getting off this ship.

The door unlocks. Shouts erupt down the corridor outside, boots thumping on wood punctuated by the clash of metal on metal. I inch my way toward the door, barely breathing, heart clattering in my chest. Is this the sign I've been waiting for? The bargain fulfilled? It must be midnight. It *must* be time. As my fingers brush the half-open door, it's yanked fully open. Pearl stands on the other side, blood splattered across the clean white, untucked shirt she's wearing.

"What are you waiting for?" she says, thrusting a similar shirt and breeches at me. "Get that ridiculous gown off! We have to get out of here!"

"Are you all right?" I ask hurriedly, ripping the dress off and pulling the shirt on over my head. "At that dinner, you looked—"

"Just trickery. Had to make them think they were winning, didn't we?" she says, grinning with those needle teeth. "But now we really have to move—we haven't got much time. I couldn't drug them all."

She winces as a shout ends in a gurgle, then a loud thump echoes through the storeroom as though a body has just hit the deck above. I pull on the breeches then accept the blade that Pearl hands me. Agnes's blade. I breathe in, gripping it in my fist. This isn't the first time I've escaped from a ship, but they're usually listing in the water. Not alive with blood-thirsty sailors.

I hurry after Pearl as she nimbly navigates the corridor, and we listen for any signs of movement beyond the doors. I'm about to follow her up the ladder steps when I feel a tug. It is a keening thing, deep in my chest, a calling. Just like the calling to my mother's chest. It pulls ceaselessly at me. My eyes snap to the far end of the corridor. The captain's cabin.

The map, the letter, and my mother's notebook are in there.

"Wait," I call to Pearl as she begins ascending the ladder steps. "Wait—we can't leave yet."

Pearl pauses, looking back over her shoulder. "You can't save him. He was never with us."

I know she means Seth. I shake my head. "No, not him. There's something I have to retrieve. Something I can't leave behind."

Pearl wavers, indecision dancing in her eyes. Finally, she nods, twisting back to follow me. "Be quick. I'll stand guard."

I find my way along the corridor, to the room at the back of the ship. I steel myself before opening the door, that tug twining around my heart like a leash. The panes of pearly glass wink darkly in the window frames, filled with shades of smoke. And in front of the glass, on the desk...

The tug, that sharp, insistent pain fills my ribs as I hurry over to it, closing my fingers around it.

My mother's map.

Beside it are her notebook and the letter, but the words shimmer faintly in the fractured moonlight, just like the mark-ings on the map. So the words, all her words and markings, were made with magic. They were made for no one but me.

I tuck it away and the sharp tug evaporates, leaving an aching warmth behind like the calm after a long winter storm. I hear angry shouts along the corridor and I whip around, hoping they aren't the crew Pearl drugged, waking up.

"Leaving so soon?"

I gasp as the door slams shut. Seth steps forward into a shifting patch of moonlight from where he was concealed behind the door. His shoulders drop as he thrusts his hands into his pockets, his shirtsleeves pushed up past his elbows. His shirt is only half-buttoned, as though he has hastily dressed in the dark. As my eyes travel up to meet his, I find them unwavering.

"You can't keep the map," I say. "You know you can't."

"I can't keep you either, it seems. You've made your choice."

I blink, shifting my attention between the sliver of metal in his hand to the door behind him. Calculating my chances if he won't let me past.

"I was never yours to begin with. I don't belong here."

He laughs bitterly, still moving closer. Now all that is between us is the table. My breath forms a knot in my chest, tightening, inch by inch.

"You aren't even willing to try. You know I didn't want to betray you. Not really. I almost didn't let you go down to that graveyard. I shouldn't have, I should have just…" He shakes his head, his intention left unuttered.

I catch the deep regret in the set of his jaw, the shape of his mouth. But he's blocking the door. I grip Agnes's blade. This isn't about him wanting me. It's about him losing the map and his mother turning on him; I'm sure of it. And however much I am sorry for that, it doesn't stop me from needing to get off this ship to save my father, with my mother's legacy safely in my possession.

"Get out of my way, Seth."

He removes his hands from his pockets and leans down to pull his own blade from where it is strapped near his boot. He places it on the table and holds up his hands to show they are empty, his eyes never leaving mine. "I won't stop you. I only wanted to talk to you before you go. This could be the last time and... I guess I just want to say for the record, I'm sorry. You don't know how sorry I am that it's ended like this between us."

I huff a breathless laugh, circling to the other side of the table. "More tricks? I can't tell anymore where the lies end and you begin."

"It's all the truth, Mira."

"I doubt that."

He looks down, curls tangling around his sharp cheek-bones, the quick breath he drags in making his chest rise then fall. A frown dimples his forehead, as though he is try-ing very hard. "That night, in the bowl of stars, I... I didn't want it to end."

My mouth goes dry, heart beating faster. At last, he's being honest. I can taste the truth in his words. "I didn't either."

I place Agnes's blade on the table, the clink as wood meets metal ringing in the near silence of the cabin. Seth's eyes rise slowly to meet mine and he swallows. I wait, barely breath-ing, hoping he'll say something else.

Something real.

"If I let you walk away now, we'll never get another night like that," he says softly. "My mother will hunt you down for that map. You'll never be rid of her. And I have to do as she says. I *have* to. I don't have a choice."

I move around the table slowly, my steps light, as though

testing how far I will go, how far I'm willing to trust him. If it's possible for us to find a way back from what he did. "Then we're both stuck, on opposite sides. Forever."

I reach out a hand hesitantly, letting my fingertips trail as a whisper over his knuckles. He closes his eyes, the frown he is wearing falling away. He stays still, so carefully still that I chance another step toward him, so my body is only inches from his.

He opens his eyes, turning his head so our lips are a breath apart. Warmth spreads through my veins, coursing through every inch of me as I bring my other hand up to his face. His eyes lock with mine, and I watch them ignite with flame. I run a finger along his jaw, where I bruised him, featherlight, barely any contact between us. Just enough to draw a jagged breath from my chest, for the warmth inside me to rise to a blaze.

I want him.

Since the moment I found him on that dying ship in the storm, I've wanted him.

His eyes stray to my mouth, then back up to my eyes. "If I kiss you now, it might be the last time I ever do."

I smile with the smallest flick of my lips. I know this is reckless. But when I'm near him, it's like my whole being is made of embers. And all I want is to burn and burn.

"You should have kissed me for longer that night in the bowl of stars, Seth."

And before I think it through, my mouth finds his. My breath hitches as he turns, arcing his body around mine. His kisses are hungry this time, harder. I gasp, unspooling as his arms wrap around me. His scent is pine and smoke, like we are lost in a forest. Just me and him, in an expanse of green and silence, exploring what we might have been.

I move my hand up, my fingers curling in his hair. He smiles against my mouth and I can't help smiling back. Then I move my mouth to his, parting his lips with mine. There is an urgency between us, a thirst that I know will not be sated. We are lost. We are a slow crashing wave, falling forever, never quite reaching the shore.

"Don't leave," he says quietly, his lips moving down, exploring my skin, tasting my throat, then farther, to the dip at the base where my pulse flutters. I feel his heartbeats mirror mine, quick and insistent as I tip my head back, leaning into him. "Stay. We'll work this out. I'll make her give me my own ship. Join me, and this will all be over."

"I can't," I gasp as his hands move from the small of my back, slowly tracing the curve of my ribs. His mouth drifts over my clavicle, leaving a trail of fire. I stifle a moan, giving in to the flames consuming me, wanting his hands to explore every inch of my skin. *Wanting* to feel his mouth everywhere, to press harder, to release this pressure that's built between us, ever since I first rescued him. I revel in it, the relief of giving in. Every nerve in my body fizzing with longing as I arch my back, letting it consume me.

Letting this fire between us burn.

Then I open my eyes and remember. The map. My escape. Seth isn't my end or my beginning and I don't belong here on this ship with him. I draw in a breath, letting the air cool me, extinguishing the flames flooding my veins. He feels it, the shift between us, and pauses. His hands fall away from my body, his mouth no longer touching my skin. We step apart, both of us wide-eyed at how we both lost control. And how much further we could have gone.

"I can't stay with you, but you can leave with me," I say, my voice a throaty gasp, still drenched in desire. "I have to go. Come with me. We can outrun her."

He looks away, already shutting himself off. Already pulling up a barrier between us. "We'd never get away. I... I have to buy you time. All of you. If I misdirect the crew, if I tell Renshaw you set a course for a different direction..."

"Seth..."

"You said it yourself. I betrayed you. We can't ever be together. But at least...at least I can help you in this."

I stumble back, picking up Agnes's blade from the table, the full force of the sacrifice he is making hitting me over and over. I walk to the door on shaking legs, placing my hand on the handle. Every inch of me burns for him. I don't look back—I can't. It will ruin everything.

I can't save us both.

"Maybe we'll meet again and everything will be different," I say.

Then I cross the threshold, leaving a piece of my heart behind.

CHAPTER
TWENTY-FIVE

I BARREL INTO PEARL IN THE CORRIDOR OUTSIDE. Her eyes flare wide in the dark and she grabs my hand quickly, tugging me toward the ladder steps. "What were you doing in there?" she hisses.

"Nothing. Just something I had to finish," I say, avoiding her eyes. Seth's kisses are still fresh on my lips, my mind muddled from his touch, his scent. A thud sounds below, angry voices rising slowly.

Pearl swears, leaping for the stairs. "I should have dropped more poison in their damn supper," she says before kicking her way through the hatch. I swing up behind her, bracing myself for what we will find in the night.

We step into a world of blood and flame.

"Shit," I breathe, dragging Pearl back quickly. A dagger thunks into the hatch, landing where my head was seconds before. I turn to Pearl, heart beating like a drum, Agnes's blade already gripped in my fist. "This is not good."

Renshaw's ship is being invaded. A vessel sits on the starboard side, hooks with trailing ropes embedded in the railings. Sailors, smugglers, men and women with knives slash and punch, fighting over the bodies already littering the deck.

"What happened?"

"Elijah happened." Pearl grins, pointing at the other ship to our right.

The hatch opens out toward the back of the ship, the three masts in a line before us. I see the invading ship, sitting sleek like a cat next to Renshaw's. It's designed to be fast, slim like a razor, and my mouth turns dry as I note the symbol emblazoned on the mainmast.

A compass.

"That's his. The *Raven's Curse*."

"Elijah?" I search my memories for that name, trying to pinpoint anything similar, any time this crew might have spoken of him. I've seen that compass symbol before. On the ring Joby wears, and painted on a woman's cheekbone in the Mermaid on Ennor. I yank back my sleeve to expose my wrist, finding that the compass point Lord Tresillian etched in my skin is luminous.

Pearl's grin widens. "You'll meet him soon enough."

"I thought you said you drugged most of them?" I ask, my thoughts crashing back to the present as a skirmish breaks out to our left. I duck to avoid a flailing arm, gripping Agnes's blade in my fist before springing back up. I recognize the man as one of Renshaw's crew and deliver a swift kick to the small of his back, sending him reeling into two women who knock him out cold.

"I did," Pearl says, crouching low to the deck. "Renshaw

has a shadow ship that trails her, just for moments like this. They're off that."

"A shadow ship?"

I weave with Pearl, following her lead as she beckons me across the deck, hopping over fallen bodies and past the fighting. She jerks her chin to the port side as we move, twisting to avoid a man with a curved sword. A woman wearing a long, sweeping jacket levels him with a look, letting a knife fly at his throat. He tumbles to the boards at our feet, and we skid to avoid him, blood gushing through his fingers. I look up at the port side and have to narrow my gaze, not believing what I'm seeing. There's a ship I didn't notice before floating on the water.

"It's silent. Unmarked, unnamed, and if her crew so much as breathe a word of it, she slaughters them. We're pretty sure she had a witch spell the wood it's crafted from. If you don't look directly at it, you wouldn't even know it exists."

"But you knew of it?" I say, shoving two men aside as they fight with bare fists.

Pearl shakes her head, as though I'm not quite getting it. "*Eli* knew about it."

We reach the railings at the front, starboard side, nothing but endless ocean before us, just as the hatch to belowdecks cracks open. Men swarm up, roaring with battle cries, and I whip around. There must be at least a dozen of them, all armed, all raging as they join the fray.

"Shit!" Pearl says. "I *told* the apothecary I needed something stronger..."

I drop back a foot, ready to fight for my life, wondering if I can get Pearl aboard the *Raven's Curse* in time. The connecting ropes are a few feet away; we have seconds to get there and climb across before we're swamped. I wipe the sweat from my face and grit my teeth.

Then without warning, Pearl pulls me over the side of the ship.

I gasp, expecting the ocean. Expecting the tumble of dark waves to greet me. But instead I land in an awkward heap, sprawled on the deck of another vessel. Pearl holds out a hand and I grasp it, letting her help me up.

"Welcome back to *Phantom*."

I look up and around, finding the *Raven's Curse* above us, Renshaw's ship looming next to it. *Phantom* was hidden. Sitting snugly on the water, waiting in the shadow of the other, bigger ships. I drop my hands to the deck, lean back and laugh.

Merryam shouts commands, gripping the wheel as Joby rushes past to unfurl the mainsail. I stand as the crew dance around me, Pearl and Joby doing the work of half a dozen sailors. Checking the map and my mother's notebook are still safely tucked under my shirt, I feel the deck tip and sway as we part ways quickly with Renshaw's ship. I spin, watching the ship as we drift farther across the inky waters. Screams and shouts rend the air, the flashes of fire and smoke pluming as a cloud above the deck.

A lean figure watches us. My breath catches as I recognize the shape of him, the angular shoulders, the bowed head.

"Seth," I whisper. The memory of his kisses burns my mouth, and I swallow, staring back at him. My heartbeat quickens, anchoring me to the spot I'm standing on. And I watch as we drift apart.

A chance slice of moonlight floods his face. His eyes are in darkness, boring into mine, his mouth set in a grim line. I'm still angry with him, furious at his betrayal. But I believe that he regrets it. That he wishes he could take it back. And those kisses… I sigh, feeling the ghost of his fingertips shivering over my skin. The hungry press of his mouth on mine. I fold my arms across my body as we sail away and look until I can no longer see him.

Until we are swallowed by the night.

"Who is Elijah to you?" I ask Pearl an hour later. We are huddled belowdecks over mugs of broth, hastily dished out by Joby. It was only when they were sure that there would be no pursuit that the others even acknowledged me. Then the tension eased and they wordlessly led me to the galley.

Pearl shifts in her seat, eyes flitting to Merryam as though asking her permission. Merryam shrugs and Pearl smiles at me. "He's who we work for. All of us. Who we're loyal to. On the Isle of Ennor, our home."

I frown, taking a small sip of broth. It's woodsy and rich, reminding me of the broth our healer on Rosevear doled out for me just before I left. Just before the watch flooded the beach and my father was taken. "And you think he boarded Renshaw's ship so we could escape?"

"We don't think—we *know*," Merryam says. "It was just as he planned. He's been in contact with Pearl the whole time, slipping her the poison she ordered from the apothecary, ensuring she had the keys she needed to sneak around unnoticed. To us, he's our leader. To the rest of the continent—the watch, the ruling council—he's Lord Tresillian."

I narrow my eyes as the steam curls around all their faces. Hiding their secrets. Obscuring their true thoughts. Lord Tresillian, *Elijah*, is the man I made a bargain with. The man who seemingly holds my father's life and mine in his hand.

"And you're taking me to him now?"

"We're taking you where we need to go," Joby says, settling his forearms on the table.

"Which is where?" I ask, eyeing each of them in turn. In my mind, there is a countdown. An hourglass, the sand slowly trickling away minute by minute. That sand grows more precious the less there is at the top, each grain marking another hour I have failed my people. I bristle, settling my own forearms on the table, prepared to fight to get back to Penscalo in time.

"We're not your enemy," Pearl says. "Nor is Elijah. But Seth…"

"Seth *is* my enemy, right?" I say, running my hand over my forehead. "You were friends with him though, weren't you?" They all stare back at me. "Did he betray you too?"

Merryam raises a small smile, settling back in her chair. "We were told to pick up Seth and whoever he had with him and take them where they asked to go. But Elijah also told us to take our time, get to know you a bit." She fixes her gaze on me, the hard flint showing at the corner. "He warned us that we might run into difficulties with Renshaw."

I grit my teeth, the past few days unspooling before my eyes. The landing at Finnikin's Way. Seth's wound and the long night at Port Trenn. My every waking moment haunted with thoughts about my father and Bryn—if they were safe and well, if they had given in to despair. If I was doing the right thing by following the coordinates.

"You could have warned me."

"Would you have dived if we had? Or would you have sneaked off when we were at the apothecary in Port Trenn?" Merryam raises her eyebrow and I look away.

Of course I would have bolted if I'd known. I had the coordinates. I would have found a way. I swallow the broth, feeling it trail all the way down my throat. Wouldn't I? Even if that meant leaving Seth with them?

"Of course not."

"That's why we didn't tell you," Joby says, a slow grin spreading across his face. "That's why you were locked in that room while we saw to Seth. Couldn't risk you escaping and finding another crew to take you onward. Not when Elijah wanted you to dive for what was down there."

I snort, placing my mug firmly back on the table. "This has all been a setup. A waste of time. My father—"

"Is not dead yet," Merryam says, her hand snaking out to grip my wrist. I look at her, the deep brown of her eye softening. Warming. "Elijah was very clear that we were to make sure you got what you came for. And that we had to stop Renshaw from taking it from you, even if that meant being captured by her."

She releases my wrist, leaning back. I dip my forehead, drawing in a slow, steady breath. "That's the problem though. It was all pointless." I hesitate, then pull out the map. Smoothing down the creases, I watch all of their faces. They range from confusion to disappointment. To them, it's just a blank piece of parchment as it appears to every human but me. "Only I can read it. So I can trade secret information with the watch, but I can't give it to them for my father's life. And if they press me, if they find out how I know where to find the secret places of the isles—" I swallow "—they'll keep me in their prison for good. They'll never let me leave."

As soon as I utter those words, an ache fills my chest. It's the truth I've known since discovering my legacy. It's a weapon, but one that can be used against me too.

I carry this ache with me as the others shuffle back on deck, or to their bunks for a few hours' sleep. Merryam sets a course that will take us back to hug the coastline of the mainland while Pearl puts some healing salve on my hands to reverse the damage the lye has done to them. It instantly cools the nettling under my skin, as though laced with something stronger than healing herbs. Probably it is from the apothecary we visited. She checks my side and finds that it is just badly bruised, already mending. Then she melts away to climb into her bunk and I realize they are all giving me space. I go up on deck, only Merryam there with me. She holds the helm, guiding us carefully through the night.

"There's something we haven't told you. Something *I* haven't told you."

I lean on the railings nearby, waiting for her to speak.

Merryam presses her lips together, then releases a small sigh. "Seth is my cousin."

"What?"

She glances at me, then back at the night-dark ocean. "My mother and I were in the family business with Renshaw. I grew up with Seth, playing on the rigging, learning the smuggling routes and the tells that the watch were onto us."

I cross my arms, studying her. Seeing all the resemblances that I had overlooked. The way their hair curls in the same way, the rangy set of their shoulders. And how she was the person he sought out on Ennor. The last puzzle piece about this crew clicks into place. When I pulled Seth from the sea with a bullet in his shoulder, Merryam was desperate to know if he was alive. She did everything, *everything* to ensure his survival, risking her own position to take him to her lord's apothecary. The son of a rival.

The son of her enemy.

"My mother died, killed at a drop gone wrong at Finnikin's Way, and Renshaw, my aunt...she *changed*. She grew more ruthless. Bitter. Like she had a bone to pick with the world. And one night, she turned on me, blamed me for her sister dying. Seth helped me leave the ship, hid me away and secured a skiff so I could escape unnoticed." She smiles, creases forming around her mouth. "I owe him my life. Just as he owes me. I pitched up on Ennor and the rest is history."

"She thinks you defected? Sold her out."

Merryam nods. "But Seth isn't like that. Or so I thought. The thing is, when you spend so much time with someone who is poisoned at the root, that poison can rub off on you. I have no doubt now that he intended to betray you, and that the plan had been in play for some time. What I'm not sure of, though, is if he regrets it. I hope he does. I hope there's still something of the person I love in there, that Renshaw hasn't killed all the good in him yet."

I consider this, weighing it against the kisses I shared with him. Against the regret he's shown since I returned from the siren's graveyard. How he sacrificed himself by not leaving with us, instead making sure we could escape. If he did lead Renshaw to chart a different course, to divert her from our trail, as soon as she realizes... I shudder. Perhaps people can change. Maybe he'll find a way to get away from her like Merryam did.

"Thank you. For telling me."

Merryam nods, her gaze trained on the waves.

"I need to make one last request, and I think you know what it is."

She smiles. "You want me to take you to Penscalo."

"Yes."

She sighs. "Look, I understand. My crew is my kin. I would do anything for them. But it wasn't part of the plan, Eli never said—"

"Please. I'll deal with him."

"You don't know what you're offering there, Mira." She grows quiet, watching the waves. "I'm loyal to Eli and he is to me. But you haven't seen what he does to his enemies. What he is capable of."

"I can take a fair guess," I say, remembering the suffocating dark, the shadow slipping down my throat. Drowning me. "Please, set a course. I'll square it with him."

She rubs a hand down her face, then looks up to the stars. She swings the helm, a quarter turn, holding *Phantom* steady as the ship shifts. The sails snap and billow overhead and I adjust my feet on the deck. "It'll get rougher. The tide's against us on the way back. He's on his way here now, so you'll have to hold her steady. Explain why we've changed course."

I step forward, placing my hands on the wheel, and feel the steady tug of the sea beneath us. Merryam points out the constellations, where I have to line them up to keep on course. She steadies the wheel as the first wave swells, showing me what to do. "Thank you."

Merryam places her hand on my shoulder before walking away. "For what it's worth, I hope you get to save your kin."

I am left alone in the endless night, mulling over all she has said. The sea turns against us, just as Merryam said she would, great waves yawning, ravenous and wide. I brace myself, the spray hitting my face like needles. But I hold the course, keeping *Phantom* sure. I don't know how many hours pass; all I know is that we're slipping closer to daylight as the moon arcs overhead, tracing a path through the night. My arms ache, head growing dim with the need for rest, but I know this is for me and me alone to do.

I pull the map from where it is concealed inside my shirt, holding it against the helm. I am alone for the first time, and this may be my only chance to study it. The sea is in a frenzy on the map, reflecting the swirl of unease around me. I narrow my eyes, finding *Phantom* in the dancing waves, and gasp. She's dark against the moonlit night and the Fortunate Isles are still a way off, but I can see that Merryam has indeed set a course for them. I trace my finger along the coastline, searching for secret ports or hidden isles, for places the watch may not know about.

As I am lost in thought, in plans of how I will rescue my father and Bryn, studying the map as I keep the helm steady, the shadows and the dark deepen around me. I hastily shove the map back into its hiding place as a voice speaks from a depthless fold of night.

"We meet again, Mira."

CHAPTER
TWENTY-SIX

"LORD TRESILLIAN," I BREATHE. HIS FOOTFALLS echo across the deck, rumbling like thunder on a distant horizon. He stops beside me, peering at the ocean. "Or is it Elijah?"

He smiles, turning toward me. "Perhaps it's both."

"So you are the lord of an isle and also the lawless boy, the Elijah who the watch are putting up Wanted posters for in Port Trenn."

"Only Port Trenn?" He raises his eyebrows, every inch a lord except for the glitter of mischief I catch in his eyes. "How offensive. I must try harder."

I laugh. "And you're also the reason I'm here and not still prisoner on Renshaw's ship. Should I be thanking you? Or are you planning on sending me up the rigging in a heavy ball gown too?"

He steps behind me, his hands reaching around me to grasp the helm. Directly over my own. The faintest patter begins under my ribs, an ember of heat flaring out. "I will never treat you as Renshaw did. I plan to earn your trust, Mira. Not squander it. May I help you guide the ship?"

My breath hitches and I blink, looking out at the night sky. "All right."

He stands behind me, his body occasionally pressing against mine, his fingertips exerting gentle pressure over my hands, guiding the ship through the night. We navigate the choppier waters together, him explaining the adjustments he's making to our course. I feel the heat in my chest feather out, flowing through me softly, gently. I lean back against him, giving in, just for a moment. And I wonder what it would feel like if his hands left the helm. If they moved down my sides, following the curve of my waist, then my hips.

I bolt upright, creating a space between our bodies once more, and clear the fog of my thoughts.

As though he can hear them, as though he knows exactly where I imagine his hands on me, he chuckles darkly and murmurs in my ear, "You know, as much as you hated it, you did look very lovely in that ball gown…"

I shake my head, ducking out from between his arms to put several feet between us. He may be charming, but I know he's dangerous. And I still hold the map and the knowledge of how to read it, which he very much wants. His grin is wolfish in the moonlight. I fold my arms, willing the flames he ignited to calm. He's toying with me, yet again.

"You're enjoying this, aren't you? Is everything a game to you? That ship, all the fighting, the blood—"

"It was necessary," he says, his grin snapping to a frown. "I had to get my crew out of her clutches. And we did make a bargain, Mira. I had to uphold my end."

I shrug noncommittally, trying to work him out. Every encounter I have had with Elijah has presented a different side. The boy who followed me on Ennor, the stranger with dangerous magic stepping from the dark, the young, arrogant lord at Renshaw's table, perfectly at ease on a ship of cutthroats. He may have helped me escape that ship, but perhaps I am in more danger now.

"Merryam told me her orders. That they were to pick me up on Ennor, then keep me occupied while they learned more about me. None of this is circumstance. It was your plan all along to find out what was hidden in the siren's graveyard."

"It was my plan to keep it from Seth and therefore Renshaw's grasp," he says smoothly. "If it's the map I believe it is, then it is far too valuable to slip into the wrong hands."

I pull it out, unfolding it. "What, this? It's just a simple map. Like any you'd find aboard a ship. How could it be valuable?"

His smile doesn't quite reach his eyes. He glances at me, blinking slowly, and that same instinct that told me to run in the storeroom shivers once more through my blood. I will the slight tremble from my fingers. Whatever this boy is—trickster, lord, liar, sailor—he is also the most dangerous person I have ever met. And yet I can't help wanting to be near him.

"We both know exactly how valuable it is. And how it makes *you* valuable too."

"As valuable as those vials of blood you had Merryam shift for you? What kind of *valuable* creature did they come from?"

"You believe me a monster?"

"You desire something from the sirens, something I now have. Would you slaughter them for their blood? For *their* magic?"

He's quiet for a moment, eyeing the dark sweep of ocean. "That blood came from a rather nasty nest of wyverns in the Spines. A whole coven's worth of hunters went after them when the witches had reports of an entire town being massacred. A *town*, Mira. Thousands of people. And wyverns don't hunt to feed. They keep their prey alive and play with them, sometimes for days. They hunt for *sport*."

I shiver, wrapping my mind around his words. This is not a detail my mother or father ever included. "What exactly are wyverns?"

"Bat-like creatures. But huge, and quite terrible. They don't breathe fire or live alone like the firedrakes. They're pack creatures. And yes, the witches used their blood for their casting—hexes, spells, curses. And I took the rest to distribute among my apothecaries and to sell on to the others." He sighs. "I suppose in my mind, it's taking something evil and making it good. That blood will be mixed into potions by the apothecaries, used to cure people and save them. And those wyverns will never terrorize another town or village again. Now, does that answer your question? Shall I change course, or would you still like to reach Penscalo?"

He runs his fingers over the helm, frowning slightly as his fingertips graze the wood, adjusting the direction of the ship. I open my mouth to reply, and close it again. When I saw those vials of blood, rows and rows of them in the hold of *Phantom*, I felt certain what it meant. That whoever owned them must be wicked, heartless, and cruel. But now I am not so sure. I rub my arms, feeling the cold as the wind suddenly whips across the deck. My mother was a siren. She was a creature, hunted for her blood. She killed people in order to survive. Does that make her monstrous?

I study him properly for the first time, sweeping my eyes up his frame, the broad shoulders, the tailored jacket hiding his muscular arms. His hair isn't just a dark brown as I first thought. It is shot through with oak and ebony, framing a sculpted jawline, lips that curve in thought. The faintest stubble flecks his face, and as my eyes travel lower, down to his casually buttoned white shirt that's partway open beneath his black jacket, I smell a faint hint of wood smoke. Of stars and shadows and deepest night. His eyes flick to mine then back to the ocean. But not before I see the true color of them. Not black at all, nor the absence of color and warmth. But a swirling deep gray, like the ocean on a calm, sunless day. The kind of day that hints of approaching tempests and the certainty of a bountiful wreck.

"What are you thinking about, Mira?" he asks, his voice low and close with, I'm sure, a hint of uncertainty. As though he knows I am weighing him up and he does not want to be found wanting.

I blink, looking directly at him, finding the barest hint of the wicked grin he wore before, as though to mask what he is truly thinking. I fumble through my own thoughts, cursing myself for being distracted by him, by the revelation that this boy might not be the dangerous stranger I first believed him to be.

"I'm thinking that you haven't told me who you really are at all," I say, my voice a little breathless. "All I know is fragments. That this is your crew, and you wanted them to take me to the end coordinates I gave them. That you don't shy from bloodshed, particularly when it comes to a rival ship. And that your magic isn't like anything I've ever seen or heard

of. You're not an apothecary. You can't be a witch. You're…
I don't even know if you're human."

He fixes his gaze on me, saying nothing. As though trying to discern my true thoughts, and what he wishes to im-
part. Then he shakes his head. "Are you? Human, Mira? It
sounds like you actually know quite a lot about me. But I'll
put your mind at rest. I won't change the course Merryam
set. I'll take you to Penscalo."

I frown, teasing out his words, wondering what the catch
will be. "No bargain this time? No demand for what I retrieved from the sirens?"

"There are two days left, yes? If we stay on course, you'll
be there by dawn tomorrow. You'll have time."

I grip the railings, my hands aching as my bones press into
the wood. The relief of knowing I can make it, that I will
be on Penscalo before my father's and Bryn's end steals my
breath. But there is always a price, I'm learning. This world
of sea and storm runs deep with bargains and blood. "Name
it. Spell out exactly what you require."

"All right," he says, eyeing me. "Promise me that you will
not give that map to the watch captain. You will not tell him
what it is, or how you came by it. And you most certainly
won't take your father's place in that prison."

I draw in a shuddering breath. The map is my leverage.
My *only* leverage. I feel through his words like the rope in a
net. Finding the knots, the weak sections. Testing the gaps to
find what I can snap. "I cannot take my father's place. And
I cannot hand over the map or explain anything about it."

"Correct."

I bite my lip, working through the wording of this new
bargain. After last time, I have learned what it may cost me

to leave a loophole in a bargain. "Why don't you want me to hand myself over? Why is that so important?"

"I have my reasons."

"Is it because I am tied to the map? You realize by now only I can read it. So you don't want all that knowledge falling into their hands."

His jaw tenses as he stares out at the water. "There is that. But that is not the only reason."

"But—"

"If you hand yourself over, you will never see daylight again. You will never see your kin, or Rosevear, or anything and anyone you hold in your heart." He says this in a rush, an edge to his voice that cracks on the final sentence. "And maybe you're not the only one on board this vessel who exists between two worlds. Maybe it's rare to meet someone like you. Maybe I don't want you to sacrifice yourself."

A hush settles over us. I release the rail, massaging the blood back into my palms. Kneading them as I consider his words. If I didn't know any better, I would say Elijah cared about whether I lived or died.

He said I couldn't give the watch captain the map. But he didn't say I couldn't offer up one or two of its secrets. There is a cove I noticed on there, a mile or so east of Port Trenn, one lonely house perched atop the cliff. The perfect place to land a haul before sending it onward across the mainland. I've never heard of such a drop point, nor have I ever seen this cove marked on any previous map. It's the ace up my sleeve, the knowledge I hope will be enough.

"All right," I say quietly, my word carried away on a sudden breeze. "I won't offer myself in exchange. And I won't tell the watch about the map." I turn to him, spit on my hand,

and hold it out for him to shake. He looks from my hand and back up to my face, a grin splitting the moody curves of his features. I want to make it clear that this is not one of *his* bargains marking my skin. This is on *my* terms. He keeps one hand on the helm, then extends his palm out toward mine. I grasp it, and feel him pull me closer.

When we are only a few inches apart, our breath mingling in the cold night, he whispers, "I could get used to making bargains with you, Mira."

I pull my hand away and dance back. There is something so unsettling about Elijah. At once alluring and yet utterly deadly. "Let's not make a habit of it."

"Why ever not?"

Because you unsettle me in a way that I do not understand. Because I've been betrayed once already. Because I'm afraid that if I get to know you, I may actually like you.

I blow out a breath, training my gaze on the ocean. "Once I've freed my father and Bryn, I intend to stay far, far away from *all* of you," I say. "After tomorrow, you'll never see me again."

CHAPTER TWENTY-SEVEN

IT TAKES ALL NIGHT TO REACH THE ISLAND WHERE the watch hold my father and Bryn.

I count the hours on deck, gripping the rail until my fingers ache. A squall sets us back and we have to cut against the wind, forcing us to crawl through the waves until it dies away.

At last I have hope that I can do this, that it is possible to free them. I have two days, a secret I have gleaned from the map to trade for their lives and my mother's legacy, tucked next to my heart. I'm almost there.

Penscalo looms like a fortress on the horizon. The buildings the watch have commandeered tower up as we draw closer, and I see the prison set farther back into the town. The housing for islanders sits on stilts over the shoreline, stretching out along the water. Penscalo wasn't always like this, or so I've been told. The people used to be like us. They used to be free.

When we disembark, I cast a look at Elijah. He stands at the helm, eyes as gray as the sea. Our gazes lock, a current passing between us that leaves a nettling under my skin. As though we have words left unspoken.

He holds up one hand in farewell before leaving me standing with the crew on the quay. "Why doesn't he leave *Phantom*?"

Pearl's laugh is like the breathy thrum of a dragonfly wing. "He can't step foot on Penscalo. Not in broad daylight anyway. I'll wager he's on every other Wanted poster plastered to the walls and windows."

"Want a bet?" Joby says, nudging Pearl's shoulder.

Her eyes light with a spark as she grins with those needle teeth. "Go on."

"I bet you five coppers I find more of his Wanted posters than you."

Pearl tilts her chin. "Count when we leave?"

He grins at her and they clasp fists. "You better have my coin ready, little ghost."

Merryam merely tuts before stalking off down the quay. We follow soon after.

The watch are everywhere, wearing scarlet coats and an air of boredom that spells trouble. The wind is thick with rumors as we walk along the quay; even the street-sellers have fallen quiet and watchful. A man buys a small bunch of white-petaled flowers, not bothering to haggle as his gaze cuts left and right to the watch close by. He hurries away, the small posy in his fingers, and I wonder if they are to celebrate a birthday, or to honor the dead.

With a nod from Mer, we split up, Merryam and Joby weaving toward the pub to catch any stray gossip, Pearl and I to scope out the hanging square.

"It's too quiet here," Pearl says, hunching her shoulders up around her ears against the morning chill. "Like all the life's been bled out of the place. Reminds me of…"

"Home?" I glance at her.

"Yeah," she says, pursing her lips as we both picture Finnikin's Way.

"It's the days before a hanging," I say, pushing on through the pressing crowd. "People travel to see it. By tomorrow night, there will be beer and blood running through the gutters."

Pearl grimaces. "It really is just like home."

We walk past a group of men spilling out from the baker's. They are carrying brown bottles and pasties, their eyes heavy lidded as they look us up and down. I figure they're off-duty members of the watch. I suppress a shudder and pull Pearl away, fighting the urge to close my hand around the blade I have hidden. They are the kind of men best avoided at any time, scarlet coats or no.

"You never told me how you got out of there the first time."

"Eli," she says, stepping past a hunched-over woman in a dirty gray shawl selling pieces of hangman's rope for luck, a copper a piece. "He was there to renegotiate his contract with my father. He was really young, a newly minted lord, can't have been more than fourteen. I watched him deal with them like an adult, never backing down, staying calm and in control. Even when Jev tried to rattle him. I was ten and I hadn't eaten in three days. Can't remember why now—it's just the way they raise us. Punishment and reward, always keeping us dangling.

"I saw my chance of a better life, or at least a decent meal, and cornered him on his way back to his ship. I looked him square in the eye and told him I wanted to work for him. He took one look at me, then at my people and agreed on the spot." She shakes her head. "I only found out later that he had to pay my father to take me away. I was just another term in the new contract. My family effectively sold me."

"That's terrible." We round a corner and the street opens up, pavements widening, shops with discreet brass plaques beside their doors. Members of the watch mill around in groups. There are a few passersby, mostly women in fussy dresses, paper packets tied with string under their arms. I imagine they are the watch's wives and daughters. The women who are bound to them. This is the smarter side of the watch's island, away from the houses on stilts. But beneath the polished veneer, it is the most deadly side.

"I got lucky," Pearl says with a shrug. "I got out. Most don't. Too many secrets woven into that place. They only allowed me to leave because they thought I didn't know any of them."

As I turn to Pearl to ask if she means the hidden route out of Finnikin's Way, a shadow looms over me. I whip around, expecting the watch, or one of those drunken men with their brown bottles. But as I reach for my blade, I see who it is.

"Kai," I choke out as his arms envelop me.

"Hello, little one," he says as I shake, tears coming over me so suddenly, I can barely catch my breath. The feeling of his arms, his scent, everything... I didn't realize how much I needed this. How much I missed this boy who is like a brother.

"Mira!" I look up just in time to find Agnes barreling toward us. "I thought... I thought—" She blinks furiously, then

punches my arm. "Don't *ever* leave me and not send word!
Never again!"

"She's been pretty unbearable," Kai says, finally releasing
me, only for Agnes to wind her arms tight around my neck.

"Don't listen to him. He's been worse than me," Agnes
murmurs into my hair. "You smell of smoke. Where have you
been? We've been here for days, trying to get in to visit them."

I push her away far enough to look her in the eye. "Have
you seen them?"

Agnes shakes her head, red hair clinging to her damp
cheeks. "They won't let us in. Family only. But we know
of others locked in there whose family haven't been granted
access either."

I set my jaw. "Bastards."

"And who is this?" Kai asks, eyeing Pearl as she slinks close
to the shadowy doorway of a shop.

She watches Kai and Agnes like a feral cat. It is my first
glimpse of who she might have been before Elijah found her
in Finnikin's Way, what she is underneath the white-blond
halo of hair and porcelain-fine skin.

"This is Pearl," I say, reaching for her. "A friend. She and
her crew brought me here."

"I'm Agnes," Agnes says, crossing her arms over her chest.
They watch each other warily, two wild creatures trapped in
human skin.

Kai steps forward and holds out his hand, grasping Pearl's
the second she offers it. He towers over her and a small smile
twitches her lips.

"I'm Kai. Any friend of Mira's gets stuck with us too. It's
the rules."

Pearl's smile widens. "I can live with that."

"Now you've all met, can you fill us in?" I say to Agnes, taking her hand in mine. "Tell me everything."

We sit huddled around a table in a pub we find just off the main street, the only one where no members of the watch are lurking. A few people are sitting at the bar itself, swapping stories with the barmaid as she polishes glasses. We choose a table at the far end, near the smoky fireplace. I don't want anyone overhearing our discussion.

"We waited three days after you'd gone," Agnes says, eyes wide and solemn. "But then Kai and I agreed that we didn't trust Seth."

"We know you said he was just navigating to Ennor for you, but it didn't sit right. There was something shifty about him," Kai says, holding out his palms.

"So we took a boat from Kai's yard and traveled to Port Trenn. Not the easiest voyage, but Kai got us there." Agnes hesitates. "That's when we heard whispers of Renshaw. Saw the Wanted posters. She looked so like Seth, with the set of her jaw, those eyes…"

"Even if we were wrong, we knew you could be in trouble," Kai adds, thanking the barmaid as she brings over our drinks. We fall silent as she sets them down, and I picture my two friends in the bustling port. How stark the contrast between our small, lonely existence on Rosevear and that web of life and color and noise. I slide a hand across the table to Agnes, silently thanking her and whatever luck brought her back to me in one piece. They could have been swallowed by ill fortune in a place like that, with no knowledge of the port or anyone to guide them. And it would have been all my fault.

Two more people that I care deeply for that have been put

in harm's way because of my foolish judgments. For trusting a boy I rescued from the sea, and for believing I could find the key to my father's freedom by listening to my instincts and shutting everyone else out. Never again.

"So, we came straight back to Rosevear, gathered the community, and made a plan to liberate Bryn and your father. Then, we were to go after you." Agnes draws a single gold coin from her pocket, placing it firmly on the table. "There's more. A whole bag. We've been secretly trading beads for the past week. We knew we couldn't afford their bail, but we thought maybe we could scrape enough together to bargain for their lives."

"If we can get you an audience with the watch captain," Kai says, taking a breath. "If he accepts the bribe, then maybe…"

I bow my head, hot tears prickling at the corners of my eyes. I screw them shut, taking a deep breath in, out. Then I hear the scrape of a chair and feel Agnes's arms around me. I lean into her, all the fear, all the despair and guilt of what has happened to Bryn and my father washing away with the tears that soak into her hair. I clutch her, sniffing, feeling the first stirrings of hope.

Hope that this might work.

Hope that they won't die.

"Thank you," I gasp. "You could have been caught, any of you. Those beads… We decided not to trade them all this fast, didn't we? Just in case…"

Agnes pulls back, her gaze locking with mine. "We would do anything for one of our own. *Anything*. Even if it meant risking getting caught by the watch ourselves. You know that. It's not all on your shoulders, Mira."

Kai reaches across the table, patting my arm as Pearl looks

on, saying nothing. As my tears dry, I allow that hope to fill me, consuming all the worry that has weighed me down. From my mother, my blood, I have what I need. The strength to find my own way through this, a glimpse into what I am under this skin.

And from my people, the tools to see it through.

"We heard about the watch's raid on Rosevear."

Kai looks out of the window. "Two cottages burned to sticks. No one harmed though. We got the families out in time. They're getting bolder. Growing in number. It was a warning, plain and simple. They mean to scare us into submission. We need Bryn back and we need your father. Every person counts if we're to get through the next winter."

I shudder, picturing the children. The mothers huddling babies to their chests.

Pearl clears her throat, speaking for the first time since we arrived. "I can get you an audience with the watch captain."

We all look at her sharply. She shrugs, that feral gleam I have seen before in her eyes. "I owe my kin on Finnikin's Way nothing. Perhaps it's time the watch learned of its secrets."

I smile slowly and Pearl grins back.

CHAPTER
TWENTY-EIGHT

WE SEND A MESSENGER TO THE WATCH'S PRISON and within the hour, we have an answer.

"Tomorrow morning at first light," Pearl says with satisfaction, showing me the short message before crumpling the paper and tossing it into the fire grate. I watch the paper curl, then catch alight. By midmorning, my father could be a free man. I would liberate him and Bryn, take them back to Rosevear, and strike a bargain with the watch.

That dream carries me into the evening as the pub slowly fills. Pearl sent word to *Phantom*, and Joby and Merryam pile in. We order food: roast pork with applesauce and loaves of bread as Agnes and Kai get to know the crew who have carried me.

We secure rooms upstairs with the barmaid, who gives us clunky iron keys and sends a boy from the kitchen off to fill our bathtubs. My limbs ache to be clean after so long at sea. To sink into blissfully hot water and a clean bed. Victory is so close now. No one will hang. And after we all return home, I can think on my mother's letter and choose the path I want to take. I can finally have a candid talk with my father and find out more about my heritage. I feel sure that now I can persuade him to allow me to come and go. That he will not try to anchor me to the island in a way that is suffocating. That I can explore the deep ocean and find out where I fit into it. All with a map that was built into my mother's blood. Her ancestral memory printed on parchment.

I blink, realizing I have been lost in the haze of hope for the future, and notice the noise. The pub has filled with sea-farers singing a shanty. I listen to them, sipping my drink, and nod to Pearl and Merryam as they disappear upstairs to their room, hands tangled together. Agnes, Joby, and Kai have joined in with the shanty and my view of the whole pub is suddenly unobscured.

That's when I see him.

Leaning up against the far wall, arms folded across his chest. My heart leaps to my throat and I push back my chair, get-ting to my feet. Seth's half smile tells me all I need to know. He has been waiting for me to notice him. He may have been watching me for some time. My blood heats as I shove my way through the crowd, aiming like an arrow for him. I lose sight of those dark curls for a moment as I round the corner of the bar, and see that he has stepped to the door. He cocks his head, checking I'm still following, then walks outside.

I know it could be a trap. There could be a dozen of Ren-shaw's crew outside, waiting to take me back to her ship and demand that I give them the map and the knowledge of how to read it.

Seth traveled with me to that underwater place and helped

unlock the fear in me of leaving my island, of finding the pieces of myself that I could never find at home.

But he also betrayed me.

He used me to uncover my mother's legacy and then left me to Renshaw's mercy. He lied to me and hid who he truly was. The son of a murderer. A smuggler, a woman with a growing empire of ships and shores, her face plastered on Wanted posters across the Fortunate Isles and beyond.

But... I have to know if that tug I feel, that tie that binds us is still there. I have to know if it means anything or if I should end him now and be done with looking over my shoulder for another foe. The kisses we have shared flutter on my lips and I take a breath, pushing those moments aside. The hunger I felt for his touch on the ship, before we escaped. He did seem truly sorry for what he did. But I can't let it obscure my judgment, not when I'm so close to saving my father.

I wade through the revelers, push open the door, and step into the cold night. The shanty singing is instantly cut off; only muffled sounds escape the heavy wooden door and granite walls. I look along the alleyway, straining my eyes against the dimly lit corners. I tremble, not from fear, but anticipation, as every shadow becomes one of Renshaw's crew in my mind. At any moment, I may have to fight my way through to Seth and demand answers.

"Quite the party in there," Seth's cool voice murmurs, and I watch as he peels from the shadows of the opposite wall. "I'm surprised you're celebrating with your father still behind bars."

"No thanks to *you*," I hiss, drawing out my blade. "You may have helped me leave Renshaw's ship, but I wouldn't have been there in the first place if you hadn't betrayed me."

"I'm not the one who abandoned me to a foundering ship after being boarded."

"You chose to stay!"

His mouth curves into a grin. "You didn't try hard enough to persuade me to leave."

An almost-smile plays at the edges of my lips. "I'm surprised you survived."

He flicks a curl out of his eyes. "Seafarers like me always survive. Unlike you islanders, it would appear."

In seconds I cross the cobbles, pinning him to the wall, my knife against his pale throat. At once any playfulness is gone, my temper sudden and blood hot. One twist and I could end him. It would be fair—he did betray me. Even if he did then feel regret later. Even if there is something between us, growing, simmering since the moment we met. He almost stole my one chance of freeing my father and Bryn, and took away the days I had left between the wreck and this moment that I could have filled with finding a way to save them. Instead, he led Renshaw to trap me. If it hadn't been for Elijah and our bargain...

I need answers. I need to know if there is still a tether between us, and if he *truly* regrets his betrayal.

"I'm here alone. She didn't send me," he says quickly, his swaggering confidence slipping.

My body is still pressed up against his and I can feel the insistent beat of his heart. Just like I could in the captain's cabin aboard Renshaw's ship. I still my breath, waiting. Waiting for that thread to tug. To feel something of the connection between us that I first felt on the wreck of the *Fair Maiden*. Anything.

There is nothing. Nothing deeper than a hunger for him.

I shove that aside, pressing it far back so it cannot obscure my judgment. I followed that tether between us, saving him from the sea, believing it to run deeper than the kisses we have shared. But perhaps that is all that was ever between us. Desire. Secrets.

Lies.

"Were you working for her all along?"

"I…" He swallows. "Yes. She found out where you lived, which island. And sent me out on that ship in the hopes that your people would wreck it."

I laugh breathlessly, darkly. "She sent you out on a doomed ship? How did she know you would survive?"

"She didn't." His eyes meet mine, a coldness to them I hadn't noticed before. Fleeting hurt creases his features before he stares back steadily. "But I agreed anyway. I wanted to find you. I wanted to find what was buried in the ocean and win favor with her. I wanted—I still want—my own ship. You know that."

I lessen the pressure of my body against his and remove my blade from his throat. "But you're her son."

He smiles bitterly. "All the more reason for me to prove myself worthy. If I am her weakness, I will find myself dead or taken." He blinks and the shadows crowd over him. "When I have my own ship, I'll have my own crew—a kin I choose who are loyal to me, not her. I'll be able to make my own way. I…I hoped you would understand that—the need to be free. To feel the rush of the wind as I hold the helm of my own vessel. And to never have to answer to her again. If I stay with her, I'll always be in her shadow. I'll never be able to be who I am, what I want to be. I envy Mer that. She got away. She found people she can trust. She forged her own family."

I breathe out steadily, releasing him. I step back, but bring my blade up between us, keeping it angled toward his throat. He slumps back against the wall, curls falling over his forehead. He wants freedom just as much as I did. He wants to find out who he truly is, without the legacy of his mother pinning him in place. He wants to carve his own path, just as I did. But...I still don't trust him.

"You were a self-serving prick. You hid your relationship to Merryam. You kept all that secret from me. There was a whole extra layer between you all, and I *felt* it, but you never showed me the whole truth."

He shrugs. "I don't deny it. But I am sorry that you got caught up in it. I didn't expect..." He looks down, kicking his foot back against the wall. "I never expected to like you."

I take a breath, looking away from him, picturing that night we slipped into the starlit water. How we floated in the bowl of iridescence and I wanted to stay there forever with him. "Why are you here, Seth? If not for Renshaw...why?"

"I want to help you. I need you to trust me again, like you did before." He laughs quietly. "That was the worst thing, watching you slip beneath the surface. Knowing that when you came back up, I would have betrayed you and that even then, I couldn't take it back. I knew you would never look at me the same way afterward."

I raise my chin, fixing my gaze on him. He stares back steadily and my heart, my reckless, treacherous heart beats faster, hotter in my chest. That hunger that I pushed away resurfaces. His lips part slightly as his gaze snags mine and I step toward him, lowering my blade again. I lift my free hand, brushing the curls away from his forehead.

I am aware of everything. The gentle flutter of his breath,

the sharp cold of the air as it creeps under my collar. The scent of his skin, like pine and wood smoke as his lips meet mine. I gasp quietly, his kisses soft, searching, as he winds his fingers through the strands of my hair. The alleyway, the town melt away as I tuck myself into him, his heart beating as hard and fast as my own.

"Does this mean you forgive me?" he says, moving his hands to my waist. "Please say you do. If I had known you for you, I never would have come to Rosevear. I swear it."

His thumbs trace circles in the small of my back, sending fiery kisses up my spine. I arch into him, wanting him. "No," I say with a smile. "I don't forgive you. Kiss me again and maybe I will."

He smiles back, his eyes darkening as they flick to my mouth, then back up to my eyes. "You need to know, she's angry. She'll come for you. She won't stop until she has you and that map in her possession."

I sigh, smoothing my hands up his chest. He told me before that she would hunt me down. If Renshaw survived Elijah's attack, then she won't only be after me for the map. She'll want revenge. It's something I'll have to figure out later, after I've freed my father and Bryn. But I need to know that Seth isn't part of her plans. "Promise me I can trust you."

"I promise, Mira."

We leave the alleyway, his hand in mine as we steal upstairs, winding up the staircase of the pub, the thump and roar of the singing beneath our feet. I lead him to my bed, one step, two steps, our feet finding their way across the floorboards.

I trace the shape of his mouth with mine, exploring him in the close darkness. His fingers find the buttons of my shirt, undoing them slowly. When the shirt falls to the floor, he steps back for a moment, taking me in. Tracing the shape of my body, the curve of my hips and chest, giving me the space to decide how far I want to go. I smile, locking my eyes with his. A shaft of moonlight glitters across the floor, and Seth's breath catches. It floods me with heat as we collide, teeth and hands and the touch of his skin against mine.

I give in to my hunger for him.

It's like falling. Falling forever through a world of stars and night. His mouth moves down my body, grazing my chest, licking and nipping, leaving a blazing trail, moving lower to my stomach. His thumbs lightly brush just under the band of my breeches, teasing the soft skin that only ever feels the sea. My heart thunders, fighting against my ribs, hungry as I pull him up to standing, parting his mouth with mine. We tangle together, breathless, falling onto the bed at his back.

He tumbles me over, his hands at my waist, pulling my body toward him.

I whisper, "Yes, yes, I'm ready," and he undoes the rest of my clothes, and his own. I slide my legs apart, his thighs against mine, and arch my back as his hand slides up my inner thigh, then gently between my legs. I gasp, moaning into his chest, my whole being on fire as he removes his hand. Then my legs and arms wind around him, pulling him closer, tightly against me. He whispers my name, blotting out the very stars, and our bodies connect in the endless, velvet dark.

There are some things I learned far too young, like how to swim out on the rope and ensure my island's survival. I learned how to hold a blade and where to cut a vein until a man would bleed to death. I learned how to hide my grief. How to bury the questions about my mother and myself, even when they burned within me.

But I never learned this. How to share a bed with someone and whisper my desires into the dark. How my very being could unravel, like I was floating once more in that warm, starry bowl of sea. I learn all this with Seth.

And as dawn arrives, beyond the window, I whisper to him, "I forgive you."

CHAPTER
TWENTY-NINE

AS THE DAWN LIGHT FILTERS LAZILY THROUGH THE curtains, I untangle myself from Seth and leave him. Tucking the map and notebook with my mother's letter inside against my chest, I push back my hair, hastily wash in the bathing room, and smooth down my shirt. I gaze into the mirror over the sink at the person I have become. Everything has changed in the last two weeks, and I feel as though it's reshaped my features. My mouth is still red and full from Seth's kisses, from us laughing together in the dark. But my face is defiant. Strong. No longer questioning everything about myself, or why I am so different.

"You can do this," I mouth, gripping the edge of the sink. "By tomorrow, we can all be back home."

I clean my teeth and give myself one final look before leaving the bathroom, hurrying down the staircase and out into the street.

★ ★ ★

I didn't want Agnes to come with me. I didn't want to put any of them at risk any more than I already have done. But in the early-dawn light, she was already waiting with that knowing look of hers, standing on the corner outside. I should have known better than to try to do this alone.

We stare up at the looming walls of the prison. Gray and endless, they stretch up, sprawling across half a street. People hurry past, buried in their own lives, casting swift glances at Agnes and me as we stand outside. No one lingers here. It's as if the life and color have been drained away, a layer of gray hopelessness coating everything. Agnes twitches her foot, staring at the old wooden door with iron studs embedded in it. The knocker is shaped like a roaring lion, the symbol of Arnhem. It's meant to define us as a fierce, proud nation but I only see it as a symbol of the ruling council. Of their law keepers.

The watch.

"According to Pearl, the offices are upstairs. They keep the prisoners at the back, by the cliffs." My voice catches on the word *prisoners*. I pull back my shoulders, trying to appear more grown-up. As if I demand an audience with the watch captain every day. "Don't breathe a word. Don't admit to anything. Actually, just stay outside, would you? I can't risk you—"

Agnes puts a hand over my mouth. "Stop that. Stop those thoughts right there. We're doing this together, or not at all."

I close my eyes as she pulls her hand away. Then I nod in acceptance. I'm glad the others didn't try to come with me. Kai, Pearl, Joby, or Merryam. For all I know, the crew of *Phantom* is wanted by the watch already, and they never take kindly to islanders. It's a wonder the watch captain agreed

to this meet. He must want to catch the people of Finnikin's
Way very badly...or his curiosity has got the better of him.

"Besides, who would get you out if you said something in-
criminating? We both know you can't charm your way out of
a cloth bag." She wrinkles her nose and grins at me.

I know what she's trying to do as she eyes my hunched
shoulders, the worry creasing my forehead. I force myself to
stand tall, to be the person Bryn and my father need me to
be. The young woman I saw reflected back in that mirror
this morning. If anything, I channel my mother.

The door creaks open, emitting a gust of cold air, and a
man in a scarlet coat sizes us up. He beckons to the two of
us, casting a quick, sweeping glance along the deserted street,
and we step inside the walls of the prison.

He looks at us both in turn and I make sure I meet his
gaze, titling up my chin. Whether he sees this as strength or
defiance, I don't know, but his features twist into arrogance.
"Only one of you. The other can stay here."

Agnes sucks in a breath, ready to argue, but I place a hand
on her arm. "She stays. I'll go."

The man's eyes light up at his small victory over us and
he jerks his head at a staircase. "Up there. Second door on
the left. Let yourself in, take a seat, and the cap will be along
when he's ready. You'll have to wait."

I swallow, my confidence crumbling just a little as I realize I am leaving Agnes with him. She leans in and whispers
in my ear, "Just focus on the meeting."

"Agnes, you should leave. I'll be fine."

She gives me a small push toward the staircase, shaking her
head. "Stop that. Go."

I ascend the staircase at a slow trudge, fighting for calm. I run through the arguments I have formulated for the watch captain and go over my plan to ensure my father's and Bryn's freedom.

The watch captain's chambers smell of wood polish and ambition. His desk sits before a window that looks down on the street, and I can see people furtively darting past toward the market square, arms laden with produce. I sit in a leather chair in front of the imposing rosewood desk and for the third time, my nerve slips and falters. A clock ticks on the mantelpiece at the far end of the room, deafening in the looming silence.

The watchman who told me to let myself in ordered me to wait. But he never said for how long. And now, every tick of the clock reminds me of the seconds slipping through my fingers, the last collection of moments and hours before my father and Bryn will walk out to the gallows. Before they will be tried and marched to their deaths.

I shove the image away. My hand creeps to the bag of gold coin on my lap. The people of Rosevear take care of our own. And right now, I am the one who has to be strong. I'm the one who has to represent us all.

The creak of the door at my back tells me he has arrived. I resist the urge to turn in my chair, waiting for him to walk slowly and purposefully toward me. His footfalls pause halfway across the room, and I imagine him scrutinizing me. Studying me for weaknesses, for tells of my courage faltering. I sit straighter, tipping up my chin.

"I apologize for keeping you waiting, miss…"

"Mira."

Captain Spencer Leggan circles the desk, sliding into his own chair. It is noticeably higher than mine so that he is look-

ing down on me. It should unnerve me, but it's such an obvious tactic that all it does is put me at ease. Because it is *his*
first tell. That he desires power. That he wants me to break
before him.

And I won't.

He is young, not much older than Kai, with straw-blond
hair and gray eyes. No, not gray, not the beautiful starkness
of the sky and sea on a winter day. His eyes are the absence
of that. They are the cold without the wild beauty. I got a
glimpse of him on the beach, full of triumph and goading
us. Those eyes regard me now and it's as if he wants to suffocate the wild from our corner of the world, and I am a rep-
resentation of that. I suppose that to him, weeds are meant
to be tamed.

Or stamped out.

"I take it they offered you tea?" he says, voice clipped and
careful, as if he measures out each of his words before utter-
ing them. He wears a scarlet coat, just like the other members
of the watch. I see the detail of it now up close, the medals
decorating his chest, the gold buttons depicting the roaring
Arnhem lion.

"They did not."

He blinks slowly, assessing me. "Would you like tea brought
in?"

I smile. "No, thank you."

"Right, well. What can I do for you today, Mira?"

"You can release my father and my friend."

He stares at me, those gray eyes like a stone wall meeting
mine. "I'm afraid you will have to elaborate. Who is your father and your friend? Are they prisoners here?"

"They are. You took them from our island, from Rosevear.

You and your men brought them here and tomorrow you are planning to hang them." I swallow, making myself hold my nerve, keeping the tremor from my voice. "And I am here to ask you to release them."

He leans back into his chair, the ghost of a smile playing on his lips. The clock ticks incessantly on the mantelpiece, louder and louder as I wait for him to speak. I try not to move, keeping myself as still as possible. The seconds tick away, feeling like minutes, hours—

"Do you know what they call me? Not Captain Leggan, but the other name."

I shake my head slowly.

He clears his throat, his smile disappearing. "Boot. When I first started out, I was in charge of the men's boots. Keeping them clean, polishing them and such. Then as I rose through the ranks, it was used in a different context." He leans forward, eyeing me down that blade of a nose. "I hear it whispered now by our prisoners. The captain brought in by the ruling council themselves. The captain who *stamps them out.* Smugglers. Wreckers. People here think they can exist above the law."

"But—"

"You can't," he snaps, suddenly vicious. "I will stamp out every nest until these waters are safe, just like the Far Isles. The merchants will fill the ports, the routes brimming with trade, and I will be lauded as the person who brought order to this lawless place. Do you think your father is above the law? Is that it?"

I grip the edge of the chair, swallowing hard. "No, I—"

"I won't tolerate it. Not here. Not on my watch. I won't rest until every last one of you is convicted and made to *pay.*"

He squeezes his right hand into a fist, the whites of his eyes showing. I tremble as all that hate, all that anger within him, bubbles over, twisting his features. I realize in that moment that this is personal. He hates the isles. This is not just a desire to rise through the ranks, to gain the power he believes is his for the taking. It's more than that.

"I can pay," I say softly, pulling the bag of coin out.

It takes all my courage. All my conviction. I weigh the bag in my palm, the price of their freedom. This gold would have been used for our survival on the island. It would have bought food for the long winters and repairs for the cottages so they don't whistle with drafts in a storm. It is more money than I have ever seen in one place, never mind held. This would have brought prosperity.

I have already used mine, Kai's and Agnes's share to get me this far, and now I am condemning our island to another winter of hunger and scraping by. I breathe heavily as the gold coins spill out on his desk. This has to work. This is all we have to offer. But fear niggles at the back of my mind, that he'll question where it came from. That he'll know with certainty what we did. But I have no choice.

I cannot offer him the siren's map, and not just because of the bargain I made with Elijah. He was right—he would take it and unleash his fury on us all. I would be made to read it and give him the information he seeks. He would discover every hidden cove, every islet that only appears when the tide allows it, and destroy the balance of it all. The Fortunate Isles would be reduced to a series of trading routes for rich merchant ships, no life to be found on the isles.

And if I told him of that secret place near Port Trenn that I found while scrutinizing it aboard *Phantom* he would never

believe that was my only information. He would never let
me leave this prison. Having listened to him now, I have the
measure of him. He is far crueler and more calculating than
I ever realized. All I have left to trade is the coin. And even
that is a terrible risk. I feel the map underneath my shirt and
keep my features as neutral as possible. He can't know of its
existence. Not now, not ever.

The captain stares at all the gold. His fist relaxes, his features unspooling into restfulness. He gazes at the pool of
wealth, blinking steadily. Then he reaches forward, brushing his knuckles over the pile. I wait, holding my breath as
he looks up at me.

He laughs.

"I deal in information as well as blood, Mira." He pulls
the gold toward him, the coins scraping against the wood. "If
they had turned informants, I would have released them. But
this…this is generous of you. I will overlook the fact it was
probably stolen. Off a ship you callously wrecked, no doubt."

"No—"

He holds up a hand to silence me. "Utter one more word
and I will take it as proof of your guilt and you will hang
alongside them tomorrow morning."

I gape as he gathers up the coins, each one plunking into
the cloth bag. "I should have known when I received the
information in the note from that girl yesterday. Finnikin's
Way." He chuckles darkly. "My predecessor allowed such
places to exist. Allowed their people to carry on smuggling
their goods, avoiding taxes, murdering and pillaging."

Plunk.

"But not me. I will weed them out. I will follow the route

your friend was so good as to tell me, to Finnikin's Way, and make them pay. I'll make them answer for everything."

Plunk.

He swipes away the last of the coin and rises to his feet. Striding across his office, he flings the door wide, motioning for me to leave. After a brief hesitation, I slide out of the chair, standing on shaking legs. My heart beats like a drum in my ears, the floor stretching and tilting as I reach the doorway.

"Be glad I'm allowing you to leave, Mira." He stares at me steadily. "If our paths cross again, it will not be the case."

Then he carefully closes the door in my face.

I walk from the prison in a daze, only just making it outside before I retch on the pavement. I lean against the wall, the biting cold of the wind waking me from my stupor. Agnes holds back my hair as the door slams shut behind us. Sealing my father's and Bryn's fate.

"No, no, no…" I moan, dropping my hands over my eyes. I have completely misjudged him. Captain Spencer Leggan isn't just stealing my father's and Bryn's lives; he has ripped away my future. The future of our entire island. Condemning us to another winter of empty bellies, one we won't all survive.

I sob, tears clawing up my throat, stinging my cheeks. I am a fool. A fool to have so readily tipped that coin onto his desk, a fool for believing the captain of the watch would play fair. There is a code, but it only keeps the watch safe, and never us. I feel Agnes's arms come around me, feel her tears on my face too. She knows without asking, it's over. We have lost.

My father and Bryn will hang in the morning, and there is nothing more I can do.

CHAPTER THIRTY

I STUMBLE BACK THROUGH THE WATCHFUL STREETS. Agnes grips my hand in hers, hiding her face in her shawl. She has always worn her heart on the outside, usually full of quiet joy. But now, she wears her sadness like a shroud. It's etched into every crease of skin and I wonder if I look just the same.

When we walk through the door of the pub, Kai is pacing before the fire. His face crumples as Agnes lets out a small sob and in two strides, he catches her. I tremble at the sight of it, my throat constricting. I don't know if they realize how much love is between them yet and it chills me that this heartbreak might be what finally draws them together, lighting the spark they share.

"Mira, sit down. There has to be a way," Kai says, blinking back tears. He loves Bryn like a father, so his pain is my pain. It's searing hot, almost impossible to think around. I sink into a chair and he tucks Agnes into his side as she cries quietly. "Tell me everything."

I begin with my mother's legacy, the map, unfolding it over the table. "It's just blank parchment to you, but that's not how it appears to me. There are so many secrets here, Kai. Coves and islets and the way the tide wends around the islands. It's everything we need to know to master the isles." I take a breath. "And it's everything that captain needs to stamp us all out for good."

Kai frowns down at it, tapping a finger on one of the folds. "This Elijah, he told you he'd help you as long as you didn't tell the watch about this map? Or give yourself over to them?"

"Yes. That was our deal for bringing me to Penscalo on time. But then when I met that captain... I realized I couldn't just give him a piece of information. He would want more and more, and I never would have been able to leave."

Kai searches my face. "You trust him though, this Elijah? Or any of the crew as much as one of us?"

I think about Seth and last night. His hands twisting in my hair, our shared breath in the close dark. Then I picture Elijah stepping from the shadows. How he boarded Renshaw's ship and drenched the deck in blood. This world, our world, isn't filled with trust. On Rosevear I would give Kai or any of them my life and know they would guard it. But beyond Rosevear's shores... I don't know. It's a world of bargains and secrets. And if I can't use the map as leverage without myself tied to it, then I don't have anything else to trade.

I put my head in my hands. "It's hopeless."

That night, alone in my bed, I can't sleep. Not while my father awaits the dawn and his fate. Not while the realization sinks in that the burden I have carried will stay with me now, forever. I will carry it with me until my final days, how I have failed him. Failed all of them. I turn over, reaching a hand across the sheet to the space Seth occupied only last night. I haven't seen him all day. Haven't shared the news of what happened in that meeting. My fingers curl into a fist and I bunch it into my chest. I don't want to seek his comfort now.

I leave my room above the pub and sneak down the stairs, creeping along the silent cobbled streets until I find the sea. It's gone midnight and just around the corner from the quay, the waves devour the rocky coastline greedily, snatching great handfuls in their haste before the tide turns. My breath catches as I watch the moonlight highlight the inky tips of the water, beckoning me in. I pull off my boots, socks and shirt and dive beneath the frothing surface. At once, my blood ignites. I breathe out in a rush of relief, feeling the heat and home I longed for. I dive farther, kissing my fingertips along the sea-bed and swim out, away from the island, the prison, and the ever-present watch.

With every second, every pull against the tide, I run through my thoughts. The way that captain looked at me. The way he condemned my kin so readily. The feel of Seth's lips on my skin, leaving a path of burning embers…

I close my eyes, a stream of bubbles escaping my mouth, and push harder, faster, as I swim farther from the shore. The water turns deepest green, closing around me like a cocoon, and I finally begin to slow. My mind is a snarl of knots, pulling tighter with every move I make. I am scattered, too full of everything that has happened to find real peace. And in a few short hours, the hanging.

Crouching on the seabed, I pull my head into my knees, lightning dancing through my body.

And I scream.

I scream inside that dark, deep cocoon of ocean where no one can hear me. Where no one can stop me. Then when my breath is spent, I kick off for the surface.

The night is dark and rich, the air so sharp with cold it burns my throat. I gather it inside me, breathing in, out, coating my lungs like flame. I close my eyes, drifting on the water as the tide pulls me farther out.

What if I don't go back? What if I just…drift? Detach myself from this world and what will happen all too soon? What if I escape to the sea forever and give in to that wild part of myself?

I shake my head, even before the thoughts fully form. I could never leave my father and Bryn to their fate. I have to face this. Face the mistakes I have made, how I have let them down. Let myself down. Face the fact that I am not the daughter my mother believed I would become. My life is so tangled now, I have lost track of what I am and what I want.

I drift, turning each plan over, each way I could rescue them. But I keep coming back to Kai's question. Who do I trust?

The only face that surfaces, to my surprise, is Elijah's. In a strange way, I believe we are the same. Whenever I am near him, I feel an ancient stirring in my blood, as familiar as my heartbeat. Like we were forged in the same way. I trust him to follow through with a deal. I trust him to uphold his end of it—he has done so once before. And I trust that what I offer will be something he wants enough that I can persuade him.

I do not trust him in the way I do Kai and Agnes. My first instinct when he stepped from those shadows was to run. I can almost sense the monster lurking under his skin, prowling behind his beautiful, storm-gray eyes. But he is my best option, even if his help comes with a steep price.

I breathe in, out, allowing the sharp air to douse the fire on my tongue. I look out in the direction of Rosevear. It's not so far away. I could swim there right now, cutting through the ocean that divides me from my home. It's close, and yet just beyond my reach. I stretch my fingers as though I can grasp it: home, safety, the familiar. Then I curl my hand into a fist. I turn my back on it, facing Penscalo and gathering my strength.

Then I head for the shore to make one final bargain.

CHAPTER
THIRTY-ONE

I SWIM BACK TO THE ISLAND WITH ALL MY FEARS still haunting me. The sea has cooled the fury, but has left me certain of one thing. How far I am willing to go to save them. How far I *have* to go. I pull myself out of the water, my skin cooling in the night. There's a steady breeze lifting my hair from my face, sending shivers dancing along my ribs. I cast a last glance at the ocean, wishing I could stay there. Wishing the weight of my people hadn't landed on my shoulders. Then I feel a presence at my back. It's the smallest shift, as though a fingernail scrapes down my spine, waking the instincts that are always just below the surface. I turn, raking the dark and knowing who I will find.

"Elijah," I breathe, as though casting a wish. "How did you know?"

"Big day tomorrow," his voice speaks from the shadows. "I take it things didn't go so well with the captain."

I wring out my hair, pulling my shirt on. I know that

voice now. I am used to the cadence of it in the velvet dark. "He is not the kind of person I can make a bargain with. But you...you are."

Elijah leans against a rock, hands in his pockets, watching as I braid my hair. He cuts a fine figure against the wash of moonlight. His dark hair is slightly ruffled, stubble shadows his jaw, and his eyes, intense and smoldering, bore into me.

"I can't just fix everything. That's not how this world works."

"I don't know what to believe," I sigh. "About you, about Seth, about the watch and that captain. The tide's turning. I can feel it. And I have a choice to make."

"You forgave Seth. That must mean you believe in him. Why aren't you seeking a bargain with him?"

I look at him sharply, hoping he can't see the blush on my cheeks. Does he know where we were last night, our limbs entwined long after midnight? "That's not something for discussion."

He grins, holding up his hands. "Of course. He's not helping you then? And you haven't traded places with your father?"

"No and no," I hiss softly, pulling on my boots. "Which I'm sure you're already aware of on both counts."

"You're pushed into a corner, Mira. No way out this time."

His words leave me cold. "I know," I say softly. "I know. Which is why I have an offer for you. Something you want, something you can't refuse."

"I have to be honest, Mira, I do feel a little like a last resort. It's the kind of thing that could hurt a person's feelings."

I snort. "Have you got any of those?"

"I thought you would at least try and flatter me," he says with a rakish grin.

"I would rather just get this over with."

He is toying with me. "Tell me what you propose and I'll think on it."

I narrow my eyes, watching him. "You'll think on it?"

"Perhaps." He leans back against the rock, crossing his arms. His muscles bulge under his white shirt, the fabric taut. He's broader than Seth, I realize.

I swallow, keeping my eyes trained on his face. Not on the steady rise and fall of his chest. He really is the most beautiful person I've ever laid eyes on, and when I need to sharpen my tongue and my wits, it's a distraction. "I need you to help me free my father and Bryn. I need you to make sure they don't hang, and that they escape back to Rosevear unharmed."

He falls silent, regarding me in the steady glow of moonlight. "And what do you offer in return, Mira?"

"I—" I take a breath and frown. "You know what I offer. What you've wanted all along. Me. And the map. My services, my loyalty."

Elijah grins wolfishly, his arms falling to his sides. He prowls toward me, stopping only inches away. I hold my nerve as his hand reaches for my face and brushes a strand of hair behind my ear. His fingertips barely touch my skin, but they leave a trail of heat in their wake. I try to stop my heart from racing.

Then he leans close, so close I can feel his breath on my throat, the hush of it pulsing through every inch of me, as he says softly, "You're right, I *do* want you, Mira. You and that map. Give yourself to me forever and I'll save the whole damn world."

I shiver, not trusting myself to speak. Every part of me prickles with heat, and as I draw in a ragged breath, he chuckles quietly. As though he knows the effect he has. I tilt my chin, gaze locking with his, and form all that heat twisting inside me into something else. Something I have control over.

"Stop it," I spit, pushing him away.

His grin only widens. "You're flushed, Mira. Do you not like my terms?"

I shrug, feigning nonchalance. Even while the blood pounds in my ears. "This is my bargain. My terms. All you offer is exactly what I am trying to avoid—trading my life for theirs. I thought you said you are nothing like Renshaw? Perhaps I am better off going back to the watch and handing myself over right now?"

He is quiet for a moment and I wonder if he will melt away. If the shadows will fold over him and I will be left alone once more, with my island balanced on my shoulders.

"I will free them both. Your father *and* Bryn. They can walk away from this, go back home to their island and live out their days. And you will be by my side."

I bite my lip, my head filling with the image of my father back at home. In our meeting house, celebrating. Smiling. Laughing with his set and making plans for the future. If Elijah can deliver on this…if there's even a slim chance it's possible…

It's tempting. Too tempting.

"You ask too much. Forever is… That's not what I offer."

Elijah steps away, his boots shifting over the shingle. My heart thumps as I try to keep myself contained, my expression neutral. If he can guarantee their safety and freedom, there is nothing I wouldn't give. *Nothing.* He could ask anything. He could ask for the world on a platter and I would give it. And if he is truly asking for me and the map, forever at his side, forever at his beck and call, all I can do is say yes.

But this is my bargain. I have to try to push him.

"Not forever, Elijah," I say again, raising my chin defiantly. "You'll get what you want. But I won't be divided from my people for the rest of my life."

He considers me, his eyes sweeping the lines of my face. "We can get to the terms. But I want you to agree to our bargain tonight and seal it with ink and blood. It will be unbreakable."

"Like a curse."

"Like a *promise*."

I draw in a breath, staring out at the moonlight on the water. I have no choice. I knew that as I screamed in the deep cocoon of the ocean. "All right. Spell it out, the exact terms you want. Don't play with me. I know what *I* want, so show me your cards, Elijah. *All* of them."

He puts his hands in his pockets again, regarding me. The shadows fall across the planes of his features, rendering his eyes unreadable. "I want you to join my crew. Come and work for me, and *only* me. I want you to leave your island behind."

I turn away from him. I knew this is what he would say. That I would have to sacrifice everything. Right when Rosevear needs protecting the most, from the watch, from the cruel Captain Leggan in his high-walled prison. I balk on instinct, spitting out, "No."

"No?"

"I can't just… I can't just *leave*. Not now," I say, turning back to him. "I don't know you. I don't even know what you do, what your crew do, other than lie and steal—"

"Oh, we do much worse than that, I assure you."

"Well, exactly. How can I possibly agree?" I run my hands over my braid, thinking, calculating. But I keep coming back to my father. That noose. The captain of the watch and his damning anger. How this is better than the map falling into his hands. "I'll give you six months. That's the bargain I'll make with you. That's what I'm offering. Me and the map."

He chuckles softly. "Three years."

"*Nine* months."

"A year." His face grows dark and serious. "You will join my crew for a year, work for me, and leave your island and your kin behind. You will do whatever work I give you. You will read that map for me and *only* me, giving me all the secrets your underwater kin have left for you. I will bind us in ink and blood. *Those* are the terms."

I lean in, fixing my eyes on his. "And *my* terms are that you'll save my father and Bryn tomorrow. They will walk free and return to Rosevear to live out their days, *Lord Tresillian*."

My heart beats wildly inside me. I can't walk away from this. From him. I know what he is capable of, what he can do. He is the only person who can free them. The way he can step in and out of shadows, materializing seemingly out of thin air. That is magic. That is *power*. Just as the ocean sweeps through my veins, darkness seems to infuse his.

But I will be giving myself over to the whims and wants of this stranger. Not only that, but if I read the map for him, then he can use me as a weapon and wield that knowledge however he chooses. Elijah may have helped me secure my mother's legacy by getting me off Renshaw's ship, but there is always a cost with him. Always a price to pay.

I've tried to find another way. I don't want to tie myself to him, but this really is the only path I can take to save them. It's the only option I have left. Even as I abandon Rosevear to the whims of the watch.

"I agree to the terms."

His eyes spark, flaring briefly in the quiet night before submitting once more to the dark. "Excellent. And I agree to yours. Give me your hand."

I step toward him, the scent of smoke lingering in the air between us. The only indication of my deep fear is the slight tremor in my fingers as I place my hand in his. His skin is warm, the pressure of his hand gentle as he turns my palm over, exposing the milky pale skin of my wrist.

"This may sting."

I bite my lip as he closes his fingers around my wrist. Searing pain explodes under my skin, threading up my veins, reaching for my chest. He looks at me, our eyes meeting, and I believe for a moment I see a question. As though he believes I can answer something that's been burning inside him for so long. As though all the toying with me, the way he snaked his arms around mine aboard *Phantom*, murmuring in my ear and heating my blood with his touch... It was all rooted in something real.

But as his lips curve upward, the picture of triumphant arrogance, I know I must have been mistaken. This is what he wanted all along. To control me and through me, the map. Not to have me close for another reason. I suddenly feel like I've made a terrible decision, but what else could I have done? He releases my wrist, a cold ache weighing it down as I cradle it to my middle. The mark is so much worse than the one he bestowed aboard Renshaw's ship. This one feels ancient and cold, gnawing at the bone beneath. As though it is tattooing my very marrow, tying the pair of us together in a way that is indeed unbreakable. The mark before has been replaced by a compass. The symbol of House Tresillian.

His mark.

"A pleasure, as always, Mira, dear," he says, stepping back, already half-encased in shadows.

"Wait!" I splutter. "What's the plan? When will you release them?"

"When the moment is right. In time, you will learn that I always keep my promises. Be ready tomorrow. Carry a blade. I shall look forward to our year together."

I trudge back through the streets of Penscalo carrying a heavy, weary heart. I had no choice, I keep telling myself. I had to make a bargain with Elijah. I think of all the people I will be leaving behind. Agnes, Kai, my father, Bryn.

And Seth.

I close my eyes briefly, picturing him, us, the way he kissed me in the dark. I swallow, bitterness coating my tongue, and hug my arms around myself. I will be leaving him behind too, just as we could have become something.

"Better than the watch," I whisper softly to myself. Although perhaps not much better. Perhaps no better at all.

Footsteps sound behind me and I turn to find a knife at my throat. I hold my breath, growing still as the man holding it thrusts a deep hood back. Exposing his features, his frown. The freckles I kissed in the dark.

"Seth," I sigh in relief, wrapping my fingers around his, and push the blade away. I smile at him, softening. But I find no warmth reflected in his stare. "You startled me."

"You're out late, Mira," he says, suspicion cutting his tone. "Your hair is damp."

I shrink away, wondering what has changed. Why the spell, so swiftly woven between us last night, has suddenly broken? I bite my lip, warring with myself. Wanting to ask him what's wrong. Why the sudden change, the sudden cold. But his stare is granite, unyielding. I begin walking again and he keeps pace with me. "I needed the sea. I needed to think."

He grabs my wrist suddenly, twisting it to expose the delicate skin. In the sheen of moonlight, the lines of Elijah's bargain mark flare like embers. Seth drops my wrist, swears and turns his back on me.

"I had no other option," I say, dragging my sleeve over it. "What could I have done?"

"You could have come to me!" Seth growls, turning quickly, grabbing my shoulders. My heart leaps in my chest, marveling at his sudden fury. "After last night, after all we spoke of—"

I shove him off. "You never offered. Not once."

"To save your father? It's not possible, Mira, not if the watch captain wants him dead." He breathes steadily, shaking his head. "Whatever Lord Tresillian has offered you, he can't deliver. He won't. Nothing will stop your father's death tomorrow."

Shock pulses through me. "You seem pretty bloody certain of that, Seth. What is it you're not telling me?"

"You don't know what you've done, Mira. What you're meddling with. It's bigger than your island. It's bigger than you and me. You should have walked away. You should have grieved."

I push him away, hard. "I will *not* grieve a father who's still alive."

"Mira, come on—"

"No," I say flatly. "Just...*no*. I said I forgave you. But if you think I would give up so easily on my kin, my *home*, then you don't know the depths I will travel. You don't know a thing about me."

I walk away, leaving Seth in the street. And when I get back to the pub, back to my bed and the quiet, he doesn't follow.

CHAPTER
THIRTY-TWO

MY WRIST BURNS AS THOUGH LACED WITH ICE. I trace the pattern etched into my skin, holding it up to the light filtering through the windows of my room. I can just make out the faint outline of the compass, paler than my skin. Under the moon and stars last night it blazed brightly. Bright enough for Seth to find it, for him to know what I had done. But under the light of the morning sun, it has almost faded completely.

It continues to burn as I ready myself for the day. It's not the bone-deep ache of the night before, but an ever-present simmer. A constant reminder of the bargain I have made and what I have given up to seal it. I'm well aware now that it's his symbol. The mark of House Tresillian. And I will have to wear it on my skin for a year, just as he wishes.

I meet Agnes and Kai in the corridor, all of us silent, ghosts in our eyes. None of us look like we slept at all. Agnes grips my hand, trying to hide her tears as we walk to the prison. I don't dare tell them of the deal I have struck. Doubt fills me, even with the kiss of the bargain's tattoo on my skin. Will Elijah truly save them both? Will he get there in time for them? He has to. I run through the wording we both used and realize I left a gap. I allowed for them both to be rescued, to live out their days on our island, but how many days will that be? Have I guaranteed their safety beyond their return to Rosevear?

The watch will ransack every cottage, burning through us until they find someone to pay with blood. I worry at my lip with my teeth, my stomach tying in knots. As we reach the looming walls of the prison, I can barely hide my anxious heart.

Seth falls into step beside me as Kai and Agnes shuffle a few steps behind. His curls fall over his forehead, his eyes shadowed with deep grooves beneath them. He takes my hand, guiding me to the side, away from the main current of the crowd. He looks haunted. Even more than I do. I frown as he turns to me, reaching for my other hand and holding them tightly. Our argument lingers between us, the words we hissed pressed into our lips.

"Mira, what I said earlier still holds. Don't do this. It's not too late to walk away," he says, staring at me. As though trying to tell me something else, something hidden. Perhaps because he knows the deep grief of losing kin as I do, and would not wish that on me today. He lost his aunt and he has never spoken of his father. And it was clear from the way he looked at Merryam that their bond as cousins had been deeply shaken when she broke with Renshaw. But even so, it's not enough. If he's trying to somehow protect me, it's too late.

"You know I can't leave," I say, peering at him. Trying to discern his thoughts. "Not even for you. I would never abandon them to their fate." I glance around, my senses on high alert, wondering when Elijah will give his signal. I focus briefly on the blade concealed at my side. Then I look back at Seth.

He nods, letting go of my hands. "I was hoping I could persuade you, hoping—I don't know—that things could be different. That we had met under different circumstances."

"What do you mean?"

"Nothing." He shrugs, smiling ruefully. "Nothing. Look, if you're going through with this, I can help. Let me help."

"Seth, I—"

"Please. There's a quay, an older quay than the one the watch use, where you can sail from back to Rosevear. It's the other side of town, and it's seldom guarded. When you've gotten your father out, you can take him there."

"You truly wish to help me?"

He takes my shoulders, angling our bodies together. "Give me a chance to earn back your trust. I'll be watching. Speak to Elijah, get him to meet there."

He ducks his face, kissing my forehead, and before I can answer, he weaves away into the crowd. I stare after him, touching the place where his mouth met my skin. Then I move along with the crowd and make my way back to Kai. He stands taller than everyone and is easy to spot in this swirling mass. I fall back into step beside Agnes and Kai as though I have always been there. And for a second, I'm sure I see a flash of red hair. Dark red hair, darker than Agnes's, by the entrance to the square, dark as the blood in the sea that day, over in an alcove, tucked away—

But when I crane to look, focusing on that exact spot, there is only an old woman with a red knitted shawl. I press my hand into my chest, willing my heart to calm. Of course, my mind is straying to memories of the day my mother died, but I have to trust that Elijah will make good on his word. And I have to forget Seth's grave eyes, his lips brushing my skin. I have to trust that he wants to make amends.

I feel rather than see a shadow darkening. It gathers in the corners like the slow trickle of a dark stream as we move farther inside the walls of the prison, to the hanging square in its center. The crowd bunches around us, gossip mingling with a low rumble of expectation. I breathe through my nose, eyes only for the gallows, as that shadow deepens, lending the air a scent of frost. Then it dissipates in the corner of my vision and the scent of frost evaporates, leaving Elijah standing beside me.

"A fine day, Mira," he says, voice deep like the coaxing notes of a summer storm.

"But not for a hanging."

He smiles, the slightest dimple appearing in his left cheek. "Never for that."

I breathe out through my mouth, willing my heart to stop racing. Willing myself to believe it will all be fine. My head fills with stars, too dizzy, whirling faster and faster.

His hand finds mine. I still instantly, the touch of his skin warm against the jagged cold of my own. "Follow my voice, Mira. Steady breaths. Pretend you're about to swim out to a wreck."

I close my eyes, doing as he says. I listen for the flickering low notes in his voice, lingering on the way he forms my name in his mouth. Then slowly, as his thumb rubs a steady circle in the creases of my palm, I drown everything else out. The noise of the crowd. The scent of death looming over the square from hangings past. And I focus on the feel of his hand wrapped around mine.

"Await my signal, then tell your two friends to be ready to run," he says. "The others are in position. The plan is already in motion."

"Joby, Pearl, Mer?"

"Yes," he says, his voice brushing my ear, just like last night. "And a couple of others you haven't met yet. I need you to get up on the platform and cut the prisoners free. I may not have time to free them all myself. Then *you* must run. I will get them out of the square, but I can't take you too. You have to be ready to move. Do you understand?"

I swallow, my gaze fixed on the gallows.

"Elijah, I want you to take them to the old quay. Ready *Phantom* there. Can you do that?"

He is quiet for a second. "If that's what you wish, Mira. I'll spread the word through my crew."

There is suddenly an absence, a void at my side, and I turn sharply, seeking him. But he is gone.

I look around, wondering if anyone else noticed how he appeared then melted into the shadows. But no one around me seems to have seen him. Kai's eyes meet mine, worry etched in every line of his face, and I lean over, placing my hand on Agnes's arm. "Get ready to run when I say. Trust me."

"Mira..." Kai starts.

"Trust me," I say again, squeezing Agnes's shoulder before turning back to the gallows. "There is a plan. Go to the old quay on the other side of town, the one the watch rarely use."

"Why does it worry me how you say that?" Kai says quietly, searching my face. I know what he's looking for. Some sign that I have sacrificed myself. Traded my own life for theirs. "Mira, what have you done? Promise me you didn't…"

I reach for his arm, trying to reassure him. "I've done what I had to. I'm not trading places with them. I promise."

Kai opens his mouth to say more, but at that moment, the crowd roars. It begins in the far east corner, ripping through the gathering, pummeling us with the force of it. I whirl to see what is happening, heart in my mouth as the scarlet coats of the watch form a line.

There. There is my father. He and Bryn and two other men, all gray as dust, all shuffling with bowed, broken heads and backs. Even from here I can see the jut of his cheekbones, how the skin hangs from him in a sorry web. He's a flicker of his former self. The watch and their captain have reduced him to ash and bone.

A sob forces its way up my throat and I clamp my jaw together. I can't cry. I won't. Not now when they need me to be strong. Quiet sweeps over everyone, as though the ghosts are whispering among us. Waiting for the next four to join them. My father. Bryn. The two other unfortunate souls destined for the noose.

"I can't look," Agnes murmurs, turning her head into Kai's shoulder.

"Any moment now…" I mutter, scanning the crowd for Elijah. Where is he?

The watch lead my father and the others up the steps to the wooden platform, each noose hanging before them. The dull thud of their boots echoes like a death knell, each footfall counting down their final, precious moments. I can't breathe.

The watch captain strides out, mounting the platform with quick steps, and walks back and forth, surveying the crowd.

Any mutterings fall deathly silent. Any merriment long ago extinguished. I bunch my hands into fists at my sides, longing to throw a blade at him. I can see the gleam of triumph in his eye, even from half a crowd away. He has won. He is victorious over us islanders. He has stamped out the vile wreckers of Rosevear.

"These men have been tried and found guilty of pillaging, plunder and—" he gazes around "—murder."

Gasps pepper the audience. I plant my feet, wanting to tackle him to the ground and beat him senseless. I picture our people. The children. The hungry bellies that will surely now follow. This is what he wants: he wants us scared. He wants us dead. My desperation grows claws as I rake my gaze back and forth, willing Elijah to fulfil his side of the bargain.

A seed of doubt grows in my mind, needling me. I can't see him. The nooses are mere inches from my father's and Bryn's noses. Death, in all her silent glory, lingers on that platform. I begin to push my way through the crowd, heart in my throat, keeping my sight set on my father, hoping he will look up, hoping he will see I am coming for him.

A dash of blond hair catches my eye. I whip around, following that slip of white gold, just in time to catch a wink.

Pearl.

The air seems to thicken, the very world turning to treacle.

I turn back just in time to see the platform darkening, shadows settling over the men like shrouds. The watch captain starts talking again, his voice turning nasal as he realizes he has lost the crowd. Cries of panic fracture the square, fingers pointing up at the gallows. My father's eyes snag on mine, growing wide and fearful. I push forward, needing to reach him, needing to tell him to hold on. His mouth opens in a scream—

Then an explosion rips through the square.

CHAPTER
THIRTY-THREE

I CHOKE ON A CRY AS SMOKE BILLOWS UP, dousing all of us in thick, impenetrable gray. But not before I see a new figure on the platform, standing just behind my father.

Elijah.

This is the signal. I have to get up on that platform. And Kai and Agnes have to run. I turn, but I can't see them. Panic squeezes my chest as thick smoke covers the square, fires igniting everywhere from the explosion.

"Agnes…" I cough, pushing my way back. "Kai…" I hold my arm up to cover my mouth and nose as my eyes burn. Flame licks at the corners, the crowd scattering, running for the exits. I search for Agnes, calling her name until a hand grips my arm. It's Kai. I release the breath I was holding as I see they are both intact, relief washing over me. Agnes is gripped in his other hand, her eyes streaming from the smoke.

"Is that the signal?" she grates out, fighting against a round of coughing. "What's happening?"

I push them toward the nearest exit, not bothering to be gentle. We instantly fall into our roles as three of the seven when we swim out to a wreck, Agnes pulling out her blade, Kai sweeping the space around us for other survivors. But there's no time for that. I need them to save themselves.

"You both have to run! I'll find you. Get to the old quay. Get to the ship now. Go!"

Kai wavers for a moment, as if to argue, then braces his hand on my shoulder before letting me go. A look passes between us, still as the sea at low tide. We both know who he would save, who Kai will protect with his lifeblood. He throws his arm around Agnes's waist, leading her away. They both melt into nothing, devoured by the smoke, and I turn to the platform, blade already in my fist.

I dodge past flailing limbs, jumping fallen debris as cries rend the square. I reach the platform, scramble over the edge, and drop to a crouch. When I see the steps are empty, no watch crowding nearby, I leap up, crossing to the gallows. Elijah is cutting away the ropes from my father, who is doubled over, wheezing and coughing. I want to help him, but then I see Bryn.

"Mira," he croaks, his old steely eyes meeting mine. I flick my blade to saw at the ropes binding his hands at his back, then the noose that lies slack around his throat. Each slice cuts the cords of the thick rope agonizingly slowly. Too slowly.

I hear a shout, the watch reassembling behind me. I have seconds, if that. My breath forms ragged bursts, heart drumming in my ears as the final piece of rope falls away, leaving Bryn a free man. I turn, searching for the other two prisoners. But they're gone. Already escaped into the smoke.

"I'll take them. Now, get to the exit," Elijah says, gripping my father's shoulder. "I can only take two at a time, so you have to go. *Now.*"

I nod, eyeing my father and Bryn, seeing how gaunt they are from their short time in this prison. How many years it has stolen from them. Death still lingers nearby, ready to lead them away. Bitterness swirls in my belly as my eyes find Elijah.

"Thank you," I say, and he jerks his head in a nod.

"Just get yourself to the old quay. Don't want to break our bargain now, do you?"

I swear I see fear in the depths of his stare, as though he feels death's presence too. As though I mean more to him than the year of service I have agreed to. I remember the look he gave me, the unspoken question as the bargain mark bit into my flesh. But there's no time to unravel it as the shadows darken, weaving around the three of them. He steps back, folding into them, my father's face brimming with terror.

Then they are gone.

I turn, leaping off the platform, darting for the exit with the last of the crowd. The smoke is thinning, revealing flashes of scarlet everywhere. The watch. I gulp, stumbling over an abandoned tray of rock buns, trying to avoid the red coats, the rifles. But I'm surrounded. Two members of the watch emerge from the smoke, blocking the exit I was aiming for. I veer off to the left, hoping to find another along the thick wall that borders the street. My pulse drums in my ears, drowning everything out but the need, the desperate need to escape.

"You're trapped!" A familiar voice cracks like a whip across the square. I whirl, finding them everywhere. The watch, hemming me in. Rifles in hand, grim faces coated in ash and blood. Fire burns all around us, people screaming as the crowd steadily disperses. A man slumps to the ground, clutching his

belly where his guts should be. But there's a hole in him and
dimly I realize that he's been shot. And at close range—it's
torn him in half. I stare, trapped with my fear, my horror, as
a figure peels from the gloom, rifle aimed at my chest.

Captain Spencer Leggan.

I take a jagged, panicked breath, searching in vain for an
escape route. Any way out of this square and away from him.
But there's nowhere. Nowhere to run to. Nowhere to hide. A
bitter thought emerges. After I was so unsure he would uphold his end of the deal, *I* will be the one to break the bargain with Elijah.

"I thought you and your friends might try something
today," he says, voice filled with granite, like the walls of his
prison. He picks his way over a fallen body, kicking aside the
dying man one of them shot. My heart twists with fury and
fear, eyes darting to meet him. He takes another step, keeping his rifle trained on me.

"I brought in extra watchmen. Posted them throughout
the town. There's nowhere you can hide now, Mira. You and
your island are finished."

I search desperately for a shadow, for any sign of Elijah
coming back for me.

"Did you know I was in the Far Isles when they fell?" His
grin is manic, too wide for his face. "I'm sure you've heard
what happened. The islanders came to heel. Came to understand that there was no other way. That wrecking, smuggling,
lawlessness is a crime. And you *will* be punished. Made to pay."

I slink back, tripping on a plank of wood. Scrambling, I
stand again, realizing this is it. I'm not going to make it. I hope
more than anything that Elijah got my father out. That Kai
and Agnes made it to the quay. I look up, finding the watery

wedge of sun in all the gray, and wonder if it's better to be captured, or killed right now. I picture my mother. The place where she was forged. I bring my hand to my heart, where her map and letter are tucked against my chest. A single tear travels down my cheekbone and I close my eyes, wondering if I will see her again. Wondering if she will be there waiting, on the other side...

A shout, high-pitched with terror, gutters out suddenly. I blink my eyes open, casting my gaze back to earth, back to the square as the watch captain turns, his gaze raking across the smoke. Then another gurgle, the sound of a body dropping to the ground. He whirls, searching his other side, barking orders to stay in formation. The watchmen surrounding me glance around, uneasy.

Then I see him.

Joby.

And the fire in my heart reignites.

A stream of people, civilians in wool dresses and shirts, cry in panic, engulfing the watch. I blink, gasping at the sudden mass of people, the watchmen trying to fight through them, to keep me in their sights. Then Joby is next to me, battering his way through the crowd, grabbing my arm to drag me deeper into the smoke. "He told you to get on that platform then run. That was the damn signal!"

"I didn't... There were too many of them." I cough, swearing before my throat closes up.

Joby pushes me toward a small door, set deep in the wall of the prison square, and with a firm kick, it screeches open. "He's already got your father on the old quay. The others are safe. *You* are not. He'd never forgive me if you were lost."

I look up and over his shoulder as three men in scarlet

coats surge toward us. I can hear Captain Leggan screeching at them, telling them to find me. To take me alive, to weed me out, wherever I'm hiding. I freeze, listening to the hatred, the guttural loathing in his commands.

Joby gives me a shove, forcing me toward the escape route, to freedom. *"Run."*

I fall against the doorway and turn to do as he says, but realize Joby has stopped. I look at the doorway, then back to the square. I can't leave, not yet. I can't leave Joby here. The watch captain wants blood. He wants to stamp us out. He wants a *hanging*. And Joby… I swear softly, feeling for my blade.

I never leave a soul behind.

I leap from the doorway, knocking into the watchman on the right. He stumbles, hat tumbling back as I bring my fist up to his jaw. He falls, spluttering, and I kick his rifle away from his hands, into the smoky gloom. Before he can rise, I turn to see Joby barreling into another watchman, while a third hastily reloads his rifle, shouting for backup. I kick at the rifle with a feral scream, sending it spinning away, and as the man turns, scarlet coat swinging, I jab at his face. My fist connects with a crunch, pain splintering down my arm as he falls to the ground. Knocked out cold. I shake out my hand, turning to look for Joby and find him, rifle in hand, grinning at me.

He spits blood from his mouth and jerks his chin at the doorway. "Do you ever do as you're told?"

"Only when it's the right thing to do," I answer, following him out of the square and back on to the street. "We'll be on Wanted posters from here to the Far Isles for that."

He laughs as we start to run, aiming for the old quay. "It'll be an honor. I hope the bastards put a decent price on my head."

The streets are deserted. The only sound from the whole town is the crackling blaze as the flames devour the gallows in the hanging square. Every now and again I hear shouting, the pounding of insistent footfalls. I hasten my steps, not wanting to tarry. Picturing my father, alive and well. Warmth fills me, bathing me in a glow I haven't felt since before he was taken. He's a free man, and so is Bryn.

They are no longer destined for the gallows.

CHAPTER THIRTY-FOUR

"THEY'LL BE AT THE NORTH END OF THE QUAY, nearest *Phantom*," Joby says as we round a corner. We slow our steps, hiding our faces as we approach a pocket of people. The rumors have already started—I can hear them sharp with fear as they are carried to us on the wind. The explosion, the escape. The fury of the watch and their captain. My pulse drums an insistent beat, spurring me on. I just need to see my father now. To hug him and get him off Penscalo.

"At last," I hear a voice say, and an arm comes around my shoulders. I look up at Seth, his face grim under flecks of blood. "Got tangled up with a few of them on the way out. Sorry I'm late."

"I think you're right on time," says Joby, giving him a nod. "Mer will be ecstatic."

They exchange a grin and I know what Joby means. Merryam must have been waiting years for her cousin to defect. And finally, now Seth has done it.

The north end of the quay is shrouded in mist. We shoulder our way through the milling crowd and I spy Merryam, foot propped up against the wall of the old harbormaster's offices, head dipped low to avoid anyone recognizing her. When she sees us, she tips up her chin, relief flaring up her features as her eye travels over Seth. Then she moves off, just ahead of us. Guiding us through the milling people.

I catch up to her, murmuring in her ear. "Were they followed? Are they safe?"

"Everyone's safe," she says, glancing over her shoulder at me with a wink. "The perfect escape." Then she nods at Seth. "For all of us."

I breathe out, releasing an inch of tension, my shoulders dropping. We are nearly there. So close to freedom for us all, and this nightmare finally behind us. Even Seth has found a way to escape Renshaw, and perhaps if I can persuade him, he can join me on Ennor. Suddenly, my hope soars, eclipsing all my fears.

We reach the far end of the quay, the crowd dissipating. And in the midst of the swirling mist, I find her mast, at last.

"Phantom," I whisper, a smile growing on my lips. There was never a more welcome sight than her, sails unfurled, ready to embark. Flame and victory dance through my middle and I cross my arms over my stomach, holding all that joy in, desperate now to see my father safe, to see him well.

To see him free.

Seth moves away, muttering something. I turn from him, scanning the crowd, searching every face for the one I need.

Elijah materializes in front of us, emerging from a pocket of shadow. After him steps Bryn, looking around with mistrust and uncertainty. And then…my father.

I barrel into him.

"Mira," he says faintly, his arms wrapping around me just as mine come around him. My whole body shakes, crying and laughing all at once as his old fisherman's hands smooth down my wayward hair. "You did this?"

I loosen my grip on him, shifting back so I can see his face. He has aged in such a short time, trapped in that prison with death hanging over him. But he is free now. Free to live in the open air, on the sea wrapping our island. Just as it should be.

"I did. I'm sorry it took so long."

His face creases into a tired smile, his eyes blazing in the folds of his skin. "Just like your mother. She would have shattered the world to break me out too."

"About her... I opened it, the chest."

His smile falters, his hands clasping my shoulders. "You opened it?"

I nod.

He breathes out. "I should have told you. So many things. I should have warned you of all that is to come. I should have prepared you... I thought about it in my cell. I should have let you have the key long ago and never hidden her true nature from you. I was afraid, Mira. Afraid of what you would become, what you might ask—"

"We have time," I say fiercely, gripping his arms. "It's all right. We have all the time in the world. You can tell me all about her. You can tell me everything."

He smiles once more, and I sniff, grinning through my tears.

"I never wanted to lose you to the sea," he says softly.

"Father, you won't."

"We need to get moving," Agnes chips in quietly and I

look around, seeing her propping up Bryn on one side, Kai on the other. Their faces are etched with worry. "Bryn's not in great shape."

I nod, reluctantly stepping away from my father. Now I have him, I don't want to let him go until we get back to Rosevear and the safety of our shores.

I turn to Elijah. "Are you not returning with us?"

He smiles and shakes his head. "No. My crew will escort you. I have…business to attend to. We may need to hide your father and Bryn once you have your reunion. They are wanted men."

I hold his gaze for a moment, wanting suddenly to say more. But the words stick in my throat. How can anything I say express all I feel inside? The tight knot of emotions exploding inside me, wearing away the worry, the despair of the last two weeks. Leaving only blazing hope.

"Thank you," I say fiercely as my father hobbles over to Bryn and the others, assembling to board *Phantom*. "I can never repay what you've done."

He fixes his gaze on me, the cool dark of his eyes like twin oceans, depthless and full of secrets. "Remember our bargain. I will come for you at the next full moon."

I bow my head, reaching instinctively for my wrist, for the markings hidden under my sleeve. "I will be ready."

He nods, just once, then opens his mouth, as though about to say more. But as he looks up, his face freezes. "Renshaw."

I whirl, searching the mist for where his gaze has landed. And out of the cold, smoky white, I see a flash of auburn hair. I take a step forward, eyes darting to my father and Bryn, just boarding *Phantom*. Then back to her as she walks toward us, surrounded now by her crew. My heart pounds, once, twice, drowning everything out. She smirks, as though she's won, and I can't understand why. But then…then I see him. I see him beside her, matching her pace. And the drowning sound, the rushing screams louder in my head—

It can't be.

It's Seth.

Seth is at her side. I blink at him, frowning, heat and cold crashing through me, the shock closing over me. I don't understand.

"Seth?"

His face is an impassive mask as he stares stonily back. "I tried to warn you. I tried to make you see sense. But you wouldn't hear of it, would you? We're here to trade."

I feel Elijah stiffen at my side and catch Merryam's breath hitch, her expression crumbling to devastation before she melts away into the mist.

Seth is by Renshaw's side. It can only mean one thing.

Joby positions himself beside *Phantom*. Pearl is already on board, hand on the knot that holds her fast to the quay. Bryn is also on board, eyes wide with shock as Pearl stops him from moving back to the quay. I swallow, realizing what order Elijah must have given in that small slip of silence when Renshaw appeared. If this goes south, they are to run. Run and leave Elijah to deal with Renshaw and her crew alone. Agnes and Kai already have their blades in their fists. The mist hangs low, cloaking everything in quiet. It is just us and them, alone on this stretch of stone.

My eyes fix on Seth, desperately seeking the person I have grown to care for. The boy I might even have grown to love.

"You know how I like to shoot the shit with you, Renshaw…" Elijah says casually, checking his pocket watch. "But I'm in a bit of a rush."

She smiles. "The trade is not with *you*, Lord Tresillian. Although I should really pay you back in kind for what you did to my ship." She gestures at me. "It's with her."

I blink again, feeling for my blade. Out of the corner of my eye, I see more of her crew emerge from the mist, silent as ghosts. There are at least twelve of them, all armed.

We are surrounded.

"Me?" I say, stepping forward. I hope their attention will stay on me so my father can join Bryn aboard *Phantom* and sail safely away. Fear curdles in my chest. I gulp, trying to mask it.

"*You.* My son tells me you've been a little naughty, stopping that hanging from going ahead." She chuckles. "And I don't doubt it, given what you *stole* from me. Now I find it's actually you I needed all along. That I can't have the map without *you* to read it. So if you come with us now, quietly, *willingly*… I'll leave the rest of your merry party alone."

I look at Seth, who stares back at me. I picture our night together. His mouth on mine, tracing slow circles over my skin… I blink in confusion, pain building slowly, pressing into my chest, the comprehension of what's happening dawning. He told us to use this quay. He made sure I would be here.

"Why?"

His face slips for a second before he gathers himself. "It was you all along, Mira. If you'd only come away with me this morning, we wouldn't need to do this here. I could have spared you this. If you'd only *listened*."

I inhale sharply, the betrayal cutting deeper than a knife. "You…you led us here. You brought us here for Renshaw to ambush us. Twice now, Seth," I say quietly, the flint filling my voice. I pin my gaze to his as the truth unspools before my eyes. The truth of what he is. What he's done. "Twice now I have trusted you. And you betrayed me. You promised. You *promised* I could trust you. I thought… I thought it meant something. I thought we—" My voice rises steadily before I stutter to a halt, realizing the lengths he has gone to. And how far I have followed him into the trap he was setting.

He only followed me up those stairs so I would trust him. So I would let him in, so he could lure me away… I shudder, the feel of his hands on my skin changing, twisting in my mind. He never cared for me. He only wanted me for the map, wanted what Renshaw would give him in exchange for me. Maybe they hoped I would read it willingly, spill all its secrets if he could make me believe that he cared for me. But now, now he is threatening my father, my friends. I seethe, fury like poison burning in my veins.

I look at him, this boy with dark curls, all the constellations of the sky on his face. My first. The one I could have handed my heart to, given time. Perhaps that was what he was hoping for, although he never would have given his in return. I press a fist to my chest, feeling my heart splinter. Knowing what I gave to him. Knowing now that all along, he was lying.

Anger—the cold, quiet kind—floods me, quenching the poison of his betrayal. "I won't make the same mistake a third time."

His lip curls at the corner. "I don't need you to."

"My son will make a fine captain, wouldn't you say?" Renshaw says. "A fine trade. His own ship, for you. And what a prize you are."

"I am not a *prize*," I hiss. "I am not a *thing*."

The anger hardens me further, building under my skin

like a winter tide. He told me he wanted his own ship. He *wanted* to get away from her. But he never told me that I was the key to his freedom. That he was willing to sacrifice *me*, the girl who might have loved him.

"All along," I say, my voice deceptively calm now. "Every moment. Every decision you made, making me trust you, making me—"

"I told you what I wanted," he snaps, losing his composure. "I told you I wanted my own ship. I never lied about that."

"No," I say bitterly, the fury seeping deep within me, settling into my bones. "Just everything else."

He looks away, not meeting my eyes, and in that moment, another piece of myself fractures and dies. I handed this boy my forgiveness, my trust. And he *lied*. He discarded it as if it meant nothing to him. As if *I* meant nothing.

Renshaw snaps her fingers. "Take her. Make sure she has the map."

I shuffle back as Renshaw's men close in. Elijah moves forward, blocking their path, and I ready my knife, gripping it in my fist. I wasn't born an islander for nothing. I won't become Renshaw's pawn. And she can burn before I give her a single secret from my mother's map. Kai, Agnes, and Joby fan out, squaring up to groups of Renshaw's crew. Elijah's gaze swivels to me, then back to the rival crew in front of him. He bares his teeth and I see the true predator prowling under his skin. The man directly before him, one of Renshaw's thugs, takes a step back, eyes widening in sudden fear.

Merryam rushes out of the mist, a cry in her throat. Swift as a needle, she threads through them with steel and we're unleashed. Joby's fists fly, taking down one of the crew with a punch to the jaw to my right, then shouting as another clips his shoulder. Two of Renshaw's men slip past Elijah toward me as he swings for a third, quickly becoming surrounded. Agnes and Kai team up, fighting back-to-back, a woman already clutching her middle at their feet, blood gushing as she gasps.

The mist seems to deepen, hiding even them from me. I grip my blade tighter and prepare to defend myself and my kin with everything I have.

The man with gray eyes emerges from the mist.

I drop a foot back, measuring my chances. He won't take me. He's twice my size, but he's grinning like he's already won. I shift my weight, preparing to spring—

But a hand grips my arm. I flinch, spinning around, hissing when I find whose hand it is, the harsh lines in his gaze.

Seth.

He sets his jaw and I tense, ready to fight, ready to draw blood.

Somebody stumbles before me, blocking my path. My father. My horror leaves me motionless for a beat, two... I thought he was on board *Phantom* already. I thought he was safe.

His eyes meet mine as he steadies himself, the rasp of his breath too harsh and insistent. As though the fight, the islander inside, has left him. But he raises his chin as he fixes his gaze on Seth, squeezing every last inch of strength from his ravaged body. "You can't have her. Get behind me, Mira. Give me your blade."

I shake my head, fury beating in my temples as I place my hand on his arm, trying to push him behind me. Away from Seth and the shouts of the crews in this mist. Away from the blades and danger and *death*.

"No. *Never*," I hiss. "They're not hurting you."

A scream splinters the air and I whip back and forth, trying to place where it came from. Elijah is a few paces away, grappling with a man. He twists the man's arm until it snaps, pulling him into the shadows as he howls. Seconds later, the shadows spit the man out and he falls to the ground unmoving. Elijah appears a second later behind three others and they scatter. Merryam is there, nimble as a dancer, slicing for their throats.

As the mist thins I catch sight of Joby and Kai homing in on Renshaw. Agnes is pulling her blade on a woman with gold hair, and I realize that only Pearl is guarding *Phantom*. They're spread too thin over the quay. Fear curls inside me for them, for what might happen to them.

"This shouldn't end in bloodshed," my father says weakly, grasping my arms, his voice cracking over the words. "It shouldn't end this way."

I grip his arms too, losing sight of Seth, of all of them. The fighting fades away around us, dissipating into the mist. I only have eyes for him. I need him to get on board *Phantom*. I need him *safe*, away from this. "I have crossed the *ocean* for you. You are not placing yourself in harm's way for me. Not now, not ever. I've only just saved you. I'm not ready to let you go."

His face softens, one hand pressed to my cheek. "You are ready. You—"

His eyes, his soft, sea-blue eyes, contort.

"Father!"

His legs drop from under him, the weight of his body pulling me down. I breathe hard, watching as the blood blooms across his chest. Right where a bullet has pierced him. "No, no, no..."

I press my hands over it, willing it to stop. Willing the warmth to stay inside him, for his soul to stay intact.

But there's so much blood. Too much, pouring from him, I can't stop it. I can't—

A sob rakes up my throat as his features relax. I hold him in my arms, cradling his head, and listen to his final whispers. "I should have let you leave Rosevear long ago, Mira. You were never meant to stay on our island. It's time. It's *time*, my dearest one. The sea gives. The sea takes."

I shake my head, holding him tighter. "No, it's not your time. We'll get you aboard *Phantom*. It's not your—"

"I love you."

Then the light in his eyes gutters out.

CHAPTER
THIRTY-FIVE

I HOLD HIM TIGHT TO ME. I CALL HIS NAME. I WILL life back into him, for someone, *anyone* to give him back. It isn't his time, it isn't, it isn't.

"Mira, I…I tried to warn you."

I look up, my eyes a blur, and behold Seth's face, staring down at me. Haunted. Haunted by what he has inflicted.

"It could have been your rifle. Your bullet. It's as if you shot him *yourself*," I say quietly, pain cracking me in two. And out of that pain pours my wrath. All of it, focused on him. "You did this. *You*."

My rage sharpens to a point. I'm yelling now. *Screaming* at him. I reach for my blade, gripping it, my hands slick with my father's blood—

And throw.

It connects with Seth's shoulder, right where that bullet tore through him in the sea at Finnikin's Way. He barks with pain, dropping his own knife. His hand reaches up for my blade, embedded deep inside him. He staggers back and I stand slowly, blood soaking into my clothes, my skin, as I stalk toward him. He shrinks from me, paling as I near him and babbling incoherently.

"Are you afraid, Seth?" I say softly, delighting in his fear.

I am the sea in human form.

All her anger.

All her storms.

"Do you understand what you've done?"

His eyes widen, as if seeing me for the first time. Seeing into my soul and finding the truth in it. That I'm not quite human. That I was born of tide as much as land.

That my kin drown the likes of him in the deep.

Any feelings I had for him are severed with steel. He is nothing. Nothing but a liar and a thief, the reason my father's blood is smeared over me. The reason my father is dead only a few feet away.

I grip the handle of my blade, ripping it from his shoulder. He goes down on his knees, all the color draining from him, and real fear, *true* fear dawns over his features. He stares up at me, showing the whites of his eyes.

I saved him twice, this boy who twists the truth like a poet. But this time, he will have to be saved from *me*. I bend low, so he can hear me. So every word I utter is like a burning brand as I angle my blade at his throat.

"I will *never* forget this. Not as long as I live. Mark me. Mark my face. I will be your undoing. I will take *everything* from you."

He mumbles, his words mingling and blurring as I flick my wrist up, ready to spill his blood.

"Mira, no." A hand grips my arm, wrenching me away. I

look up, finding the one person who could make me hesitate. Whose face is a picture of devastation as she shoves Seth away from my blade.

Merryam.

I turn, finding them all staring at me. Renshaw and her crew. Elijah and his. Agnes and Kai, blood smeared across both of them.

Seth staggers away, whimpering as the few remaining of Renshaw's men reach for him, all of them backing away down the quay. I realize with a jolt that Elijah and the others have delivered most of them to an early grave. Their bodies are strewed over the old stone of the quay, only three left to stand with Seth and Renshaw as the mist begins to recede, floating out to sea.

Renshaw tips her head at me, fixing me for a moment with something akin to horror. "Look at you. Just like your mother. Just as wild. Just as *feral*."

I show her my teeth, wanting her to know just how like my mother I can be. That she has preyed on the wrong person. I shift forward, blood coursing through me like a tempest, hot and jagged with all my fury ready to pounce, to cut her beating heart from her chest—

Rifle fire cracks across the quay. Renshaw shrieks, clutching her head as more shots rip through the air. I gasp, stumbling back as a wave, a *tide* of the watch swarm toward us from the mist.

"Mira," Elijah says. I whip around to find him sinking to the ground beside my father. His eyes seek mine urgently. "Mira, it's over. Your father needs you. We have to go. *Now*."

The tempest inside me cools instantly, lining my veins with frost. I stumble back to my father, a bullet whistling past my ear. My blood churns like poison as I sink down beside him. His body looks so small now, so vulnerable on the cold stone. I gather him into my arms as Bryn falls on his knees beside me. A keening sound breaks from me and I bow my head, even as Elijah is scooping up my father's body, shouting at me to move. The salt of my tears, the salt of the ocean drowns everything else out. My mother, and now my father too.

All my kin ripped away.

I don't know how I get up from the ground. All I know is the steady hands of Elijah when he comes back for me, the planks of *Phantom* beneath my feet as we escape. I turn, just as we sail from the quay, to see Captain Leggan staring back. His gaze pierces mine, marking me like a curse as men with rifles line up to shoot.

I hold my breath as I sink to the deck, sure this is the end.

Shots fire, raining down on us, whistling and thrumming. I cover my ears, close my eyes, and bury my face in the deck.

Then the sharp cold of the wind whips around us, filling the sails and whisking us beyond reach.

I release that breath, turning to Agnes and Kai. To my father's body, carefully laid out beside them on the deck. And silently, they bring their arms around me.

I stare without seeing, watching the waves and mist consume Penscalo until all I see is blue. I can't move. My mind is a blank sheet. I keep replaying over and over the moment when his body falters and falls. It doesn't seem real. It is too final. Too absolute.

My father, my anchor, is gone.

CHAPTER
THIRTY-SIX

WE DRESS HIM IN WHITE AND COVER THE HOLE in his chest. We gather at the meeting house, just as we do for every celebration. For every death. We wait two days before we bury him, before we are ready to. And in that time, Agnes rarely leaves my side. She stays in my cottage, whispering stories when I can't sleep. She makes tea and sits with me in the silence. She helps me make sense of it. She reminds me that I am not alone.

And then, on the third day, Kai brings my father's coffin to the meeting house. I tremble when I see it, the terrible beauty of it. The care he has poured into carving out my father's story. The waves of the sea, the delicate sea thrift drifting at the edges. The eyes etched in the side, my mother's eyes. I begin to cry for the first time in days, a torrent of tears that could drown us all. I grip the side of the coffin and carry the weight of it with the others who go out on the rope to the wrecks. My sisters and brothers of the storm. The seven of us, working as one again. We carry him to the edge of the cliffs of Rosevear. To where the sea thrift grows and he can always look out to the ocean. Bryn leads the way, still frail from his time in the prison. He speaks softly of my father's bravery. Of how he has protected us all.

Tears track down my cheeks as we all pick up our shovels, pouring the earth over him. Burying the coffin, etched with my father's story, deep in the ground. Then Agnes squeezes my hand and they leave me alone with him.

For our final goodbye.

I stare out at the ocean, the wind whipping my hair around my face. I am still a blank sheet. An unfurled sail, drifting without an anchor to hold me. All the rage, all my pain has died with him. I am numb. As though Seth and Renshaw have taken everything, robbed me of even the most essential ingredients of myself. Every part of me is a stranger now.

After a while, I am aware of the shadow standing beside me. Staring out to sea with me.

"I failed," I say, my voice full of gravel.

Elijah sighs. "No. I failed. You did exactly as you were meant to. I should have anticipated Renshaw's trickery."

"Still, he's dead. He's dead and it didn't work."

"Mira, there is no blame here." He turns me toward him, lifting my chin with a gentle hand. I look into his eyes, finding regret. Truth. A hint of fear. "This is important. You are not to blame. Do you understand?"

I close my eyes, wanting the world to fade away. Wanting to fade away along with it.

His grip hardens on my chin. "But we have a deal, remember? You made a bargain."

My eyes snap open.

"You agreed to work for me. A year, Mira. Give me a year. Do not fall apart now. I forbid you to fall apart."

I sniff, tearing myself away from him, and glance down at the mound of earth. I don't say that this bargain is broken. That we failed and my greatest fear has been realized. He's dead.

"You have to get up and keep going."

I breathe in, the cold searing my lungs. Burning everything away, making them clean and new. Giving me the clarity I desperately need. I turn to Elijah, taking in his grim expression, his wide-set shoulders. The secrets folded in the shadows surrounding him.

"The watch will come for us again. And soon. Everything's changed and we're not safe. I need you to protect Bryn, to get him away from here for a while. Can I trust you to do that?"

His eyes sharpen, boring into mine. "You can trust me."

I nod, knowing that somehow, I can. This does not need to be part of a deal. He was the one I could trust all along. "Perhaps it's time to make a new bargain between us."

He sets his jaw, as though ready to fight me on this. Not wanting to concede. We both know that what was agreed before has been shattered. However much he wants that year with me that was promised. "I'm listening."

"I want..." I swallow, planting my feet. "My father protected me. He kept me here on this island and made sure I was safe. He worried every time I swam out to a wreck. Every time I willingly put myself in danger. And I never..." I steady myself. I need to get this out. "I fought him on it. Every damn day, I wanted to cut away that tie. I wanted... I wanted to be free. But now—"

"Now that tie has gone."

"And I don't feel free."

He waits.

"So now, I want more than our original bargain. I want you to protect Rosevear and my people. The watch, the captain's ambition…it's vast. They're growing in power and I don't know if we can hold out." I take a breath. "I will work with you. I will read the map for you and give up its secrets. But as long as I work with you, I want my island protected from the watch. And I want Renshaw and Seth to know how this feels, to be untethered. To be hounded and haunted like we're no more than beasts. I want them to have everything stripped from them. She took my father from me. I want *vengeance*."

He stares at me steadily. "I can agree to bringing Rosevear under my protection. I will ensure Bryn is safe and hidden. But the other term…" He hesitates. "Are you sure?"

I nod. "It also perfectly aligns with what *you* want. Renshaw has been a thorn in your side for too long."

A shadow passes across his features, extinguished in a moment. His face turns thoughtful. Then he holds out his hand. "If you follow this path, Mira, there is no return. And you may never find the peace you are seeking."

I put my hand in his, watching as he turns my palm upward, exposing the soft skin on my wrist. The delicate veins tracking up toward my palm. "I'm ready."

"Then I will make a new bargain between us."

I watch as the compass etched under my skin flares silver, fire igniting in my veins. I tense as his fingers close over it, his eyes holding mine. Burning into me. Holding a question I still don't quite understand.

When he releases me, I look down at my wrist, watching a new symbol weave over the compass.

A blade.

"Mira, I bind you to me. I offer you a place at my side in order to fulfil your wish, and mine." He takes a breath, our eyes locking. "To use your knowledge to defeat Renshaw and her kin. To bring an end to her dynasty and her hold over the sea. And to protect Rosevear and all you hold dear."

I smile, that same fire I feel when I am deep in the ocean washing through me.

I am no longer a blank sail, unmoored in a great tempest. I have a purpose, a plan. I will make them pay for what has been stolen from me. I may not long for blood as my mother did. But I will not be sated until I have revenge.

They say we aren't human. That we thirst and plunder and kill. And yes, it's true what they say.

But I call it survival.

★ ★ ★ ★ ★

ACKNOWLEDGMENTS

FOREVER AND ALWAYS, JOE, ROSIE, AND IZZY. YOU are my favorite people in the entire world. Also to my family and friends, particularly those on Scilly—Angie, Mark, Lucy, Rob, Liam, Siân, and Helena; every meal, every time you took my wildlings off on an adventure, meant a little more of this story got written. I appreciate you all so much.

To my critique partners Cyla Panin and Marina Green, for the endless voice notes, swapped manuscripts, friendship, and wisdom. Someday I will come over to Canada and we'll explore together.

Thank you to my critique circle on the WWTS retreat—Shirsten, Alex, Marina, Sam, O.E., Katie, and Bec—for reading the first chapter of this book and giving me hope that it wasn't so terrible. Thank you for your insightful comments, and to Adrienne for being so encouraging. To Isabel Ibanez for listening to the entirety of the idea for this book and assuring me that it was compelling. You're right, *Wrecker Girl* would have made a cool title, too.

To Maddalena Cavaciuti—Spurs fan, fast talker, book builder. Mads, from the very beginning, you've been all in. A constant, steady support, the first editor of my stories, there by my side at every meeting, every time I took the next step. I couldn't have done this without you, and I wouldn't have wanted to. Thank you for fighting for my stories.

Megan Reid, thank you for being the kind of editor every writer should have. You picked up this story, championed it relentlessly (in your own calm, thoughtful way), and carved a path for it to not only be published but to soar. Olivia Valcarce, I am endlessly glad you joined the crew, saw the beating heart of this book, and really got it. What an absolute dream team to work with.

Allison Cole, Olivia Hickman, and Camille Burns at DHA, thank you for reading the early manuscript, for your time and critique—especially demanding more romance. Thank you as always to the whole team at DHA for all the behind-the-scenes work that gets books made. You're the best.

To the whole team at HarperCollins Children's Books, your passion and dedication are incredible. Thank you for making this story into a book. Without you, this would not be in the hands of readers. Special thanks to Cally Poplak, Nick Lake, Jane Baldock, Matthew Kelly, Tina Mories, Debora Wilton, Nicole Linhardt-Rich, Sarah Lough, and my copy editor, Jane Tait.

To my US publisher, Inkyard Press, and my team across the Atlantic—Bess Braswell, Brittany Mitchell, Kamille Carreras Pereira, Heather Connor, Cadence King, Greg Stephenson, and the wonderful cover illustrator, Jim Tierney, as well as the many people who lifted this book up, gave me my first hardcover edition (!), and made a huge dream come true—thank you. Thank you, thank you.

To Daisy Davis, islander and talented creator of the incredible map for the world of the Fortunate Isles and beyond, I'm so glad you wanted to work on this book.

Compass and Blade was inspired by the islands I live on, the ones I've called home for my whole adult life. It's the kind of place that feels like it belongs in a story, surrounded by shipwrecks, covered in burial mounds and ancient field boundaries, where gig races happen twice a week in the season, and if you know where to look, you'll find puffins in the spring. The Isles of Scilly is special to so many people, including me. Thank you to all the people and organizations that keep it special and the mindful visitors who come back year after year that keep our community going. If you want to feel like you're walking across Rosevear, staring up at the star-shaped Ennor Castle, swimming beside Mira, or stood on the deck of the *Phantom*, Scilly is where you will find the real magic of our world.